Rae
Kennedy

make me dream of you

rae kennedy

FIRST EDITION

RAKE Publishing

Cover design: Steamy Designs

Editing: Evil Eye Editing

Interior formatting: Torie Jean

www.raekennedyauthor.com

ISBN: 978-1-7333189-9-0

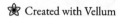 Created with Vellum

To Jo,
without whose soul-crushing honesty and fierce support,
this book would have been much shittier

AUTHOR'S NOTE AND CONTENT WARNINGS

My goal as an author is first and foremost, to bring the reader joy. Romance as a genre is inherently comforting and uplifting—the happy ever after is literally guaranteed.

For many readers, myself included, Romance novels are an escape. As such, I try to keep the content of my books safe and lighthearted.

But life isn't all sunshine, not even in Romance novels. Experiencing lows is not only realistic, but it makes the highs that much better.

My promise is that these potentially stressful situations will be brief and non-gratuitous, and I hope you trust me to tell you this story.

This book contains mentions of loss of family members, including siblings and parents. A past car accident and struggles with depression. Drowning, tattoo needles, and (unapologetically) many, many uses of adult language and explicit sex scenes.

CHAPTER 1

LIVVY

Thirteen-year-old me would be screaming, crying, throwing up.

I've only been at the bar a few minutes, waiting for my sister and her roommate. Just enough time to get a drink from the bartender, Riley. He's wearing a crop top and as soon as I tell him I'm Bex's sister he gives me a discount and starts calling me "hunny."

The bar is dim. Toward the back people dance in the anonymity of the dark to the barely recognizable techno-remix version of a pop song.

A figure emerges from the shadows to my left and joins me at the bar. Something about it—big, male, all in black, the faint musky scent, the body heat—makes my heart rate increase.

I see his hand first.

Long fingers wrapped around an empty glass. A stag is tattooed on the back of his hand, only partially visible as it disappears into his long black shirt sleeve. The sharp tips of the antlers follow the sinewy lines of his hand, pointing to his fingers clad in silver rings and knuckles tattooed with roman numerals.

And then, his deep, velvety voice. "Gin and tonic."

A chill trickles down my spine, goosebumps rising along my neck.

Daring to glance up, I'm met with more black tattoos that spill out of his shirt collar. A skull on his throat. Black roses up the side of his neck, cutting along and highlighting the sharp angle of his jaw.

His face is all hard lines, cheekbones, a sloped nose with the tiniest bump on the end. Thick brows with dark, sunken eye sockets that make his eyes look black. Lifeless. And yet, his lips are full. Soft.

It's the most hauntingly beautiful face I've ever seen. But I've seen it before. Fitting, really. Since it's haunted my dreams for the last eight years.

Noah Dixon.

He's older, obviously. Still tall. But before he was long and lanky, and now he's filled out a bit. Muscular. His neck is thicker. Jaw squarer. He didn't have tattoos when he was a senior in high school, but he was still the kid from the school across town. Mysterious.

But even though he looks different, older, and is now covered in tattoos, I'd still recognize him in a second.

My heart pounds wildly, loud in my ears. The same reaction I'd have had as that thirteen-year-old girl with the biggest, dumbest crush. Dumb, not only because he was hot and mysterious and eighteen, and I was—well—a little girl he never even noticed, but also because he was Bex's boyfriend.

They dated her junior year, his senior, and every time he would come around our house, I would spy on them. Make up imaginary scenarios where he was secretly in love with me and just dating her to get close. Go write in my diary about our future and all the times I thought he looked my direction and that one time he said "hey, Little Livvy" to me. I'd practice signing my name in cursive, *Mrs. Olivia Dixon*, and make lists of our children's names. All the stupid things you do when you're young and have your first big, major crush.

The kind of crush that changes you, that stays with you, that you still think about from time to time.

The crush that's now standing directly next to me in a crowded bar. That perfect, yet menacing face—I'm staring at it.

I'm staring at him.

And now he's looking directly at me, seeing me staring.

His lips part, the sharp edges of his white teeth showing as he smirks.

Fuck.

I turn away instantly, my face going hot.

You're not going to do this. You're not going to be the silly little girl gawking at the gorgeous, unobtainable Noah Dixon. Not again.

"Hey," he says in that rich, low voice.

Is he talking to me? He's talking to me.

I slowly turn back, holding my breath to keep from hyperventilating. Trying to play it cool but my heart is thrashing in my chest.

I meet his eyes, those dark eyes unlike anyone else's. A deep blue, like the darkest part of the ocean before it goes black or the night just before the stars come out. I've sketched them over and over. Dreamt of them. Wished for them to see me. *Really* see me.

And now they are on me. Pointedly so. Sharp enough to pierce.

His gaze trails down my collarbone to my tight-fitted tank top then further to my crossed legs, clad in my favorite pair of jeans with the rips in the thighs.

He's taking his time, looking me over slowly, not even hiding it, like he doesn't even care—no, that he *wants* me to know he's looking.

I didn't think I was showing that much skin, but with Noah Dixon's eyes on me, I'm painfully aware of every single exposed inch, now burning red hot.

He's looking at me—like a woman. Like he likes what he sees. And then his eyes are back on mine. Full, unrelenting eye contact.

Okay, twenty-one-year-old me might scream, cry, and throw up, too.

"Hi," I manage to squeak out. Fuck.

His smirk grows. "Can I sit here?"

I nod, immediately reaching for my drink and sucking on the straw. Maybe if my mouth is busy, I won't embarrass myself by letting anything else come out of it.

Noah's gaze drops to my mouth. My pulse quickens.

"Can I get you another drink?" he asks.

I let the straw slip from my lips, realizing my drink is already almost empty.

"Sure." I'm really killing it with the whole conversation thing.

Get it together, Livvy.

Noah Dixon is buying me a drink. If it were any other man in this situation, I'd have the upper hand.

He obviously doesn't know who I am, which isn't a surprise. Eight years is a long time, and I don't look anything like I did at thirteen, thank god. I was a bit of an ugly duckling—in the middle of growing out bangs, full braces, chubby—not at all helped by my awkwardness and being severely introverted.

It took years to come out of my shell and gain confidence in myself and my appearance.

And here I am, reverting to that lovesick teenager the second I see him.

Riley slides a newly poured drink across the bar to Noah with a little pop in his hip. "A gin and tonic for my favorite customer."

"You say that to all the guys."

Riley scoffs.

Noah chuckles. "I won't forget your tip."

"See, that's why you're my favorite, Noah." Riley winks at him.

"Will you get the lady here whatever she likes?"

"Certainly." Riley leans toward me. "Do you want another of what you're having or something new, hunny?"

"Same, please."

"You got it."

I turn toward Noah, uncrossing and recrossing my legs and taking another sip of my drink. "So. Noah."

His eyebrow quirks when I say his name and my stomach flips.

"The bartender knows you by name. I'm guessing you come here often."

Did I just ask if he comes here often? I want to smack myself.

He turns his body toward mine, licking his upper lip. "I do." He shifts closer. "Now that you know my name, can I have yours?"

My heart pounds at the same time all the air escapes my lungs, and my chest tightens. The thoughts swirling in my head making me dizzy—or maybe it's the drinks. What if I give him my name and it jogs his memory? What if he realizes who he's been flirting with and he's mortified? Or worse. What if my name stirs nothing in his memory because I was truly that inconsequential to him?

"You'll have to work a little harder for that," I say. *Good one, Liv, stay aloof. Mysterious.*

"Gladly." His smile widens, showing more of his teeth. It's a wicked, wolfish smile. And I'm the sheep.

Oh.

Riley places my drink in front of me, removing my empty one.

"So, A Girl with No Name." Noah plays with his straw, twisting it between his teeth. "Why haven't I seen you around here before?"

"How do you know you haven't?"

"Trust me, I wouldn't forget your face."

The irony that he has already done so is not lost on me, and I laugh loud enough I'm pretty sure half the bar hears it and almost choke on my drink. But it was eight years ago. I was embarking on my first of two emo phases and had yet to experience the gift and curse of puberty. So, I'll give him a pass.

He tilts his head, his thick brow furrowing. "Why was that funny?"

Still smiling, I suck down my drink, trying to think of what to say. "I don't know. I've just always had a forgettable face, I guess." Bex was always the prettier one, the fun one, the outgoing one.

Noah clenches his jaw for a second, the hard line of it only drawing more attention to his throat tattoos. "Anyone who would forget that face, that smile, that laugh"—the tip of his tongue grazes his upper lip then teases the edge of his straw, his gaze falling to my mouth—"is a fucking idiot."

I think I might melt. Just cease to exist. Or that I've blacked out and this is an elaborate hallucination. Noah Dixon is flirting with me. Hard. My slightly inebriated brain cannot comprehend it.

I glance toward the doors just as Bex and Macy walk inside. It's a sign that I should quit while I'm ahead. The longer I talk with Noah, the higher the probability I'll say something silly or embarrassing.

"Thank you for the drink, Noah." I slide from the stool.

"You're still not even going to give me your name? What am I going to put your number under in my contacts?"

I smile. "I didn't give you my number."

"We should fix that."

"You said you come here often. I'm sure I'll see you here again. If you still want it next time, I'll give it to you."

His grin is devilish. "Deal."

I turn and walk through the growing crowd toward my sister and Macy, before my legs give out, my heart beating so hard it's about to burst out my chest, not daring to look back at him.

Holy. Fuck. What just happened?

"Livvy!" Bex squeals and scoops me into a hug like she hasn't just seen me a few hours ago. She takes my hand and leads me around to the far side of the bar.

Macy trails after us, her curly red hair bouncing against her rosy cheeks.

I glance over to where I had been sitting, but Noah isn't there anymore.

Riley spins behind the bar. "You're late," he says through a closed-tooth smile.

"Sorry!" Bex says.

"It was my fault," Macy pipes in.

"Is Chad here?"

"He's in the back somewhere." Riley shrugs then goes back to taking drink orders.

"I'll make sure to snag him for you," Bex says to me. "Sometimes he's sneaky."

"Great." My enthusiasm is implied.

It's not that I'm not grateful for Bex helping me out, I am. It's just not what I envisioned doing after graduating. I don't know exactly what I imagined doing. Graduation always seemed like a far-off thing in the distance, a problem for Future Livvy, until, well, it was here.

Because what sort of job does one get after graduating with a Fine Arts degree?

Bartending, naturally.

Bex's long, blonde hair shines in the neon pink lights behind the bar as she pours shots and pints of beer, all with a smile on her face while random men ogle her cleavage.

She bartended here through college. Worked as a paralegal for six months after graduating, then promptly returned when she realized that it was better money, better hours, and that she absolutely did not want to be a fucking paralegal.

Maybe I should have listened to my mother when she tried to talk me out of my major and into something more practical. She didn't really care what I did at school, though, as long as I found a potential husband. An absurd expectation, when factoring in I was painfully shy, awkward, and too self-conscious to even speak to a guy until this past year.

"Blueberry mojito," Bex yells over the loud music as she slides the drink across the bar to Macy on my right. "And a vodka-cran for you," she says, winking at me. "I made them both doubles, on the house."

My third drink. Exactly what I need—to be sloshed before a job interview.

"Relax!" Bex says. "Jupiter is in Taurus, and it's a new moon. A prosperous new beginning is practically guaranteed for you."

I nod and smile, even though my insides are performing some type of Cirque-du-Soleil act in my stomach, and take a big gulp of my drink.

"You'll be fine," Macy says with warm brown eyes. When she smiles her nose scrunches.

"Oh, Chad!" Bex yells, waving to a guy in a black button-up shirt who looks to be in his mid-forties. He's just emerged from the back of the bar and is now heading our way. She flashes him a big smile. "This is my sister. She applied for the open bartender position." She motions toward me. "Livvy, this is the owner, Chad."

Oh fuck.

I lean over the bar, narrowly avoiding knocking over my drink as I put out my hand. "I'm Olivia Bishop, nice to meet you."

I'm not sure he even hears me over the crowd around us.

He looks me up and down, scratching the salt-and-pepper stubble along his jaw. "If you vouch for her," he says to my sister, "she'll do. Tell Trish to get her on the books." He looks back at me. "You start training Monday. You're on your own next weekend." And then he saunters away.

That's it? On my own next weekend? I guess it's a real sink or swim situation.

I shouldn't use that analogy because I'm a terrible swimmer.

Bex shrieks. "Yay!" And then she's off pouring more drinks.

"See, what did I tell you?" Macy gives me a reassuring nudge with her elbow.

I guzzle my drink, slurping air through the straw when I hit ice.

Macy raises her eyebrows. "Goodness. Let me buy you another drink."

I start to say she doesn't need to do that—I'll get my own, but my throat is burning, and she's already flagging down Riley.

He replaces my empty glass with a new, pink vodka spritzer just as I start to really feel the buzz kicking in.

"Thank you," I say, my cheeks warming. "You didn't have to buy me a drink," I say to Macy.

"You deserve to celebrate a little," she says, waving it off.

She and Bex have already been so generous since I moved back to Seattle after graduation, letting me crash on their couch for free while I look for a job. Thank you doesn't seem like enough.

She and my sister have been best friends and roommates since their freshman year in the dorms. She's the level-headed yin to my sister's impulsive yang.

Macy's phone buzzes in her purse and she pulls it out. "Oh biscuits, it's Spencer, I need to take it." She smiles apologetically as she answers. "Hey, babe." Her smile quickly falls. She covers her other ear with her hand. "I'm sorry, it's loud in here I didn't hear your last call."

She looks at me and mouths "sorry."

"I told you I was going out with Bex and Li—" She's quiet, mouth downturned as she looks down at her lap. She nods as she listens to whatever he's saying on the other end. "Yeah, okay. I will." Another pause. "I've only had one drink, I'm not going to —" She stops abruptly then says, "Yes, you're right. Okay. Talk to you later."

She looks at her screen for a moment after the call is ended then back up to me, like she forgot I was here. Her expression back to a big smile. "Sorry about that. Where were we?" She reaches for her drink, blinking rapidly.

"Do you want to dance?" I ask. "I wouldn't mind dancing."

Macy scrunches up her face and shakes her head, but then she looks over my shoulder and shouts, "Wood!" waving someone over to us.

A blond guy in a white T-shirt walks up to us, looking like he just walked out of a damn J. Crew catalogue. He's got that muscular jock, all-American, boy-next-door thing going on with the blue eyes and tanned skin and a big smile with perfectly straight teeth. The only quirk to his ridiculously handsome face is his slightly lopsided smile.

"Mace, bro! I didn't know you were here!" He goes in for a one-armed hug. Macy dodges left and he quickly recovers, smoothly transitioning his outstretched arm up for a high five which she returns.

"Do you want to dance?" she calls out.

Wood's eyes light up, his smile widening so that dimples appear in his cheeks. Of course he has dimples, too. "Oh, heck yeah, girl. Let's go!"

"No, not with me. You know I don't dance. With her—" Macy gestures to me and he looks my direction for the first time realizing I'm here. "This is Bex's little sister, Livvy."

The smaller, lopsided smile is back on his lips as he takes me in. "Well, hi, Bex's little sister, Livvy. Nice to meet you."

He lifts a fist to me, and I bump his knuckles. Then he does a hand exploding thing and I try to copy it but end up doing a weird little jazz hand move instead.

"We'll work on that later." He winks at me then turns back to Macy. "You sure you don't want to join us? I've got two hands. I can totally handle both of you."

Macy rolls her eyes. "I'm sure you could, but I'm good. Keep her company and keep her safe and don't let any weirdos near her."

He shoots finger guns at her with a wink. "I'm your guy."

Wood and I head to the dance floor, his hand lightly on my mid-back as we weave through the crowd.

Under the flashing lights, we dance to the pulsing music, melting in with the other dancers, drunk and letting loose. He keeps a respectable distance from me, not automatically going for the rear grind like so many men do. He's making me laugh with every random, dumb dance move he can think of—the sprinkler, the shopping cart.

But the dance floor is crowded so we end up closer and closer. I'm still buzzing. The music is good. It's hot and sweat beads at my temples.

Then past Wood's shoulder, he's there. In the distance, leaning back against the wall, half in shadow. Noah. He's watching us. No —he's watching me.

His eyes are completely obscured, the hollows of his sockets black and empty. But I can feel his stare. The sensation sends a chill down my spine. A feeling of dread. Excitement. My skin heats. My pulse races.

Wood puts his hand on my hip.

Noah steps forward out of the shadows, brows furrowed, mouth set in a scowl. His eyes are, indeed, on me—and Wood's hand. If a glare could cut like daggers, his would cut to the bone. Cut to kill.

He looks like he wants to come over here, punch poor Wood in the face and take his place. I wish he would. Not the punching part, just the dancing part.

I keep dancing, trying to push the thought of Noah's hand on me out of my mind.

But the next time I glance in that direction, he's gone.

Wood taps my shoulder as he leans in, lips close to my ear. "Do you want to take a break? Maybe go grab another drink?"

"Sure."

He takes me by the hand and leads me through the throngs of people and toward the bar. Giggly and sweaty. I don't think anything of it until we squeeze up to the bar and then Noah is there. Tall, looming over me, black sleeves pushed up to his elbows revealing his tattoo-covered forearms, jaw clenched, eyes on Wood's and my entwined hands.

Wood drops my hand to clap Noah on the shoulder. "Sup, bro!"

Noah nods, his expression softening ever-so-slightly.

Are they friends?

Bex hands two bottles of beer to the guy on our right. She's put her long, blonde hair up and is almost out of breath when her bright eyes land on me.

"Oh, good," she says, "you found each other. Another drink?"

Noah glances between me and my sister, eyes darkening. "You two know each other?"

Bex laughs. "You remember my little sister, Livvy, right?"

CHAPTER 2

NOAH

W ell. Fuck.

Bex is still grinning, like the last words out of her mouth didn't hit me so hard in the chest they almost made me physically stagger backward.

Livvy. Bex's little sister.

I never would have guessed. Bex's little sister, who always hid when I came around and maybe only ever said two words to me, is the woman I've been thinking about all night? Of course, it's been a long time, and she clearly isn't a kid anymore.

She doesn't look anything like I remember. Except for the eyes. She has the same eyes. They were too big and round for her face back then, but not now. Now, they fit perfectly. Bright green in the middle, turning to emerald, then a golden brown along the edges. They're still big, surrounded by dark lashes. Exquisite. I can't decide if they're her best feature or if it's her adorably pouty mouth.

Now that I think about it, I see her and Bex's resemblance. Except for their coloring, they could be twins. Bex has blonde hair, blue eyes, and dimples. Livvy has brown hair, green eyes, and freckles. But their features are almost identical—their little sloped noses, round eyes, pouty lips, and heart-shaped faces.

I'd never forget a face like that. Again, I mean.

"Livvy, you remember Noah, right? We dated back in high school."

"Yes. Yes, I do," Livvy says to Bex.

So, she knew who I was. Interesting. She was toying with me. The idea makes my defenses prickle at the same time it brings a grin to my lips.

"Another vodka-cran?" Bex asks.

"Water for me," Livvy says.

"Me, too," I say. Wood is already chatting up some brunette at the end of the bar, putting that charming smile to work.

Bex scoops two glasses full of ice then starts filling our waters. Livvy keeps her eyes forward, watching her sister. She doesn't want to look at me. It's cute.

Bex sets the waters down, condensation already dripping down to the bar.

"I thought you lived out of state. Are you just visiting?" I ask her.

"I just graduated and moved back. I didn't realize you two still hung out." She's still only facing Bex, her words clipped. Is she annoyed with me? I almost chuckle at the thought, my smile growing.

"Just the last few years or so," I say.

"Macy and I met Wood in college, at a frat party, of all things," Bex laughs as she pours some tequila shots. "Turns out he's Noah's cousin. They live together on the top floor of this building, and Noah tattoos next door."

Bex turns, showing off the intricate tattooed cluster of flowers cascading down her shoulder. "He did this for me. He's all right." Bex smirks. "When he's not being a dick."

"And so are you," I say. "When you're not being a bitch."

We smile at each other while she flips me off and says, "Love you, too."

Livvy looks up at me, finally. "Her tattoo is gorgeous. You do really nice work."

"Thanks."

"I've been thinking about getting something for a little while, actually." She looks away after she says it, her thick lashes fanning against her pink cheeks.

"Do you have any tattoos?"

"No."

The thought of giving her her first tattoo, of marking her virgin skin, makes my chest tighten and my dick harden.

What the fuck, Dixon?

"Well, you can come by. Anytime," I say coolly, like the thought of it isn't inexplicably turning me on.

"Okay," she says. "Have you done any of your own tattoos?"

"Yes."

"Can I see?"

I run my tongue along the edges of my teeth. "They're on my thighs."

"Oh," she says, her eyes widening.

Her plump lips stay parted as her cheeks blush a light pink. And now I'm wondering what shade of pink she turns when her whole body is flushed.

Fuck.

If only she wasn't my ex's little sister.

❤ ❤ ❤

It's late when I get home, as usual. The last several days at work have been exhausting. I did a six-hour shoulder piece today. My back hurts. And I just want to talk to *her*.

I check my phone. No messages.

It's been almost a week since I've heard from her.

I toss my keys on the stainless steel countertop and slam my phone down next. The sound echoes around the kitchen and rings in my ears.

"What's up, bro?" Wood saunters out of his room. He's wearing loose gray sweats, no shirt.

"She's not online. Still."

"Ah," he says, getting a sports drink out of the fridge. "The girl of your dreams."

"A Gatorade? At midnight?"

"Got to replenish those electrolytes after cardio." He winks.

Of course. "You can't give me crap for my online girl when you have a different one every week."

"Touché." He takes a big swig of his drink. "But at least I put myself out there. Leave it to you to stay conveniently closed off to love in real life, only to become completely obsessed with some anonymous girl online."

"I'm not obsessed." I am.

"You don't even know what she looks like, bro."

"I don't have to."

"She could be, like, an old lady or something."

"Her profile says she's twenty-one." It's the only piece of personal information on either of our profiles.

"Dude. It's the internet. People lie. She could literally be a man."

I throw my keys at his head. He easily dodges, and they clash with a metallic ring on the concrete floor.

"Am I wrong?" He laughs nervously while scanning my immediate area for anything else I might throw.

I grunt.

"Instead of pouring your heart out and telling all your deepest darkest secrets to this mystery person, maybe you should, I don't know, go talk to a therapist and then go out and make a real-life connection with someone."

I glare at Wood for a good minute. "I went to a therapist for four years after the accident. It didn't help as much as talking to her the last eight months has. And I don't want a real-life connection."

I'm not even going to think about how the first woman to catch my eye in over a year turned out to be Bex's little sister, who used to spy on us making out in my car after curfew.

"I wouldn't be good for anyone right now," I add.

"Not with that attitude." He takes a last chug of Gatorade, wipes his chin with the back of his hand, then puts it back in the fridge. "Speaking of real-life connections...could you do me a favor?"

"What kind of favor?"

He lowers his voice. "I just need you to introduce yourself to my lady friend when she comes out."

"Forgot her name?"

"It's Cindy or Cynthia or something like that."

He has that pleading look—the one that's annoyingly sincere. I roll my eyes, but say, "Okay."

Cindy/Cynthia emerges from Wood's room a few minutes later in ripped jeans and a loose sweater. She looks like his usual type – tall, long hair, pretty smile.

"Ready to go?" Wood asks.

She nods then spots me sitting at the counter. She blushes when I nod her direction and then quickly looks away.

I get that reaction a lot. Sometimes I make people uncomfortable. Or they think I'm intimidating with all my tattoos. I also don't have an easygoing smile like Wood.

He jerks his chin in her direction, widening his eyes in plea.

I stand and take a step toward her, putting out my hand. "I'm Noah."

She still seems unable to make eye contact for more than a second at a time. "Um, I'm Madison."

Behind her, Wood silently snaps his fingers and mouths, "Of course!"

My phone dings on the counter. That pathetic little pang of hope surges through me. I snatch it and the screen lights up with a message notification.

It's *her*.

"I know that look," Wood says with a little chuckle in his voice.

I want to tell him to mind his own business, but he's right. I'm already grinning like an idiot at just the sight of her name—or, screen name, I guess. My heart pumps harder.

"Shut up," I say, walking toward my room as I open the app on my phone.

"Tell Angel I say hi!" he calls.

"She doesn't even know you exist."

"Dude. I'm devastated."

I shut the door behind me, my fingers unable to open her message fast enough.

ANG3L:

Hey you

2HORNED:

Oh there you are

ANG3L:

Sorry I've been MIA

2HORNED:

That's okay. I knew you were busy

ANG3L:

Yeah, moving sucks. But I'm finally settled

2HORNED:

I'm happy for you

ANG3L:

How have you been?

2HORNED:

I'm alive

ANG3L:

That's good. I'm not into necrophilia

2HORNED:

Jesus fucking Christ

I send several crying laughing emojis.

ANG3L:

What? Should I not have said that?

Just being honest *adorable shrug*

2HORNED:

You always are (honest and adorable)

I've missed you

ANG3L:

Miss me or my dirty mouth?

2HORNED:

Both. Always both

Fuck, she sends a stupid little smirking face and I'm already getting hard. She's in a playful mood and, honestly, I don't give a fuck if we sext tonight or not. I'm happy just talking and knowing she's around and hasn't ghosted me.

But I'm also not going to turn her down if she wants to take things there.

2HORNED:

I've thought about you every day

ANG3L:

> Oh yeah? And where exactly were you when you were thinking of me?

2HORNED:

> Hmm...at work. In the shower. In bed.

I adjust my hard-on as it starts getting uncomfortable, straining in the confines of my jeans.

ANG3L:

> Are you in bed now?

2HORNED:

> Yes

I unbutton my pants, throw my phone on the bed, and pull my shirt off like it's an Olympic sport. I drop trou, boxers too, my erection bobbing out in front of me, already pulsing and hot. I leap into bed, slipping between the sheets with zero grace. Zero chill. My heartbeat erratic.

ANG3L:

> Naked?

2HORNED:

> Yes ma'am

ANG3L:

> Good boy

I respond with the sweating, panting emoji.

ANG3L:

> Stroke yourself for me

2HORNED:

> I am

I'm throbbing in my hand. I squeeze the base of my shaft and give it one long stroke.

Fuck.

I hadn't realized how much it was aching until my fist slides over the tip. I groan, rubbing the end of my cock as it gets thicker and harder, the sensitive head red and swollen. What I wouldn't give to have another warm, soft body next to me right now.

2HORNED:

It'd be better if it were your hand right now

Or mouth

ANG3L:

I'd make it feel so good for you

2HORNED:

What are you doing right now?

ANG3L:

I'm in bed, too. Touching myself through my lace panties

2HORNED:

Fuck

I wish I could see her. I want to know what she looks like. Her face, her body, a fucking ankle, I don't care. If I could see her lips, parted in pleasure, hear the little sounds and gasps she makes while she touches herself, see her fingers playing between her legs—I'd never recover. Even just the idea is pushing me closer to the edge, my abs flex in anticipation of release.

But she has strict rules about remaining completely anonymous. No pictures, no videos, no sharing details that could give away our identities.

She's at my fingertips yet untouchable. Un-have-able. Maybe that's why I want her so much.

ANG3L:

Imagine me, while you're stroking yourself crawling over your body and straddling your head. Your face crushed between my thighs

2HORNED:

Yes. Sit on my face I need to taste you

ANG3L:

Should I ride your face until I come?

2HORNED:

Yes please. Use me, suffocate me

I want you to come so hard your legs shake as you drown me

ANG3L:

Fuck, you eat me out so good, my sexy devil

After I come on your face, I'm going to slide down and kiss you, taste myself on your lips

2HORNED:

I want. So fucking hot

ANG3L:

And then I'm going to sit on your cock. I'm going to make sure you watch as it disappears inside me. I'm so wet you slide in so easily

Fuck. She knows exactly what to say, what visuals to use to get me close. I usually last longer but it's been a while and the climax I've been trying to hold off has grown too big, a raging beast inside me I can no longer cage or control.

2HORNED:

You're so perfect riding my cock, Angel.

But I'm going to need to hold your hips down and fuck up into you. Hard

ANG3L:

Yes, please. Don't take it easy on me, I want to feel you so deep inside me

2HORNED:

Holy fuck. You're going to make me come

CHAPTER 3

LIVVY

2HORNED:

Holy fuck. You're going to make me come

ANG3L:

I'm going to come, too

I grab another handful of Doritos out of the bag between Bex and I on the couch.

"Who have you been texting all night?" she asks.

"Just a friend."

She raises an eyebrow, creating hairline cracks in her almost-dry avocado face mask. My mask is almost dry, too. I can't wait to wash it off. Is it supposed to be itchy?

"Bex, let her have some privacy." Macy pours the last of the white wine into her glass, sitting cross-legged on the floor by the coffee table in her big, "I hate Mondays" Garfield T-shirt and pajama pants. Her hair is up in a messy bun, matching green mask, the glow of the television lighting up the side of her face with a new true crime documentary playing in the background.

"Also," Macy says, tipping her glass to me, "you know she

won't quit until you tell her who it is and what his Sun, Moon, and Rising signs are."

"How do you even know it's a guy?" I chuckle.

They both roll their eyes at me.

"Is it Mark?" Bex asks.

"Who's Mark?"

"He's one of the bouncers from the bar. The taller, built one. He was asking about you the other day." Bex smiles, her left dimple showing.

Really? "Oh. No, it's not Mark, or anyone you know. It's a friend...from school."

"A *boy* friend?" Macy chimes in.

"Maybe," I say.

They exchange looks, both stifling smirks.

"What? He really is just a friend."

I don't know what else to say. It's not like I have any other information to give. I don't even know his name.

And I'm absolutely not about to explain to them what I started doing for money my last year of college. I stumbled upon it by accident, really. It was good money. Easy money.

I could do it anywhere, anytime, around my schedule—at the library, between classes, with multiple clients at a time while eating pizza and studying for midterm exams.

It's amazing, actually, what I can chat about without even blushing. I'd turn beet red in real life if I even whispered half the things I've typed.

But I never get even remotely aroused. They're just words. Easily written after years of media intake, reading sexy novels, and seeing porn. It comes naturally—even though I have no experience with any of those things in real life.

It seemed harmless enough, just something to do for a little money while I was in school, something I could stop at any time. Surprisingly, many of the men seemed lonely more than anything. They wanted someone to talk to.

I made sure to remain anonymous—no names, no discussing things like where we live or work, no pictures, no videos.

Beyond the anonymity, I wasn't comfortable enough to show my body anyway, thanks to always being a little heavier growing up and a healthy dose of shame in my body or anything remotely sexual, courtesy of my overly religious mother. As I got older, she didn't even have to say anything. Her silence was enough. Accompanied by her ever-present gold cross necklace.

Never have I felt more judged by an inanimate object.

And, oh boy, if that little cross only knew the filthy things some of these guys are into. And I play along. It's fun. As Angel, I am a confident, sexy, experienced woman that men worship. I don't have to be Livvy, a virgin, who only stopped being too shy to talk to men as she was almost through college.

I think being Angel has helped me with the confidence, actually. That and finally realizing I'm not that awkward, chubby tween anymore.

2HORNED:

Jesus Christ that was so hot.

Did you come?

ANG3L:

I did. It was so good

"It was the husband! It's always the fucking husband." Bex scarfs a last Dorito then licks her fingers before typing hard and fast on her phone. "He's a Sagittarius. I knew it. Total killer vibes."

"I don't know, I think it might have been the creepy neighbor who was totally stalking her," Macy says. She goes to take another sip of her wine then pouts when she realizes it's empty. "Darn. I think that's my cue to wash off this face mask and go to bed. Don't tell me who the killer is, Bex."

"I told you it's going to be the fucking husband."

Macy rolls her eyes, smiling. "Night, girls."

"I should go to bed, too," I say, getting up. *Seriously, are neither of their faces itchy?*

"Night." Bex waves, eyes still glued to the television.

She hardly ever goes to bed before three or four in the morning, thanks to years of bartending, but I cannot hang much past midnight yet. Guess I need to work on that.

I get ready for bed then get into my makeshift bed—an air mattress with several blankets and a lumpy pillow on the floor in Bex's bedroom. But it's better than the couch, especially with Bex's late hours at the bar and Macy's early hours at the hospital.

2HORNED:

Thank you. I really needed that

ANG3L:

It was my pleasure. Literally and figuratively

2HORNED:

good

ANG3L:

Have you been doing okay?

Still not sleeping?

2HORNED:

Very little sleeping. The nightmares have been worse lately

ANG3L:

The same ones?

2HORNED:

Yeah

ANG3L:

I'm sorry. I wish there was something I could do to help. If I was there I'd hold you until you fell asleep

2HORNED:

> That would be heaven

I send a string of heart emojis

2HORNED:

> Are you going to bed now?

ANG3L:

> Yep

2HORNED:

> Goodnight, Angel

I swore I was only going to do the online chatting thing while I was in school, and then I'd get a "real" job. Something I can mention at the dinner table without giving my mother a heart attack.

Maybe the bigger reason is I want to start dating. I want to meet someone, finally have a boyfriend, for fuck's sake. And, I don't know, it would probably be weird to be chatting with multiple men and sexting while trying to foster a real-life relationship, even if the guy was okay with it, which I'm guessing most wouldn't be.

So, I did. I told everyone I was dipping out and wished them well. There was just one left. Mister two-horned. My naughty devil.

I tried several times to type out my goodbye, but I could never hit send. I've been silent for a week trying to figure out how to say it. So, I'm just not going to.

Yet.

I will.

Soon.

Soon-ish.

I sincerely enjoy talking with him. Hell, half the time we chat —we don't even touch the topic of sex. Don't get me wrong, he's fun to sext with, too. But we talk about so many things, struggles and fears and wishes and dreams that it feels like I know him on a deeper level. I genuinely consider him a friend.

He seems lonely, too.

His profile says he's twenty-six, but for all I know, he could be a forty-year-old dude living in his mom's basement.

I don't really care about that, though. He's a good person. And it doesn't really matter.

It's not like I'm ever going to meet him in real life.

♥ ♥ ♥

I've spent all week at the bar during the day, the "boring hours," as Bex refers to them, she and Riley switching off training me. And even though I've only worked the slow times, it's still kicking my ass.

Tomorrow night I'll be on my own with the chaotic Saturday night crowd. But tonight, I have off, and I have other plans.

I put away the list of standard cocktail and bar specialty drink recipes I'm supposed to have memorized and open my sketchbook instead.

I've been working on this charcoal drawing of angel wings all week and I finally got the vibe just right. There's a soft and ethereal quality to it, but the wings are also dynamic, almost like they're in motion. I hope it's good enough.

The sky hovers somewhere between blue and black, the lights of downtown Seattle just coming to life. I stand in front of the door, the open sign glowing neon pink in the almost dark. To the right is the bar and to the left is a coffee shop, all the lights off and chairs up on the tables for the night.

You can do this.

I push the door to Black Ink, Inc., except it's a pull. Shit. Okay, regroup. Hopefully no one saw that.

I *pull* open the door the Black Ink, Inc., my insides a jittery mess, my sketchbook tucked under my arm.

As soon as I do, a bell attached to the door rattles, the ringing echoing through the space.

The shop is bigger than I expected—not that I have anything to compare it to. The back wall is weathered red and brown brick. The side walls are all black, covered in white chalk drawings and words. There are giant, industrial-sized metal light fixtures hanging from the ceiling and each station is separated with metal and glass hanging screens.

There are people in a few of the stations, the buzzing of tattoo guns drowning out the sound of the music playing overhead.

A woman looks up from behind a counter as I walk in. She has black hair except for two bright blue streaks around her face, a septum piercing, and thick, black winged eyeliner.

I walk past a large black leather couch toward her. "Hi."

She blinks. "Do you have an appointment?"

Fuck. Did I need an appointment?

"No."

She sighs. "Take a seat. I'll see if anyone has time to take a walk-in."

"Oh, thank you. I was actually wondering if Noah was available."

"Noah." She looks at me with half-lidded eyes and pursed lips. "Yes?"

She rolls her eyes. "It's almost impossible to get an appointment with the owner. He has a year-long waitlist."

Noah's the owner?

"Oh." Something inside me deflates but I try to keep an easy-going smile on my face. "I guess put me on his waitlist, then."

"I can't just put your name down. Noah has to approve new clients first."

Smile officially gone.

"I'll take her," that familiar, velvety voice says, and I look up just as Noah is walking out from a back office. He's wearing black jeans and a threadbare white T-shirt, the tattoos covering his entire torso just visible through the fabric. "Livvy's an old friend," he says to the girl at the counter, but his eyes are on me.

She rolls her eyes and goes back to whatever she was working on before.

He smiles, his lips parting just enough to show the tip of one cuspid. And just that little smirk and the way he hasn't taken his gaze away from me has my entire face burning.

"Do you know what you're wanting to get?" he asks.

"Um. Yeah. I sketched something. It's rough."

"Come on back and let's take a look at it."

I follow him around the counter and back through the door he came out of a minute ago. It's an office with a small desk in the center and a couple of chairs, black metal cabinets along the back wall, and all black-painted walls. But these black walls are covered in large, framed photographs of intricate tattoo pieces.

Noah leans back against the desk, gripping the edge of it with his hands, the muscles in his forearms flexing under his black tattoos.

"Is your drawing in there?" He gestures to the sketchbook clutched in my arms.

Right. "Yeah."

I fumble with my sketchbook, turning to the page with the finalized angel wings. I lay it down on the desk, open to my sketch. He leans over to look at it, his thumb grazing the spine, his expression unchanging.

Why did I think this sketch was good enough to tattoo? It's obviously dumb. I'm about to snatch the book back and just say never mind when he picks it up.

"Wow, this drawing is beautiful," he says.

"Thank you," I say in a weird, way-too-breathy way. "It's nothing, really."

"No, seriously, I love how they don't feel static, and you have a great attention to detail. Do you have other sketches in here? Can I see?" He lifts the corner of the page to turn it.

"No!"

He pauses and we look at each other. Standing here while my cheeks get hot, pretending I didn't just almost freak out over nothing.

Not exactly nothing, I may or may not have sketches of his eyes in there. *His eyeballs.* If he sees those and realizes it's him, I'll vomit.

"Another time, then?" he asks.

"Yeah, totally."

"Do you want the tattoo around the same size as the sketch?"

I nod. "One on each hip."

"Show me where."

My jeans are too snug to pull them down enough without unbuttoning them. The sound of the snap and me unzipping my jeans echoes around the office in the most mortifying way possible. All the while, Noah's watching as I shimmy my pants down my hips, exposing the top of my pink, cotton panties. *Why didn't I wear cuter panties?*

I pull the boring pink underwear down on one side, just enough to expose the little bit of skin along the front of my hipbone where I want the tattoo.

"Right here," I say quietly.

He lifts his eyes up slowly to me. "Okay." He clears his throat. "I've got some time right now. A client cancelled. If you're up for it."

"Yeah, I mean, yes. Let's do it."

Let's do it? My cheeks are on fire.

His demeanor, thankfully, is professional. "I'm going to go trace your drawing. It should only take a few minutes—I'm just going to get the lines marked out then I'll use your sketch as a reference while I'm inking. Can I get you anything? Water?"

"No, thanks. I'm fine."

Five minutes is a short amount of time in pretty much any circumstance, except for in microwave minutes and when you're waiting alone in a room right before you're about to get tattooed, apparently.

"Hey."

I jump at his voice. He chuckles darkly.

"Follow me."

I follow him back to a private room. The temperature drops instantly at least ten degrees when I walk in. The walls are all white instead of black, music plays softly from overhead. In the center is a black tattoo table, a little stool on wheels, and a metal tray.

He closes the door behind us. "I thought you'd prefer it in here. It's where I take clients when they're getting work done on" —he pauses, taking in a sharp breath—"more private areas. But if you're more comfortable not being in here alone with me, we can—"

"No, this is good."

"Good." His dark eyes lock on mine and my heart pounds like a drum in my ears. "So here's what I have." He shows me the stencil he made of my sketch. "I bolded some of the lines up a little, just so the tattoo holds up better over time. Some of those fine lines tend to blur and fade after a while, unless you want to be coming in for a touch-up every year or so."

He says it like a joke, like of course I wouldn't want that, but it doesn't sound so bad to me.

"Looks great," I say.

"All right, so placement." He chews on his soft lower lip for a second. "Normally we'd consult first and I'd tell you to come back for your appointment wearing a loose-fitting dress or skirt so we could move the material around where needed. This will be a little trickier. So, tell me at any time if you're uncomfortable or want to wait. I can always put you on the schedule for another day."

"The girl up front said you were booked out a year," I say quietly.

He holds my gaze for a beat, his voice is husky when he says, "I'd come in on a day off to give you your first tattoo."

Oh. "I don't want to wait."

He nods. "Here's what I'm going to have you do." He gets a white, folded piece of fabric out of a cabinet and hands it to me as he opens it up. "I'll have you unzip your jeans again, then hold this drape against yourself while I place the stencils."

"Okay."

I do as told, then he kneels to the floor.

Noah Dixon is on his knees, in front of me, eye level with my belly button. So close I can feel the heat from his skin, hear him breathing, smell his hair.

He looks up at me and holy shit. Teen Livvy would die.

The light catches on the angles of his face, his dark blue eyes framed in thick, black lashes, reducing me to a melty mess.

The tip of his tongue wets his lips and then he says, "I'm going to pull these down now, if that's okay." He places his fingers lightly on the waistband of my jeans.

"Yes," I say, trying to keep my voice steady.

I hold the drape over my pubic area between where his hands are on my hips, clutching it tightly with sweaty hands. Noah's fingertips brush my skin ever so softly as he guides my jeans down my hips and to my midthigh.

"Okay, now these." He touches the trim of my cotton panties. "You still good?"

"Uh huh." Holy. Shit.

He pulls my panties down my hips a few inches. Goosebumps raise on my skin in the wake of his touch. I'm dizzy with adrenaline.

The snap of a latex glove makes me open my eyes. He holds my hip with a gloved hand and cleans my skin with a disinfecting wipe with the other.

My skin burns under his scrutiny as he concentrates on his task. Wherever he touches me, instantly on fire, as he places one stencil on the skin just inside my hipbone and then the other. He takes his time, carefully making sure they match up evenly.

He holds up a hand mirror. "How's the placement?"

I examine them in the mirror for a minute, holy shit, this is really happening. I'm getting tattooed. By Noah Dixon.

"Good," I manage to squeak out.

"Good." He gives me the hint of a smirk. "Go lie down on the table and put the drape wherever is most comfortable for you."

I lie down as he's turned away, getting his gun ready and unbagging needles and filling a little cup full of black ink.

He swivels around, wheels squeaking across the floor, and picks up the tattoo gun with a black-gloved hand. "Ready?"

Nope. "Yep."

"Remember to breathe," he says.

Am I not breathing? I'm not. I let out a breath and unclench my fists.

"You'll do great," he says, scooting in closer. He adjusts the drape, covering me up more and sort of tucking it around to keep it in place. He does it with care and gentleness, like my comfort and modesty are important to him. It makes me feel safe. At the same time, it reminds me he doesn't see me as anything but a client or friend and my ears burn as I think I wouldn't mind at all if he accidentally saw more of me. If he wanted to see more of me...

"Here we go, Livvy."

I like the way he says my name. "Okay." I close my eyes.

The sound of the tattoo gun is more jarring than the first touch of the needle to my skin.

I try to focus on my breathing, slow and steady. But I keep getting distracted by his touch—the way his wrist is resting against my bare thigh as he tattoos, how his gloved hand is firm on my hip, helping me stay still while reassuring me at the same time. And every time he wipes ink away, his fingers grazing over that sensitive skin no man has touched before, my heartrate skyrockets.

"When did you start drawing?" Noah asks, head down, pulling long lines with the needle.

It's like he's dragging a knife through my skin while vibrating my bones. I try to concentrate on the question. It hurts but somehow, not as much as I'd imagined it would.

"I don't know. Always? I got really into it in middle school, I guess. I didn't have many friends, so during breaks and lunch I secluded myself away with a notebook instead of socializing." That's probably why I continued not to make new friends in high school.

"You're very talented."

This is the part where I should speak up and tell him about my art degree and how I love to paint and how my dream is to have a solo show in a real gallery. But instead, I say, "Thank you."

I'm sweating. Not sure if it's from the adrenaline or the fact that Noah's breath is warm against my skin or the way his thumb swipes over my hipbone.

"I should have you design something for me to get tattooed," he says.

"Really?"

"Really."

Oh.

"How are you doing?" he asks.

"I'm okay." I think.

He's quiet for a while and I zone out, letting him focus, finding the steady buzz of the tattoo gun almost hypnotizing.

I don't know how much time has passed when he speaks again.

"I did the line work on this one. I'm going to move to the other side. Let me know if you need a break." He gives my hand a reassuring squeeze, then rolls the stool and tray to the other side of the table.

Noah adjusts the drape over to expose my other hip. The fabric sweeps over my sensitive skin, gathering a bit between my legs and I stifle a whimper before he gets back to work.

Part of me wants to close my eyes, go away to another place in my mind, think about anything other than the needle. But the other part doesn't want to miss a second of watching him. The way his tattoos ripple with each arm movement. How that little piece of dark hair has fallen over his forehead. The way his thick brows are furrowed in concentration, his mouth almost in a scowl. The hint of his cologne as he swivels back and forth between me and the tray. And how, every couple of minutes, he glances up at me, his serious expression softening for a split second before he looks back down.

"You're sitting so good," he says low as he wipes ink away, his hand gentle over my hip, barely brushing my upper thigh in the process.

My inner thighs tingle. An unbidden ache between my legs begs me to squeeze them together to relieve it, but I don't dare move.

"So good," he whispers again, soothing.

And the thought of him calling me a good girl wedges its way into my brain. No, *his* good girl. And now the ache is worse. Fuck.

"Are you okay? You've been sitting really still and now you're squirming a bit."

Jesus Fuck.

My face has never erupted into flames faster.

CHAPTER 4
NOAH

"I 'm fine," Livvy says, even though her breathing is ragged, and her entire chest, neck, and cheeks are flushed.

I'm done outlining so I cover her with the sheet and insist we take a little break. We share a snack and drink some water and she tells me about how she started working at the bar but she's afraid she's terrible at it. I kind of want to just keep talking, but it's getting late.

"Ready?" I ask.

She nods, taking a deep breath and lies back down.

I adjust the fabric to expose her skin, trying not to graze her hip or thigh any more than necessary, hating that the thought of doing so makes my dick twitch.

Her breath catches when I pick up the tattoo gun and I have the overwhelming desire to comfort her. I want to hold her hand, rub her side. It's odd, especially since she's been sitting so well and not acting overly stressed.

Something about her is getting to me. I can usually zone out a bit when I tattoo, get in a rhythm, block everything else out and just concentrate on the tattoo, but I'm distracted.

I've tattooed women in more intimate spots than this, so it's not that.

There's something about the way she breathes and her little whimpers every time the needle touches her. The way tiny goosebumps form on her skin. Even the way she smells—like fresh strawberries, dripping with sweetness—it's all getting to me.

I can't keep my eyes off her face.

That sweet, angelic face.

Angel wings are fitting for her. The feathers are pretty and delicate. They're sweet. Innocent.

I'm attracted to her—can't deny that. But it's more than that.

I want to protect her. The thought of hurting her is stressing me out. Everything inside me is screaming to be gentle with her. Be careful. Give her extra assurance and praise.

I take longer with the shading than normal. I want the tattoos to be perfect. And she's sitting like a champ. An hour goes by. Then two. Everything about her laying here on my table, getting her virgin skin marked by me, is perfect.

I wipe away some ink then gently squeeze her calf. "Almost done. You're doing so good, sitting so perfectly for me. Such a good girl."

A sharp little gasp of air whistles through her lips when I say it.

The sound makes my cock immediately react. Fuck, I didn't mean to say that out loud. But I did. And she liked it. That fact isn't encouraging my dick to soften.

Ignoring it, I finish up the shading and add a few white highlights.

"All done," I say, giving a final wipe to make sure the skin is clean and all the lines are crisp and beautiful before I show her.

She squeals, "Oh my god!" when I hold up the mirror for her. "They are exactly what I wanted. I love them. Thank you."

Her smile lights up her face.

That face. Big, green eyes and pouty lips, her delicate chin, with the faintest spattering of freckles across her cheeks and the bridge of her refined nose—she really is stunning.

The exuberance in her smile is infectious and I smile back.

I never smile. I sometimes smirk or grin in amusement, but she has me full-on, face-splitting, cheek-hurting smiling.

Fuck is wrong with me?

I apply ointment over her freshly inked skin, cover the tattoos with Tegaderm, and go over aftercare instructions with her. Then I wait outside the room so she can get dressed and I can walk her out since everyone has already left for the night.

"How much do I owe you?" she asks when she comes out.

Her cheeks are still a pretty rose color and I will not let my mind wander to the fact that now I know what shade of pink she turns when her whole body is flushed.

"This one's on me."

"Oh! No. I mean, I didn't come here expecting... I can pay."

"I know. Consider it a graduation present. Plus, you're going to design my next tattoo for me, so I'm the one getting the better deal here."

"But—"

"It's already done. I'm not taking your money."

"Noah." Her eyes are narrowed at me and I'm sure she would be infuriated to learn that instead of being intimidating, she looks even cuter.

I like how she says my name. I like how her voice drops a little lower on the 'o' part. And, no, I am not thinking about her little breathy moans combined with 'ohs' now. I'm not.

"Let me give you this gift. Please."

Livvy looks up at me with those big, beautiful eyes. "Okay. I —" She blinks rapidly. "Thank you."

She lifts up onto her tiptoes and before I register what's happening, her arms are around my shoulders. Instinctively, my hands go to her waist. Then she presses against my chest, hooking her elbows around my neck at the same time I wrap my arms around her, ratcheting her closer.

Her body melts against mine as I exhale.

I can't remember that last time I was hugged. Genuinely hugged. Years. Probably at the funeral.

It's a peace, a comfort, a softness I miss. So I let myself enjoy this feeling and the scent of strawberries in her hair a few moments longer than I ought to.

♥ ♥ ♥

ANG3L:

Can I ask you for some advice? I need a guy's perspective

2HORNED:

Of course

ANG3L:

And don't bullshit me, be brutally honest

2HORNED:

That's a lot of pressure for 9am on a Saturday morning, but shoot

I like that she's coming to me for this, whatever it is. It feels like I'm her person. Or, at least, one of them. I want to be her person.

ANG3L:

There's this guy I like and I want to get his attention without being obvious I'm trying to get his attention. If you know what I mean

I take it back. I don't like that she's coming to me for this. I don't like it at all. And I don't know who "this guy" is but I already hate him. Irrational? Sure. It's not like she and I are dating.

She's not mine. But in some ways, she's more mine than anyone else in my life is. And I'm hers.

I'm, pathetically, all hers.

> **2HORNED:**
> You want my real advice?

ANG3L:
Duh

> **2HORNED:**
> The best way to get his attention is to stop trying to get his attention. Forget about him. Move on. Be yourself. Be happy. Hang out with friends. Go out with guys who do give you attention.

ANG3L:
Forget about him? That's easier said than done. It's been years and I can't shake this crush

> **2HORNED:**
> It's not your job to make someone want you. He'll either take notice or he won't. And if he doesn't, he's not the right guy.
>
> And, I hate to be this guy, but you said you wanted brutal honesty. Guys are generally straightforward. If it's been years and he hasn't shown interest, it's probably because he's not interested

ANG3L:
Oh

> **2HORNED:**
> I'm sorry

ANG3L:
It's okay. That's what I needed. Thank you

Was telling her to move on from the guy she likes a little self-serving? Maybe. But it was still good advice. It's advice I should probably take myself. Move on.

I've been focused on my career and growing my shop the last five years. I haven't had a girlfriend in about that amount of time, too—fuck, I haven't even had sex in over a year. And being enamored with a conveniently unavailable stranger on the internet definitely hasn't helped motivate me to want to go out and meet someone.

I want to meet someone. In theory.

I also don't want to at all.

And yet, when I close up the shop a little after eleven—a bit early for a Saturday night—I find myself wandering over to the bar next door. Wood would be proud. I'm putting myself out there.

I stand back against the wall, away from all the people.

Baby steps.

It's better in the shadows—away from the strobe lights on the dance floor, not that I dance, and away from the speakers blasting remix after remix until the beat echoes in your eardrums. It really is a terrible place to meet and talk to anyone.

Almost everyone here looks coupled up already, minus a few groups and a couple guys standing by themselves around the bar. A large group of women with pink sashes and tiaras are taking shots, all huddled around one in a white sash, signaling the bride-to-be.

This was a bad idea.

I should go upstairs to my apartment. I can have a drink there for free without the headache or having to navigate a crowd of drunk idiots.

But then I spot Livvy behind the bar. A little beacon of sunshine, bright-eyed and flashing a big, toothy smile at everyone she talks to. It's not the same smile she gave me last night after getting her tattoo. It's tinged with something else I can't quite put my finger on.

Whatever it is, I don't like it. The muscles in my neck tighten.

And even though she's surrounded by customers, and I know she's busy working, I start walking toward her. Just to say hi. Order a drink. I can ask her how her tattoos are feeling so far.

But when I make it to the bar, I can't even get close to the end she's tending. It's backed up three rows deep. I wedge myself into a seat at the other end.

"Hi, stranger." Riley sidles across from me, already getting a highball glass down from the rack. "Gin and tonic?"

"And that's why you're my favorite bartender."

"Mm hm." He rolls his eyes as he loudly plunks ice into my glass. "That's why you've been eyeing Livvy this whole time."

I'd like to deny that, but I can't. So I grunt noncommittally instead. "How's she doing?"

"Hunny, it's her first weekend shift. She's overwhelmed. But she's handling it well."

I sip my gin, that feeling in my neck and shoulders gnawing away at me again. It's Livvy's smile. It's forced. And around the corners, it's starting to slip.

Even though Bex is with her at that end of the bar, the crowd of people waiting for drinks keeps growing. She pours one drink for every three Bex does, and there's way too much head on her beer pours.

On top of that, several of the men seem to be trying to get her to chat with them. She's got a great figure and a cute face—beautiful, actually. It's no wonder she's getting a lot of attention, but my brothers in Christ, she's working. She's being nice because it's her job, not because she's interested in you.

One of the guys, camping out on a stool in front of her, hands her some cash. She takes it, smiling and mouths "thank you" and he reaches out with his other hand and touches her elbow.

My stomach lurches.

Something inside me wants to growl *don't touch her*. But on the outside, I remain still and stoic. Watching.

He pulls his hand away after a second. My jaw hurts and I realize I've been clenching it.

It's not my style to butt into situations or play the white knight. I know women can handle themselves for the most part. Hell, Bex is more likely to punch someone for touching her sister than I am. But I wouldn't hesitate to lay a fucker out if I need to.

Maybe I'll go tell one of the bouncers to keep an eye on that guy, just in case he gets any more handsy or decides to wait around outside after the girls get off their shift.

I scan around the place for the younger, real muscle-y one. Mark, I think is his name.

Riley slides another gin and tonic in front of me. I hadn't realized I'd emptied my first one.

"Thanks," I say as I stand, taking my drink with me.

I slink back into the shadows to finish my drink in the corner where it's a little quieter.

My eyes keep going back to her. Livvy. That same guy is still sitting at the bar, nursing the same beer. I obviously can't leave until he does.

Does that mean I might be standing here watching them all night? I will if I need to.

It's called brooding.

I'm just being protective. She brings out the primal need in me for whatever reason. It's probably those round eyes and pouty lips. She's too pure. Too pretty. Too precious and trusting.

I push thoughts of my younger brother out of my head. I couldn't protect him, but I will protect her.

So I sip my drink and keep watching.

CHAPTER 5

LIVVY

The sink or swim analogy turned out to be prophetically appropriate, because, similarly to swimming, I am terrible at bartending.

I confused a mojito with a mai tai—but that could happen to anyone, right?

Right?

I ran out of limes and had to go steal some from Riley. I got beer all over my jeans when I spilled one on the counter. The only reason the guy wasn't pissed is because he got a free drink out of it and then was distracted looking down my shirt when I had to lean over the bar to clean it up. Actually, it's Bex's shirt. I don't own any tank tops this small.

I'm tired of smiling. I'm tired of being asked when I get off later. Three out of four times that question is accompanied by an extra off-putting eyebrow wiggle.

Bex told me to be flirty—it gets you better tips—but to also hold my ground and not take shit. I'm supposed to signal one of the bouncers, Dan or Mark, if anyone gets unmanageable.

"How're you doing?" Bex asks, carrying a fresh bin of limes to my station.

I give her an unconvincing thumbs up.

"It takes a little while to get the hang of it. You're doing great," she says, then immediately turns and starts taking drink orders.

"Hey. You there." A guy in a jacket and thinning hair snaps at me. Literally, snaps his fingers to get my attention.

I keep a big smile plastered on my face. "Hi there. What can I get you?"

"Finally. I've been waiting here for ten minutes."

"Yeah. It's busy here on a Saturday night." I shrug and offer a little giggle to lighten the mood.

He rolls his eyes. "Whatever, sweetheart. Can I just get a fucking beer?"

"Sure. What kind do you want?"

"I don't care. Whatever you have on tap that's not too hoppy."

Fuck.

"Um. The Sam Adams Summer Ale is pretty popular—"

"I ask for not hoppy and she's offering me an IPA. Un-fucking-believable." He looks over and around me to the other end of the bar and raises his voice. "Can I get some help from someone who actually knows what they're doing?"

"Is there a problem over here?" Bex asks, her customer service voice extra on point and the dimple in her left cheek on full display.

"Yeah." He throws up his hands. "A bartender who doesn't know the first thing about beer."

My throat might as well be full of cotton as I try to swallow.

"Just give me whatever lager you have on tap," the man sneers.

Bex nods over to me. "The Boston," she says, then turns back to him. "It's her first week. Giver her a break."

"Maybe hire someone who isn't an idiot, then. Or learn how to train them."

My blood is coursing fast and hard through my body. I pause filling the beer glass to search through the crowd for a bouncer.

Luckily, Mark is standing between me and the dance floor and we make brief eye contact.

I put up three fingers, our signal that we need assistance, and he strides toward me immediately.

When I glance back at Bex, she has both hands planted on the bar, eyes deadlocked on the guy. "How about you go have a time out and think? Come back when you can act like a big boy with manners."

The guy scoffs, blinking dumbly for a moment before he can speak. "You can't talk to me like that. I'm the customer."

"You're not anymore. I'm not serving you."

"You can't do that."

"We reserve the right to not serve assholes," Bex says, smile still in place but a different kind of smile altogether.

He turns a shade of purple I've never seen before. Just as he opens his mouth, Mark taps him on the shoulder.

"Sounds like you've been told to leave," Mark says with a bored expression. "I can assist you with that if you need it."

The man goes to retort, but promptly thinks better of it when he sees Mark's arms crossed over his chest, his biceps the circumference of basketballs.

"You know what, just forget it. See if I ever come to this bar again." He storms off and Mark follows him out.

Bex yells after them, "And the Sam Adams is a wheat ale, not an IPA, dumbass."

I'm shaking, the adrenaline subsiding, heat replaced by ice cold sweats.

Before I realize what's happened, the glass I've just filled with beer slips and crashes to the floor. Liquid splashes on our feet and legs. Jagged shards of glass spread everywhere.

I forgot I'd been holding it.

"Oh my god, I'm so sorry!" I look around for something, I don't know what—I can't remember where any of the towels are.

My eyelids sting and my vision blurs and I'm breathing too fast.

"It's okay, it happens," Bex says.

Riley rushes over. "Don't move. Let me get the dustpan and clean up this glass."

"I'm sorry," is all I can say. Hot tears hit both my cheeks.

"Don't worry about it. It's not a big deal," Bex reassures me with a smile.

Riley comes out and starts sweeping up the glass along with one of the barbacks who's ready with a mop.

"How about you go take one of your breaks? Go get some fresh air. We'll take care of this," Bex says with a nod.

I look around the crowded bar. People are standing around, gawking, restless, waiting to be served. "Are you sure?"

"We've got this," Riley says.

"Take however long you need," Bex adds.

I push out the back door into the darkness of the alley behind the bar. A singular fixture splashes yellow light across the brick building. Traffic buzzes in the distance.

And I finally let out the sob I've been holding in.

The air is cool against my skin. It's the first week of June, but not quite summer. I'm thankful for it. The breeze feels nice as it dries my tears.

"Hey."

His voice makes me jump and turn abruptly. I recognized it instantly, but it's still surprising to see him standing there by the door. Noah.

He's dressed all in black. The solitary light casts harsh shadows across his face giving him an eerily similar look to the skull tattooed on his throat.

I wipe my eyes with my wrists. "Oh. Hi."

"I'm sorry, I didn't mean to startle you. I saw you come out here and I just wanted to make sure you're okay. And, I don't know, I didn't like the idea of you being out here alone, in the alley at midnight."

"You're right. I should probably go back inside now. Thank you, but I'm okay." I muster the best smile I can.

He steps closer, lowering his head, brows knitted together. "Are you sure?"

Guess that smile was unconvincing.

Another tear slips down my face. Damnit.

"Yes. No." An unhinged little giggle escapes my throat. "I don't think I'm cut out to be a bartender."

He reaches over and brushes his thumb across my cheek, catching my last tear. My chest tightens at the contact.

"I think you were doing all right," he says quietly.

My stomach drops realizing he witnessed my catastrophe.

"I don't want to go back in there," I say, my voice quivering an embarrassing amount.

We're somehow even closer. I look up at him and a chill twists its way down my limbs.

"Then don't," he says.

"I can't. I kind of need this job, and Bex stuck her neck out for me, and—"

"Bex will be fine, and you can find another job. Something you'll like better."

I don't know what to say, so instead of saying anything I just start crying harder.

"Shh." Noah's deep tone is low and before I know it, he's pulled me against him, fingers in my hair holding my head to his chest.

And I cry, I cry into Noah Dixon's chest like a little baby, and I don't know if I'm more embarrassed or relieved. But it feels good. He feels good. Solid.

After a few minutes, the tears subside.

Noah strokes my hair. "Would you want to come work for me instead?"

"What?" I look up at him.

He's staring intensely down at me. Mouth fixed. No hint of laughter or joking. "I've been looking for a second person to work the front desk for a while. Taryn's been taking more and more clients."

I'm not sure how to respond. "You're offering me a job?"

"If you want it, yes."

♥   ♥   ♥

So, I'm starting a new job.

Again.

Is it a bad idea to be working for the man who was the subject of all my sexual awakening fantasies through puberty? Probably, yes.

Should I stop staring at him from across the shop as he's tattooing and focus on what Taryn is saying? Also, probably, yes.

But the way the muscles in his back move and the way his triceps flex as he works is mesmerizing. The line of his thick neck, covered in tattoos—the way they highlight the sharp angle of his jaw, the way he's deep in concentration, such a stern expression, and yet his mouth is still softly downturned—it's all too much.

Taryn tucks a lock of bright blue hair behind her ear and sighs. "I'm going to go get a coffee, then I have someone coming in for a bridge piercing." She looks at me with half-lidded eyes and a blank expression. "If someone walks in, maybe stop staring at the boss long enough to help them?"

My face goes hot. And knowing she can see the color in my cheeks makes it worse.

"I wasn't—"

She rolls her eyes. "Bet." Then walks out the door, the little bell clanking against the glass.

"Don't let Taryn intimidate you," a guy in a red muscle tank says, elbows on the counter, leaning over as he steals a pen from me.

He's one of the tattoo artists but we haven't met yet.

"She's kind of a bitch to everyone. Until you get to know her. I mean, she's still a bitch after you get to know her, too, but—" He scratches behind his ear where his hair is buzzed and squints an eye. "I forgot where I was going with that. I'm Anthony, by the way."

He reaches over the counter, and I shake his hand.

"Olivia—or Livvy. Everyone calls me Livvy, except for my mother."

"That's a pretty name for a pretty girl."

I laugh it off like a joke, but he doesn't laugh with me. Still shaking my hand and staring at me unblinkingly.

"Thanks," I say, ending the handshake.

"Shouldn't you be working?" Noah's low voice pulls my attention away, but his dark gaze is fixed on Anthony.

Anthony shrugs with a light-hearted grin. "Hey, I was just waiting on my next client."

"Go wait somewhere else."

"You got it, boss." He gives me a sly wink. "Later, Livvy."

Anthony walks back to his station and then Noah's eyes are on me, dark and sunken in shadow, they almost look black.

"Feel free to tell Anthony to fuck off if he's bothering you." His voice is rougher than normal when he says it, his mouth set in a hard line.

"Oh no, he wasn't bothering me."

Noah's scowl deepens. "I was wondering if you could help me with something. A project." His expression is unchanging.

"Sure. What kind of project?"

He hands me an iPad I hadn't noticed he was holding until right now, then comes around to sit next to me. "I haven't had the time to update my digital portfolio in a while." He opens his current portfolio of work and then a second folder filled with hundreds of photos. "I was wondering if you could replace some of the older ones with my newer work. It needs to show my range in styles and subjects, but not be too overwhelming for new clients to look through."

"Yeah, I can do that."

I start scrolling through the photo album, pretending my ears aren't getting warm from his nearness and the scent of his cologne.

"Noah, these are so good. All of them are fantastic. This is actually going to be challenging," I say with a light laugh.

His eyes soften and his lips part so subtly it's barely noticeable.

"Seriously, the drawing skills needed for some of these is amazing."

"Thanks," he says, rubbing the back of his head, his little smirk growing.

"I mean it. Half the people in my fine arts program didn't have talent like this."

"You studied fine arts?" He tilts his head as he leans in even closer, a lopsided grin playing on his lips.

"Oh, um, yes?"

"Yes?" He chuckles. "What kind of art do you do? What medium?"

"I mostly focused on oil painting, oil pastels, charcoal drawing."

"Now I really want to see in that sketchbook."

Heat blossoms in my cheeks, and I really wish it would stop doing that already.

If he notices, he doesn't say anything. But he has to notice because he's looking right at me, not even sitting a foot away. He twists one of the rings on his fingers.

"Do you have a favorite painting?" he asks.

His eyes are like the night sky.

"Livvy?"

Shit. His question, right. *Stop being awkward as fuck, Livvy.*

"I don't have a favorite one, no. I love so many. But the most famous one I like is The Kiss by Gustav Klimt. It's in Vienna. I'd love to go see it one day. Do you have a favorite painting or piece of art?"

Great, now I'm rambling. Is my face getting hotter? Fuck.

He shakes his head. "No. But now I feel like I need to figure that out." He chuckles.

Before he has a chance to ask me anything else and add to what is certainly my beet-red complexion, I pick up the iPad and start scrolling. "What's your favorite tattoo you've done?"

"Hm." He runs a tattooed finger along his sharp jaw. "Probably this half sleeve I did a few months back. I'll show you." He takes the iPad and swipes to the right spot in the gallery then hands it back.

It's a forest of black trees with twisted roots exposed. But on closer look, the shapes and shadows of the gnarled tree roots form eerie skulls.

"That is gorgeous. And creepy. I love it."

He laughs, a low rumble in his chest. "Thanks, it was a fun piece."

His arm brushes mine as he scrolls through more pictures, showing me the ones he's most proud of, telling me stories of past clients—both funny and horrific.

Slowly, everyone else trickles out of the shop but I've barely noticed the time passing. I can't believe it's already eleven at night. I could listen to him talk for hours.

"What's your least favorite thing you've tattooed?" I ask.

He groans. "Probably any pinup I've ever done. I dread those."

"Why?" I see a couple on the screen. "These look good."

"I don't want anything I do to be good. I want it to be great. It's the whole body proportions and the perfect position. It's never exactly right. Even when I trace a reference, any slight tweak or change in lighting can throw it off. They're the bane of my tattooing existence. In fact, I have a pin-up scheduled next week. I'm dreading the fuck out of it."

"Anatomy can be challenging. The most helpful thing I found for figure drawing is using real life models. I had a class where almost the whole semester was devoted to drawing live, nude models."

He raises an eyebrow, and a silly little laugh escapes my lips. I should stop talking.

"That sounds...interesting," he says with a devilish grin.

"It was really only weird the first twenty minutes or so, then you sort of forget there's a naked person in front of you, and you're just focused on the drawing and the form. It's really the best way to learn—drawing the same position from slightly different angles, figuring out how people sit and lean and slouch."

"Always nude?" he asks.

"Yeah. Clothes hide too much. You need to be able to see the musculature and things like where the hip bone sits in relation to the spine."

I glance at him and he's watching me, his cheek leaning against his hand. Those eyes surrounded by dark lashes are pulling me in again.

"So, I should find some nude models? Got it," he says with a grin. "Maybe that should be my new pick-up line at the bar."

I smile and nod, but at the same time, a knot forms in my stomach. I hate it. Even just the mention of it as a joke. Was he joking? He was probably joking. Hopefully.

I'm being stupid, I know. He's been with women, obviously. And he's seen them naked. But the idea of him seeking out someone new—of drawing them—irks me. Even though it's irrational.

"I'll pose for you." The words are out of my mouth before I even think them.

What are you doing, Livvy?

He looks at me, a tiny crease between his brows. Blood is rocketing through my veins.

"Really?" he asks.

"Yeah. Why not?"

Why not? What the actual fuck, Livvy?

He licks his bottom lip and there's silence for a beat. Then another. Oh my god what did I do?

"Okay," he says, low. "When were you thinking?"

I want to scream, *I wasn't thinking!* But instead, I say, as cooly as possible, "When's the next night we both have off?"

He stills, mouth slightly open. Me too, Noah. Me too.

"Uh, Thursday, I think," he says.

"Thursday, then," I say.

"All right," he says, nodding.

And we just kind of look at each other and he's so beautiful and I think I'm going to throw up.

The chime of the bell breaks the stillness in the air.

We look toward the door at the same time, not expecting anyone this late on a Monday night. In fact, we should have locked up half an hour ago.

Mark, the bouncer from the bar, walks in, giving me a small smile and a wave.

"The fuck?" Noah mutters under his breath.

"Oh!" Right. Shoot! I completely forgot. "Hi," I say, standing up.

Noah stands with me, that crease between his brows deepening.

"Hey, you ready?" Mark asks.

"Yep."

Noah leans in and whispers, "What's going on?"

"He's picking me up for a date."

Mark had shyly come up to me Saturday after I said I was quitting and asked for my number.

"A date?" Noah checks the time. "Isn't it a little late for a date? On a Monday?"

I glance at my phone. It's eleven-thirty. Exactly when he said he'd swing by after his shift at the bar.

I shrug. "It's late, but we both work at night, so that's how it worked out."

It's almost like a shadow passes over Noah's face, the way his expression darkens.

"What are you even going to do at eleven-thirty on a first date?"

"What's with all the questions?" I peek over at Mark, who's still standing by the door, shifting onto the balls of his feet and looking around the shop. "Hey, sorry, I'll be right there!" I call over to him.

I lower my voice. "He's going to cook me some food at his place," I say to Noah.

"You're going to his place?" he hisses.

I cross my arms.

"Sorry," he says. "It's just—it's just that I want you to be safe. I feel protective over you. It's hard not to see you as that little girl I first met."

Ouch.

"I'm not a little girl. I can take care of myself," I say, trying not to dwell on how much that sentence sounds like something a defiant child would say.

"You're right. You're an adult. I know that. I'm sorry."

I pick up my bag from under the desk and move toward Mark but as I pass Noah, he grabs my arm. Not hard, but firm enough to stop me in my tracks.

He leans down, his breath at my cheek and lips at my ear. "Call me. If you need anything. For any reason. Any time. Got it? I gave you my number, right?" He looks into my eyes, his face all angles and hard lines.

I'm not breathing. I nod. "Okay," I say as I exhale.

He lets go of my arm.

Mark holds the door open for me, and as I walk out, I look back over my shoulder to where Noah is still watching me. The intensity in his stare makes me shiver.

CHAPTER 6

NOAH

So how are things going with that guy you like?

ANG3L:

The same, mostly

Oh! But I did take your advice and go out on a date with someone else

'm instantly gutted. I hate that I can't just be happy for her. Wood likes to remind me that I'm avoiding a real connection by putting so much energy into this one. But this is real for me. I'd be happy to stay home and chat with her every night.

And I'm sad she doesn't feel the same.

2HORNED:

Oh?

ANG3L:

Yeah, he's really nice

Sucker punch.

2HORNED:

Cool. How did it go?

Please say it was terrible. Horrible. Boring. Just sort of okay. Anything but that it was great and you had amazing sex.

ANG3L:

It was fine

2HORNED:

Just fine?

ANG3L:

Yeah. I mean, it was okay. I had a nice time and he's nice, but we didn't have much to talk about so it was a little awkward at times

2HORNED:

I see. Was there a goodnight kiss?

I have instant regret. Why the fuck did I ask that?

ANG3L:

Yes, actually

Absolutely did not want to know that. I'd have rather been slapped in the face. Should I ask her how it was? Congratulate her? How the fuck did I get here?

ANG3L:

But there was no chemistry. No sparks

2HORNED:

No nothing?

ANG3L:

Nope

2HORNED:

That's too bad

I'm grinning from ear to ear.

A knock at my office door pulls my attention away from my phone. Livvy opens the door just enough to poke her head in.

"Your four o'clock appointment is here," she says in her soft voice.

"Great. Tell them I'll be right out."

She nods and shuts the door.

> **2HORNED:**
>
> Does the guy you like know about the date?

> **ANG3L:**
>
> Yes, he does. And he was not happy about it. But not because he was jealous, he thought I wasn't being safe. I think he thinks of me like a little sister

> **2HORNED:**
>
> Fuck. That sucks.

That reminds me, I need to ask Livvy how her date with Mark the body builder went. They can't have anything in common, right? Like, what would they even talk about? She's so sweet and smart and likes art history and he looks like his deepest thoughts are about whether the chocolate or peanut butter protein powder flavor is the best.

I'm being judgmental, I know. I don't know why. I'm sure he's nice. Sometimes I wish I was nice. He just doesn't seem right for her.

> **ANG3L:**
>
> What should I tell him about the date if he asks?

> **2HORNED:**
>
> Tell him it was great

Jimmy's a regular so I tell him to head on down to my station when I get out to the lobby.

Livvy smiles up at me from the front desk and I try to return it in as naturally as possible.

But acting natural around her these last two days has been impossible, because every time I talk to her, or pass her, or see her in my periphery, or even just think her name, I'm thinking about her naked.

I mean, I'm not imagining her naked, but thinking about how I'm going to see her naked. It feels like kind of a big deal, but she's acting like it's no big deal, so I can't act like it's a big deal either. Right?

"Hey," I say. "Thanks for the work you did updating my portfolio. It looks great."

"Thanks. It was fun." She smiles so sweetly and she's so damn pretty.

"How's it going up here? Good? No problems?"

"No problems." She's probably wondering why I'm hovering.

I'm stalling. Fuck.

"So...uh..." I clear my throat. "We still on for tomorrow?"

"Oh, yeah. I was thinking around nine? Bex will be working so we'll have a good few hours of privacy." She looks up at me with those big, innocent hazel eyes.

A few hours?

My cock throbs of its own volition and I slide my hands into my jean pockets so my now half-chub isn't noticeable.

"Cool," I say. See, she's chill. I'm chill.

I should get back to work.

"Oh," I say as I turn to go to my station. "I forgot to ask...how did your date go with Mark?"

Her face lights up at my question and now I wish I'd never asked.

"It was great!" she says.

It was fucking great?

"Great." I nod and smile through clenched teeth and walk away.

But the entire rest of the day I'm in a weird mood. I'm irritable. Distracted.

I keep glancing toward the front where she's sitting and trying not to think about tomorrow. But every time I try not to think about her naked, I think about her naked.

♥ ♥ ♥

She's naked under that robe.

It's obvious the instant Livvy opens the door. I knocked at two minutes after nine because it took me three minutes to work up to it.

Her silk robe is thin and clings to the curve of her hips and breasts and pebbled nipples...

Fuck. *Look at her face, jackass.*

"Hi," I say.

"Come on in." She steps aside so I can enter and closes the door behind me. "Macy's asleep, so we need to be a little quiet."

I nod and follow her through the living room, down the hall, and into a bedroom, hands stuffed in my pockets, heart pounding like a bass drum the whole time.

I close the door behind us, latching it softly. The room is dim, only lit by a few candles scattered throughout the space and the ambient light from the night sky through the window.

"Is this all right?" she asks, playing with the sash of her robe.

My throat constricts as I try to swallow. "Yeah. This is good. Are you—are you good with this?"

"Of course." There's a slight wobble in her voice but she's smiling.

Maybe I imagined it.

"My easel is all set up here." She walks over to the corner by a bookshelf, and I follow. "There's plenty of paper," she continues, "and different pencils—I didn't know if you had a lead preference

—and some charcoals if you want to use those. Have you used charcoals before? They're my favorite for figure drawing. I mean, if you *want* to use this stuff, it's here, but you don't *have* to use it. Sorry, I'm rambling."

I chuckle, glad I'm not the only one who's a little nervous. "You're fine, Livvy. I brought my iPad to sketch on if that's okay."

Her cheeks turn pink when I say her name.

I like that.

"No, yeah, that's great. Perfect." She breaks our eye contact and goes to the easel. "Sorry, I was painting earlier and didn't get it totally cleaned up." She takes a canvas off the easel and sets it on the floor facing the wall then moves some oil paints and a jar of mineral spirits to the side.

I want to see what she's been working on, but I stay quiet.

"Is there enough light for you?" she asks, placing another candle next to the easel. "I thought the softer light might be more relaxing, and I wouldn't be so...um...on display, but I can turn the overhead light on if you want."

She strikes a match along the edge of the box, but it doesn't light. Again, with a slight tremble in her hand, and no flame.

"No, this is nice." I take the matchbox from her, our fingertips brushing as she hands me the unspent match. "Whatever makes you most comfortable."

I strike the match and light the candle, then shake it, watching the orange flame die out to be replaced by a wisp of smoke. It lingers in the air between us.

"Should we get started?" she whispers.

I nod, the word *yes* getting caught in my throat.

But neither of us makes a move. She twists the end of the robe tie, looking down at the silky fabric between her fingers. I have that urge to comfort her again. I step toward her and reach out to touch her shoulder but stop short.

She looks up at me with her round eyes, her pupils dilated in the dim light.

"How about we warm up for a bit, with the robe on?" I say.

"Okay," she says quietly, a smile growing on her lips. The sight of it makes something flutter in my chest.

Livvy sits on the bed, then tucks her feet up and scoots back, bouncing a little on the mattress, a soft little giggle escaping her lips.

I'm not noticing her tits bounce, too. I'm *not noticing her tits bounce.* And I'm *definitely not* imagining jumping on the bed with her, making her bounce and laugh even more. Tell that to my cock which is already twitching.

I take out my iPad and stylus and open my sketching app, stealing glances at Livvy trying to get into a comfortable pose.

I don't wait for her to settle. I start sketching. Her profile, the slope of her nose, her jaw. The line of her back, her hair. Her smile.

She looks up at me. "Hey, you're not supposed to start, I'm not ready yet!" But there's laughter in her voice and my chest vibrates with my own deep chuckle.

I try to capture this expression, the one where she's trying to look serious, lips parted in frustration, but her eyes are bright, happy.

I can't do it justice.

Finally, she settles in a spot, legs tucked in, hands in her lap. "Okay, now you can start. For real," she says with a forced scowl.

It makes me smile. "Got it."

I start a new blank page and start sketching out her form, trying to keep it loose. Just warming up. Reminding myself it doesn't have to be perfect.

"Stop squirming," I say.

She bites her lips, shoulders bouncing. "I'm sorry, it's hard to sit still this long." She stretches an arm and tilts her head from side to side, her neck looking delicate and soft.

Fuck.

I start a new page as she repositions herself, this time with her back to me, legs bent off to one side. But when I look back up, she's slipping the robe down her shoulders.

My heart pounds.

The silk falls off her shoulders and down her back, puddling around her waist.

She's still and I don't dare move or break the quiet.

The warm candlelight flickers and dances on her skin, every curve and line. So smooth, so pretty.

She turns her head to rest her chin on her bare shoulder, finally glancing at me. "I'm ready," she says, her voice low and huskier than usual.

I can't figure out what it is about her—this thing that makes me act like I've never had a naked woman in front of me before. Hell, I can only see her back and bare shoulders and it's like I've just discovered girls don't have cooties. Looking at her like this and the way my body physically reacts to her, feels wrong. Maybe that's what it is. The forbidden.

I need to be professional. She's Bex's little sister and now my employee. Fuck.

So I put my head down and sketch. She's shapes and lines and shadows—not a gorgeous naked woman with perfect lips I just want to—

This time when I look back up at her, she's pulled the robe away from around her waist. Still facing away from me, she tosses it casually to the floor.

I keep my eyes trained on her hair and her shoulders, not letting them trail down the crevice of her spine to her...

No, I will remain respectful.

Respectfully admiring her perfect ass.

Fuck.

She looks over her shoulder. "What position do you want me in?"

My dick swells and does she have no idea what she's doing to me right now?

She looks at me with those big eyes and pouty lips, the soft light glowing all around her painting the most angelic picture I've ever seen.

No, no she has no idea what she's doing to me. I can think of many positions I'd like to put her in, and they are all very bad. Bad for many reasons.

I shake the images out of my mind.

"Whatever is most comfortable for you." I keep my expression calm, my voice level and detached.

"Okay," she says.

I fidget with the stylus as she gets into position, keeping my head down while the sounds of her sliding against the duvet and the vague movement of her limbs in my periphery pull at my resolve.

"How's this?" she asks.

I look up.

Holy fuck.

It's like all the air has left my lungs and I can't figure out how to take another breath.

She's stretched out on the bed, feet dangling over the edge. I can't take my eyes off her. Up her legs to the soft lines of her stomach and the curve of her hips. The perfect place to grip onto.

Stop imagining digging your fingertips into her, Noah. Jesus.

"It's good," I choke out.

She smiles and looks out the window. Serene. She's still and I'm still. Except for the slight bounce in her breasts every time she breathes. I might not have noticed but her breaths are coming more rapidly.

Me too, Livvy. Me too.

"You're beautiful," I say.

She turns, lips parted. Her chest heaves. That was a stupid thing to say. I was trying to make her feel more at ease.

"Thank you," she says.

"I mean it. Gorgeous."

Get a fucking grip.

I'm making an ass out of myself. I create a new page and start to block out her figure. Map out the shapes. Get the lines right, the angles.

Her breasts are fucking perfect and it's not helping my hard-on subside. They're on the smaller side, perky, round little orbs with soft pink tips.

My mouth is watering.

Keep drawing.

I layer in shadows to give the shapes dimension. I work quickly, focusing on the proportions and trying not to linger too long on her thighs, the arch of her back, the fullness of her breasts, the shadowed area between her legs...

Her breathing has slowed. That's good.

Look away from her nipples, you creep.

Her face. I slow when I get to her face. I want to get it just right, the angle of her chin, her cute little nose, her round eyes and long lashes. Her pouty mouth. That mouth is too luscious, too soft to do it justice in any medium.

"How are you doing?" I ask.

"I'm good." Her voice is low and breathy, and I wish the lighting was just a little better so I could see any of the more subtle changes in her micro expressions.

"I'm done with this one. Do you want to change positions?"

"Oh good, my left butt cheek was falling asleep."

I don't miss the pink hue her chest and neck turn when she says it.

"Sorry, was that too much information?" She looks at the ceiling as she lets out a little high-pitched giggle.

"No, you're fine." I chuckle along with her. No, too much information would be telling her that the way her breasts jiggled when she laughed and the way her skin brightened has me imagining all sorts of scenarios where I'm the one making them bounce, but harder. I'm the one making her flush, but darker. I'm the one making her breathless.

I've been in a constant state of semi-arousal since I entered the apartment, but my erection is full on at the moment.

Maybe my celibacy is becoming a problem.

She twists to her right, facing me this time. I draw her again.

We take water breaks and talk a little here and there, both finally relaxed, but mostly we're quiet and I sketch and shade and get into the rhythm of it.

She shifts to a three-quarter view the next time. I draw her again. And again. I draw her hands. Her feet. Her backside. Her face. Her hair.

Her face again.

Each one with more detail, trying to get her likeness where I want it. Each time, falling just short of conveying her beauty.

The orange and honeysuckle scented candle next to me has gone liquid, warming my arm. My hand aches. But I don't want to stop.

"What time is it?" she asks, yawning.

"It's half past eleven." I had no idea that much time had passed. "One more?"

Livvy nods. "One more."

She was right, the nerves are gone and it's almost like we've forgotten that she's naked.

Almost.

I take a sip of water and glance over just as she's scooting up the bed. She shifts her legs from one side to the other and just for a second the candlelight catches on the prettiest, little pink lips between her legs.

Water goes down the wrong pipe and I cough and gasp for air.

"Are you okay?" Livvy asks.

I nod but I can't speak from the choking. My eyes are watering and I reach for my water bottle but instead I knock over her jar of mineral spirits, which splatters across the floor and up onto the wall at the same time my elbow smacks against the candle.

It all happens in slow motion but I can't stop it.

The candle falls, landing on the spilt mineral spirits and the carpet ignites into flames.

CHAPTER 7

LIVVY

"**F**uck!" Noah shouts.

"Oh my god!" I scramble off the bed.

The fire alarm screams to life, so shrill and high-pitched I can't even think straight.

Noah yanks the comforter off the bed and throws it over the fire. But the flames have spread to an area bigger than the blanket. I grab a pillow and try to stamp it out before it reaches to the door.

Smoke starts to fill the room.

The sprinkler heads in the ceiling rattle and then water pours down on us with a hiss.

"We've got to get out of here," Noah says. He gestures for me to follow him to the door, but I turn back to get my robe and phone from the other side of the bed.

Just as I snatch them up, Noah's tattooed arm snakes around my waist and he hoists me up over his shoulder. I shriek, clutching the robe against my body as my phone slips under my arm.

I lunge for it, narrowly catching it before it falls, but as I do my whole side smacks into the door frame as Noah carries me out of the room. There's a sickening thwap and crunching sound as I yelp.

My scream is drowned out by the blaring smoke alarm.

Macy runs out of her room, hair a mess of ringlets around her face as Noah rushes me out of the apartment.

"What is going on?" she yells when we get out into hall.

Noah sets me down as I frantically try to put my robe back on.

Macy averts her eyes.

"It's not what it looks like," I say, tying the robe tight, my face hot.

Noah runs off to the end of the hall, then darts back into the apartment wielding a fire extinguisher while Macy stares at me with crossed arms.

"There was an incident with the solvent for my oil paints and a candle," I say.

The alarm shuts off and Noah comes out, breathing heavily, soaking wet.

"It's out," he says. "The sprinklers had it mostly out and kept it from spreading."

Neighbors are filtering into the hallway, grouping up and starting to talk and point.

I shiver. The thin material of the robe clings to my wet skin, between my thighs to the valley of my breasts and my protruding nipples. I cover my chest with my arms.

"Fuck," Noah mutters under his breath as he undoes the buttons of his flannel shirt. He wraps it over my shoulders and closes it over me, brows furrowed, scowling.

I look up at him, not sure if I should say thank you or sorry.

And now he's standing here, shirtless, all long, lean muscle covered in black ink.

"I'm glad no one's hurt," Macy says, her voice shaking. She looks at me. "But you're not even supposed to be living with us. There are going to be questions. I'll get it sorted out but might be better if you're not around."

"We'll go to my place," Noah says.

"I'll text Bex," I add.

Macy nods. "I'll stay with Spencer tonight. You better get going before management shows up."

♥ ♥ ♥

I don't know what I expected Noah and Wood's apartment to look like, but it's not this. Not an industrial loft that looks like it came out of *Architectural Digest*.

The walls are weathered red brick that contrast against the sleek, concrete floors. The kitchen is a wall of flat, modern black cabinets with professional grade appliances and a huge stainless steel work island in front of them.

The living room furniture is all arranged perfectly in front of the giant black arched iron windows that stretch from floor to ceiling—which is at least twenty feet tall. A black metal staircase is silhouetted against the back wall, leading to a loft area above the kitchen.

It's dark except for the nightglow coming in from the three large arched windows. They overlook downtown Seattle to the left and Puget Sound to the right. The city lights barely compete with the reflection of the moon off the water.

Wood comes out of the hallway as we walk in.

"Hey." He stops abruptly, looking us up and down. "Wow, you two look...rough. What happened?"

"We'll explain later," Noah says. "The girls are going to be staying with us, at least for tonight."

"The girls?" Wood's light blue eyes widen. "Macy, too?"

"No, just me and Bex. Macy's staying at Spencer's."

Wood's shoulders droop. "Right. Yeah, that makes sense."

Noah places his hand lightly on the small of my back and leans in. "Let's get you out of those wet clothes and cleaned up. Do you want a shower?"

"That'd be great," I say. Not only does my hair have a slight smokey scent, but the water in those sprinklers had a distinct stale smell that I can't wait to wash off me.

"Bathroom's this way," Noah says. We walk past the kitchen to the hall. The bathroom is in the middle. "Wood's room is down there, door opposite of the bathroom is a closet, and my room is over here. You can sleep there tonight. I'll take the couch upstairs."

He flips the light on in the bathroom after I enter, his tall frame and broad shoulders filling out the doorway. "I'll get you some clean clothes and a towel. Let me know if you need anything else."

"Okay, thanks."

He backs away, hand on the doorknob.

"Oh, here," I say, unbuttoning his flannel shirt. I peel it off my shoulders and take it off with a little grunt, realizing how tender my side is.

It's wet and heavy and I grimace when I go to hand it to him.

He rushes in, dropping to a knee. "Are you hurt?" He searches my face, eyes wild.

"Only a little. I hit my side on the door when you were carrying me out of the room."

"Fuck." Noah's face goes pale. "I'm so sorry. I was in such a hurry to get you out of there—"

"It wasn't your fault. It was mine."

"Where are you hurt? Can I see it?"

I hesitate. I'll have to untie my robe to show him.

"I'm sorry, you don't have to—"

"No, it's okay," I say. I'm being silly. He's already seen me very naked at this point.

But as I untie my robe, it's different. Earlier, it was for art, all business. I was across the room—a room I made sure was very dimly lit. When I dropped my robe four hours ago, it was terrifying but empowering. I was filled with adrenaline and nerves, yet I felt like a goddess. Powerful.

This is another feeling altogether. He's inches from me in the bright white light bouncing off all the shiny surfaces of the bathroom. His gaze is heavy, hot on me as my heart beats hard.

I open one side of the robe, the air chilling my skin, one breast exposed, my nipple hardening instantly.

He sucks in a breath through his teeth.

I lift my arm with a quiet groan. "Here, along my ribs," I whisper.

"Shit." He gets closer, the worry deepening in his forehead. He looks up at me. "Liv," he whispers, "I'm so fucking sorry."

He brings a hand up to where my skin is already darkened and starting to purple, the tips of his fingers stopping just short of touching.

"Can I?" he asks.

I swallow and nod.

He brushes the spot gently. My breath catches.

"Does it hurt when I do this?" He presses the palm of his hand against my ribs.

"A little."

"And this?" He presses more firmly.

I whimper. "Yes."

"Fuck. Is it a sharp pain or dull?"

"Dull."

"That's good, I'd be worried if it were sharp. How about when you take a deep breath?"

I breathe in, filling my lungs, and shakily exhale. "No, not too much."

"Good, I don't think there's a break." He stands, but his fingertips linger on my side. He slides his hand down. Slowly. Barely touching until he reaches my hip bone, caressing over the angel wing. "Your tattoo is healing nicely."

His voice is thick and my pulse is so loud in my head I barely register his words.

"Oh. Right, yeah. They're doing good. Past the itchy stage and not much peeling."

He pulls his hand away, but my hip is burning where his fingers were.

We stand in the quiet of the small space for a moment. Him, still shirtless and me with my robe half open, no words, just eye contact. Fuck, he's so pretty.

His gaze flickers down to my mouth for a second, then lower before he looks away quickly.

"Let me get this water started for you." He turns, pulls back the shower curtain, the rings screeching against the rod, and turns the knob. Water pelts the tub, mist billowing into the air.

I'm anxious to get this sticky robe off. I start to disrobe as he shuffles out of the bathroom, eyes averted, the tips of his ears pink.

I step in as the door latches closed, letting the hot water cascade over my face. I wash my hair and body with his soap. It smells like him.

When I get out of the shower, a pair of his sweatpants and one of his T-shirts are folded on the counter next to a clean towel.

I'm wearing Noah Dixon's clothes, smelling of his soap, in his apartment. It's unreal.

I pad barefoot out of the bathroom to the main living area. Wood is in the kitchen. No Noah.

The doorbell buzzes and Wood opens it to Macy, standing in the hall with frazzled hair and a small bag.

"Mace," Wood says, his voice jumping an octave.

"Hi." She smiles, eyes shifting. "Um, can I stay here tonight?"

He moves aside, sweeping her inside. "Of course you can, girl."

"Thanks." She tucks a lock of hair behind her ears. "Spencer has an early surgery tomorrow and he really needs his full eight hours of sleep for it."

Wood takes her bag, and she stands in the living room, looking out the windows, her smile unmoving.

"It was silly, really, me bothering him this late at night. I should have known better. He's a surgeon. It's literally life and death. He has to be focused and dedicated. It's really what I love and admire about him."

I'm not sure if she's talking to us or herself at this point.

Noah comes out, hair wet, black sweats, shirtless, towel over his shoulders.

"Oh good, you're out of my bathroom," Wood says. He turns to Macy with a big, lopsided grin, his straight, white teeth bright against his tanned skin. "I'll go make up my bed for you with clean sheets and blankets so you can stay there tonight."

Macy doesn't turn to look at him. "Thank you, but I'd rather just sleep on the couch." Her usual sweet voice flat and filled with exhaustion. I can't blame her.

"Oh, right. Okay." Wood only looks crestfallen for a second before that smile is back, if less lopsided than before. "I'll go get you some blankets and a pillow. Do you like a more firm or soft pillow?"

"Whatever is fine." Macy slumps onto the couch, closing her eyes and rubbing at her temples.

Wood rushes off down the hall past Noah.

"Shit, I should change my bedding for you," Noah says, combing his fingers through his damp hair.

How do I say I don't mind sleeping in his used sheets that smell like him without sounding like a total weirdo? Right. I don't.

"I'll help you," I say.

"Nah, you stay here. I'll be right back."

He retreats as Wood reappears, carrying a heap of white bedding, his arms full up to his chin, and goes over to Macy, who's slumped down on the couch.

"I just brought both a firm and a softer pillow, so you have the option. And this heavy blanket is my favorite, but if it gets too warm there's this lighter one—"

"Wood. Thank you, but I can do it myself." She takes the blankets from him and shoos him off as she gets started laying them across the couch.

His smile droops, his attempts at being helpful foiled—again.

"Can I get you anything else?" he asks her.

"Just some quiet so I can sleep. I'm so tired."

"Got it—" Wood stops himself, then whispers, "Got it."

Macy lies down and pulls the blanket over her head.

Wood tiptoes over to the kitchen, fills a glass of water and grabs a banana then places both gingerly on the table next to Macy as she sleeps.

Wood points at me. "What do you like for breakfast?" he half asks, half mouths as he walks back to the kitchen.

"Um, I don't need anything special. Just whatever you have will be fine."

"No, no I'm putting in a grocery order right now." He holds up his phone with the app open. "What's your favorite? You're our guest."

"Oh. Okay, um...waffles?"

"Nice choice, girl," he whisper-yells and then does a silent, long-distance high five. "Don't leave me hanging, bro."

I complete it with a stifled laugh and he gives me an excited little fist pump.

"Liv." Noah's voice catches me off guard and I turn to him, standing in the hall, half in shadow. He beckons me over to him. "Ready for bed?"

"Night!" Wood whisper shouts as I follow Noah down the hall to his room.

He leads me inside and closes the door behind us.

Dark curtains are drawn over the large, floor-to-ceiling window. Only the light of the moon reflecting off the water shining through the small gap lights the room, washing everything in a hazy shade of gray—the concrete floors, his large bed pushed up against a chunky brick wall.

The bed is done up with light sheets, big pillows, and a fluffy charcoal comforter that's doubled over.

"This okay?"

"Yeah, thank you. I feel kind of bad kicking you out of your bed, though."

"Don't be. I'm the one who started the fire." He rubs the back of his neck, his biceps flexing. "Come on."

He folds the comforter back and looks at me through dark lashes, drawing me to him silently in the dark. And I go, slipping in between the sheets while my heartbeat thrums in my chest.

I get in gingerly, trying not to wince when I lie on my left side.

A growl rumbles in his chest.

He pulls the covers up to my chin and kneels next to the bed, tucking the blankets around my shoulders.

His face is so close to mine when he whispers, "Good night." His arm resting against mine.

I study the bump in his nose and the way his lower lip is plumper than the top.

The scent of his shampoo lingers in his hair and in his pillow under my head. I'm surrounded by him.

This is a chance, an intimate moment. It's moments like this I wish Angel wasn't just some internet persona. I wish I was her. She would say something funny, or sexy. Make him smile, lighten the mood, make him want to stay. But I'm not her. I'm me.

And all I can say is, "Good night," and watch him leave.

I blame rolling around in his sheets, on his mattress, snuggling into his pillow, and breathing in his scent all night for my dreams.

Every dream, Noah.

His eyes.

Watching me.

Smirking at me.

Touching my naked body.

And when a warm body slides into bed next to me, in my half-asleep fog, I roll toward him, cuddling up close.

Bex giggles. "Hello, there."

"Oh." I yawn and roll back to my side. "Sorry." I glance at my phone. It's after three in the morning.

"I didn't mean to wake you," she whispers.

"It's okay. I'm sorry about the fire. It was my oil paint—"

"Don't worry about it." She touches my shoulder. "Macy said it wasn't that bad. The sprinklers actually did more damage than the fire. That's what insurance is for. We'll figure it out. Besides, we were going to be looking for a new three-bedroom place anyway, right?"

"Right."

She's mostly shapes in the dark, but I can make out her blonde hair.

"Oh hey," she says, "we haven't shared a bed like this since we were little."

"We used to sleep together all the time."

"Yep. Like when you were six and you snuck into my room every night for a year because you were afraid ET was hiding in your closet." She laughs.

"Hey, he was terrifying." I still think he is if I'm being honest.

"I always thought he was cute."

"Nightmare fuel."

She shifts on her side to face me. "Speaking of cute... Mark was asking about you tonight at the bar."

Oh, right. Mark.

"He said he texted you after your date, but he hasn't heard back," she says casually.

Yikes.

"Yeah. I meant to reply but I've been busy."

"Date wasn't great?"

"It was...okay."

The bed bounces with Bex's silent laughter. "You're not feeling it. It happens. Don't worry about it. You're young. Date as much and as many people as you want. Play the field. Have fun. You don't owe anybody anything. Oh my god! You know what you should do?"

She scoots closer and leans up on her elbow.

"What?"

"You should totally go out with Wood. He's super nice, and he's crazy hot, and he hooked up with Bethany—who used to work at the bar—a little while back and she said he's amazing in bed. Like, life changing." She waggles her eyebrows at me.

I laugh. "Why don't *you* date him, then?"

She rolls onto her back and sighs. "Wood would be a fun little fling, but he's still in the revolving door stage of dating. It's fine for when you're still figuring out what you like, and as long as you go in with your eyes open, so you don't get hurt. But I think I'm past that part of my life. Noah started off my rebellion bad-boy phase. Do you remember? Mom hated him." She chuckles softly. "That was half of his appeal. I have love for him now, but he was kind of a shitty boyfriend at eighteen. He hasn't had any long-term girl-friends since we reconnected as far as I know, either, so maybe he still is. Anyway, Wood and I—even if he wanted something serious —I could never."

"Why not?"

She scoffs. "I mean, he's Noah's cousin. You never date an ex's family member, or a family member's ex. That's code."

A heavy feeling settles in my stomach. "Even though you and Noah dated so long ago and are cool with each other now?"

"Yep. There's no statute of limitations on that code. I mean, maybe if they weren't all that close—but they're not just cousins, they're roommates and best friends. It would be hella awkward. What if it worked out, and Wood and I got married, and we'd all know that the bride and best man have slept together? It'd be too weird."

I nod, even though she probably can't see.

She's right. If Noah and I hooked up, it could get extremely awkward. Worse, it might hurt her. He's my boss now, anyway. I really need to let go of this silly crush I have on him and move on.

Noah Dixon is officially off limits.

CHAPTER 8

NOAH

Waking up to the sound of clanking pots and pans accompanied by Wood's stellar rendition of "Shake it Off" by Taylor Swift in the kitchen hits different when you've had less than three hours of sleep. It's okay. Less time with my bad dreams.

I trudge downstairs from the loft where I slept—or tried to—last night.

Wood's got eggs scrambling and bacon frying. Coffee is brewing. It looks like he ordered an entire bakery with the assortment of pastries, donuts, muffins, and bagels in baskets around the kitchen. There's also a large bowl of fruit on the table that wasn't there last night.

Oblivious, he flits around, shaking his hips and bobbing his head, a kitchen towel thrown over his shoulder. He gets out a large mixing bowl and whisk, then starts digging to the back of one of the cabinets.

"What are you making now?" I ask.

There's a low thud and then an "ow" from inside the cabinet. Wood steps back, rubbing the back of his head with one hand and holding a waffle iron in the other. "Livvy requested waffles," he says with a smile.

Macy bursts out of the hall bathroom, still in her clothes from last night, messy bun, permanent creases in her forehead as she looks around for something. Wood practically leaps over the island to get to her, a full plate of food in one hand, a basket of pastries in the other.

"Breakfast? I wasn't sure what you'd want, so I kind of got everything."

She barely looks at him. "No, I'll just grab some coffee." She looks down at her phone. "I'm going to be late. Has anyone seen my purse?"

"Your purse is by the front door," Wood says, somehow already at the coffee pot pouring some into a travel mug.

He intercepts her on the way to the door and hands her the mug, which she takes with stunned silence.

"You really do need to eat," Wood says in a stern tone I've never heard from him.

She sighs, checking her phone again. "Okay, yeah, you're right. Um—" Somehow that little crease in her forehead gets deeper. "I need to go check my levels and stuff." She retreats back to the bathroom. When she returns a few minutes later, she takes an apple and a couple slices of bacon.

"I could give you a ride—if you want," Wood offers.

"No, I'm fine," Macy says as she slings her purse over her shoulder and swings open the door. "I'm just glad I have an extra pair of scrubs at the hospital."

He slinks back to the kitchen after she leaves.

"Give it up, brother. I think she's the only girl on the planet immune to your charms. Plus, she's got a boyfriend."

Wood pours flour into the mixing bowl, a white cloud of flour billowing over onto the countertop. "I'm well aware," he says.

I steal a slice of bacon from the paper towel-lined plate while he cracks an egg open and separates the yolk and the white into two bowls. By the second egg, he's already humming Taylor Swift again. Mid chorus he sing-songs, "Morning, girl!" then goes right back to singing and whisking.

I glance over my shoulder to where Livvy is walking out.

Her brown hair is messy around her face, golden in the sunlight pouring in from the windows behind her.

"Morning," she says with a yawn and sleepy smile.

She's wearing my T-shirt and gray sweatpants. They hang off her hips, way too long and baggy. She looks adorable in my clothes.

Mine.

I don't know where that intrusive thought came from. Some feral, primitive part of my brain thinks seeing her in my clothes means she's mine.

I know she's not.

"How'd you sleep?" I ask.

"Good." She smooths a wild lock of hair behind her ear, her cheeks rosy, and comes to sit at the bar stool next to me. "How about you?"

I got very little sleep, as usual. Didn't fall until almost three and then was woken up by Bex getting in late and spent most of the rest of the night fitfully tossing and turning, in and out of the same old nightmares, finally falling back asleep around five only to be woken by Mr. Morning Wood himself at six forty-five.

"Good," I say.

"Your Belgian waffle is coming right up," Wood says, scooping batter into the hot iron.

"What about my waffle?" I ask.

He points the measuring cup at me, a drop of batter hitting the counter. "I am not your mother. I'll make it next." He looks back to Livvy. "I didn't know what you like on your waffle, I have fresh strawberries, bananas, maple syrup, blueberry syrup, and whipped cream. Oh shoot, I didn't even think about chocolate chips! Do you want chocolate chips? We might have some chocolate chips. Hold on, let me look."

"It's fine, it's fine." Livvy laughs. "Strawberries and whipped cream is perfect. But really, I wasn't expecting all this. You didn't have to go to all this trouble."

Wood waves her off. "It was no trouble. Coffee? Tea? Juice? I can squeeze some oranges."

"Coffee will be great, thank you."

"I'll get it for you." I stand before Wood can beat me to it.

He's handing her a plate with a steaming waffle, eggs, and bacon when I get back with her cup of coffee.

"Thanks," she says, looking between the both of us.

She covers her waffle with strawberries and then whipped cream. A lot of whipped cream. Then, when she thinks I'm not looking, she squirts the whipped cream into her coffee cup creating a steep mound, overflowing the mug.

"Oh my god, Wood, these are so good," she says, after her first bite, licking some whipped cream off her lower lip.

"Thanks. It's our grandma's recipe. The secret is lots of melted butter and beating the egg whites separately."

I get my waffle and cover it in butter and syrup. We eat and Wood serenades us, "Dancing Queen" by Abba this time, while he makes more waffles, bobs around the kitchen, puts dishes in the sink and eats bacon.

"How does your side feel this morning? Better?" I ask.

"I don't know. How does it look?" Livvy turns her side toward me and lifts her shirt up to her ribs.

Worse. It looks so much worse. Last night it was red and swollen, just starting to purple. Today it's doubled in size, black and blue, purple and green around the edges.

Fuck.

"Is it that bad?" She's looking at my face, a worry line between her brows. She twists to see for herself and her eyes go big. "Oh."

"Dude, that's gnarly looking," Wood says, forgetting what he's doing and overflowing the waffle iron with batter.

Livvy grimaces and I reach over and pull her shirt back down. I don't like Wood's eyes on her.

"How'd that happen?" he asks.

My chest tightens. "It was my fault," I say through gritted teeth.

"It was an accident," Livvy insists, touching my arm softly.

"You don't have to go to work today. You should stay home and rest."

She waves me off. "I'm fine. Really. It's nothing that would keep me from working. As long as I don't get banged into any more walls."

Wood side-eyes me as he takes a huge bite of waffle. I roll my eyes.

♥ ♥ ♥

At work, I make sure to check on her regularly to see if she needs any extra breaks. She insists she's fine.

But what if it's more than a bruise? What if something's broken? I'd never forgive myself.

I'm probably being too protective. But her injury is my fault. She's staying at my place. She's sleeping in my bed. How could I not be? How could I not do everything and anything to make sure she's okay?

I can hardly concentrate when I'm in the middle of the back piece I'm doing. I keep looking toward the front desk, expecting to see her grabbing her side, her face twisted in pain. But she looks fine. She's smiling, even.

Smiling too much. At Anthony. He keeps going up there. It seems every chance and break he has he's using it to chat her up, leaning over the desk, showing her his half sleeve, laughing too loud, getting too close.

I resist the urge to growl at him to get back to work.

I'm having to resist more and more urges these days.

Over the next week, Livvy and I get into a nice rhythm of living and working together. We hang out with Wood in the mornings and go to work after lunch. If she's noticed that I've made sure all our days on and off are the same, she hasn't said anything.

Sometimes we'll go take our breaks together at the little coffee shop next door to the shop.

I get us takeout for dinner, and we eat it together in my office. My desk turns into a mess of boxes and bags and napkins and sauce packets, and she always wants to try "a bite" of whatever I have, and I watch her take three.

Livvy doesn't strike me as shy, but she's...quiet—around me, at least. She doesn't seem to be around Anthony or Wood. Maybe it's me. Maybe I'm intimidating. Maybe it's because I'm technically her boss now. Maybe it's because I knew her when she was a tween going through her awkward stage.

I don't know why, but I want her to open up to me.

She loves to talk about art. So we talk about art. I've been studying up on it at night, while I'm up in the loft while everyone else is sleeping. I'm learning about Dali and Degas at four in the morning. I can't really explain why, but I want to know what she's talking about when she references their works, see what she's seeing.

It's late when we get off work. Wood's usually out on a date, sometimes he's home, uh, entertaining that date. Bex is in and out. She works late and sleeps during the day plus has an active social life. I hardly even see her. I spend more time with Livvy than I have with anyone else in a long time.

Thursday night, she's officially been living here a week, but it feels like she's been with us longer. I was going to ask her if she wanted to hang out on our night off. Maybe go walk somewhere to get food or go down to the bar for a bit or maybe just hang out here and see if there's a good movie to stream or she can put on that ridiculous reality dating show she likes to watch, and we can order food in.

But as I'm sipping on a beer in the kitchen, scrolling through my latest messages with Angel, Livvy walks out, Wood on her heels, and she's all dressed up.

She looks so goddamn pretty.

"I'm glad we went with the open-toed shoes instead of the pumps, aren't you?" Wood asks.

She lets out a high laugh. "Yes, you have excellent taste."

He smiles his lopsided smile. Wood holds his hand up for a high five. She returns it and then they do this little handshake-back-clap-fist-bump-exploding thing. Interesting.

And just as they finish this new handshake ritual they've developed, she glances my way.

"What's going on?" I ask, trying to sound nonchalant.

"Oh, I thought I mentioned it." She smiles, but her eyes are shifty. "I have a date tonight."

She definitely did not mention it. I grunt. "With Mark again?"

"Um, no. Not Mark." She bites her lip.

The door buzzes.

I stay in the kitchen nursing my beer as she heads for the door. Little purse over her shoulder. A short cream dress that shows off her legs. And lipstick—she's wearing bright red lipstick and I know her date is going to be staring at her mouth all night. And she'll be smiling and laughing and touching his arm and—

I take a sip of my beer, the glass bottle cold against my lips.

My stomach is in knots.

I'm not prepared for those knots to turn to a red-hot ball of inexplicable fury when she opens the front door to my apartment and Anthony is standing on the other side.

"Hey, gorgeous," he says, looking her up and down. Too slowly, too appreciatively.

I stand, and clear my throat, almost knocking over my beer. "Livvy, can I talk to you real quick, before you leave?"

She turns, hand still on the doorknob, brows furrowed. "Okay. I'll be right back," she says to Anthony, smiling.

I jerk my chin to the right and walk to my room where she follows.

She's between me and the door when I shut it, my arm over her head. Her eyes are greener than normal as she looks up at me.

"Anthony? You're going out with Anthony? Really?"

"Yes. He seems nice and he asked me out. What's wrong with that?"

"First of all, you work together. That always gets messy. And, I don't know, he dates around a lot—"

"Is that a crime?" She narrows a glare at me.

"No, I guess not. But you're also still injured."

"I'm fine. What kind of physical activity do you think we're going to be doing on a first date? Rock climbing?"

I wasn't thinking about rock climbing. Why was I thinking about her *not* rock climbing with Anthony? I don't know. It's not like I'm jealous of him.

I don't say anything for a beat.

Her cheeks deepen to a dark crimson. "Oh." she says suddenly. "That's none of your business or concern, Noah."

Fuck. "You're right."

I'm breathing rapidly. I'm standing too close. I can smell her perfume mixed with the strawberry scent of her hair.

"Obviously." She crosses her arms and quirks an eyebrow.

"Also, he's so loud and you're so... you're so—"

"I'm so what?" She doesn't break eye contact. She's even more adorable when she scowls. And it draws attention to her pouty red lips...

I drag my gaze back up from her mouth. "You're so..." Shit. "Quiet and reserved. It just doesn't make sense, you two."

"Well, it's a good thing it doesn't need to make sense to you, then." She twists the knob behind her, and I almost stumble when she opens the door I've been leaning on. "Good night, Noah. Don't wait up for me."

♥ ♥ ♥

I'm not waiting up for her.

I'm not.

I'm simply up in the loft at one in the morning taking notes on the difference between Monet and Manet. And, no, I didn't know there was a contemporary of Monet named Manet who was also a French impressionist painter until fifteen minutes ago, either.

Keys rattle in the door downstairs, and then it opens with the sounds of laughter.

Bex is at work, and it's too early for her, anyway. It could be Wood coming home with his date. But I already know—I know that laugh is Livvy's.

I start down the steps to, I don't know, greet her? See if she's still mad at me? To say sorry?

But they're there, standing in front of the door, arms wrapped around each other. He's kissing her. And she's kissing him back. More than a peck. More than a simple good night kiss. It's a probably-leading-to-more kiss.

It's a they-don't-want-me-around kiss.

I don't want to be around for it, either.

So, I turn to go back up to the loft to give them privacy.

But then Livvy lets out a low grunt and says, "Ow. That hurts."

Black seeps in around the edges of my vision and I'm crossing the apartment toward them. I don't even recall going down the steps.

In an instant I'm between them, pushing Anthony away and keeping Livvy at my back.

I yank at his shirt and pull him up to my face.

Pulse pounding. Blood red hot in my veins.

Fist shaking.

I can barely think.

Barely talk.

Anthony looks up at me in shock.

I look him dead in the eye. "I don't care if you are my friend. You hurt her—I will end you."

CHAPTER 9

LIVVY

"**N**oah, stop! Let him go!"

The color has drained from Anthony's face, his hands up in surrender. "I didn't do anything, I swear!"

I put my hand on Noah's arm—it's hot and hard, flexed, holding onto Anthony's shirt.

"He didn't hurt me," I say.

His grip on Anthony's collar loosens and he turns slowly around, his scowl melting away and his face softening when he looks at me. Though his chest is still puffed up.

"He just didn't know about my bruised ribs, and we were—" I swallow, my throat suddenly dry and ears warm. "It was an accident."

He lets go of Anthony, who takes a couple steps back. "Jesus Christ, dude. What the fuck?"

Noah ignores him, eyes trained on me, he quiets his voice. "You're okay? Are you sure?"

"Yes."

"All right." He nods, running his fingers through his hair, still shaking a little. "I'm sorry." He turns to Anthony. "I'm sorry, man, I just—I thought—"

"I get it. Whatever, man." Anthony looks at me. "I guess I better go, then." He takes a step toward me, but Noah makes no move to step aside, staying between us.

I'm not sure what to say or do—the whole situation changed so fast.

Anthony shoots a glare at Noah before looking back at me. "Good night. I'll call you."

I wave as he leaves.

Once he's gone, it's silent in the apartment.

"I can't believe you did that," I say.

"Livvy, I'm so sorry. I heard you say he was hurting you, and I lost it."

"That wasn't okay. You scared me."

"I'm sorry, I—fuck." He rakes both hands over his head, his hair a mess. "Are you sure you're okay? Can I look at your side?"

"No, you may not." I turn and head toward his room without another word and shut the door firmly behind me.

The audacity of that man. Thinking he can act that way—like I'm his to protect. Or that he has the right to see my body.

My head is still spinning, body buzzing. I won't be able to sleep for a while.

I change out of my dress then casually reach for the T-shirt I've been wearing to bed. Noah's T-shirt he gave me the first night. I should have given it back, but he never asked for it, and I like sleeping in it.

Leaving the shirt, I instead go to my bag. Thankfully, we were able to go to the apartment and get most of our things earlier this week while repairs are being done. I dig out my sleep tank and shorts then head to the bathroom to wash my face and brush my teeth.

Of course, Noah is in there. He's at the singular sink, brushing his teeth. I swear to god, he's the only person who could make brushing his teeth look sexy. His jaw sharp against his flexing, tattooed neck. The veins in his hand bulging under the ink.

Stop looking at him, Livvy! You're still mad at him. Don't even acknowledge him.

He steps aside silently as I turn on the water to wash my face. He rinses his toothbrush while I dry off, looking straight ahead in the mirror and *not* at him. But his eyes are on me. My traitorous body reacts to his attention. Heart beating faster. Nipples hardening. Oh shit, I forgot how thin this tank top was. And these shorts are so short.

"You're not wearing my T-shirt," he says as he puts his toothbrush away.

"Yeah, I've been meaning to give it back to you." I get my toothbrush out, still not making eye contact.

"You don't have to." He hands me the toothpaste. "I like you wearing it," he says, quieter.

I don't respond, vigorously brushing my teeth instead, and he leaves.

Son of a bitch. I told myself I wasn't going to let him frazzle me anymore. I had another guy's tongue in my mouth tonight, for Christ's sake.

I flop onto the bed. It's almost two in the morning and I'm wide awake. I check my phone. I have a message from Anthony saying he had a nice night. I'll reply tomorrow.

Going into the app, I look for a message from him, and there it is, from earlier tonight.

2HORNED:

> Are you around tonight? I'm a bit lonely

I find myself smiling at his message. I don't know why, but he's the only person I want to talk to right now. Maybe because I don't have to be the Livvy everyone thinks I am or expects me to be with him. I can just...be. And I don't have to worry about my reputation or how I'm perceived. I can be sad or stressed or say dirty jokes or straight up ask him to call me his whore and he never judges.

ANG3L:

Hey, I just saw this. I know it's late but I'm here now. I could use some company too.

Are you still up?

2HORNED:

Hey, you. Yeah, I'm up

ANG3L:

Can't sleep still? The nightmares?

2HORNED:

They've been not as bad. No, tonight I sort of fucked up with a friend and now she's mad at me. It's going to keep me up

ANG3L:

I'm sorry. I've had a weird night too. I'm sure she'll forgive you if you apologize sincerely

2HORNED:

I hope so. I really fucked up

ANG3L:

You should get her a gift

2HORNED:

A gift?

ANG3L:

Yes, but not some generic scented candle or lotion or that bath salt shit, something that shows you pay attention to her

2HORNED:

I thought girls liked that stuff

ANG3L:

No

2HORNED:

> Shit. Okay. I think I know something that might work. I don't want to lose her friendship over this

He is so sweet and sincere. And, no, my stomach didn't at all flip when he said his friend was a girl. And I didn't automatically wonder if he's closer with her than he is with me. He knows her in real life—he's probably closer to her. As it should be.

But...he has said he doesn't tell other people the things he talks about with me. And I bet he doesn't sext with this friend either. Unless maybe they're more than friends. I should be happy for him if that's the case, but I'm not.

ANG3L:

> Can I help take your mind off of it?

2HORNED:

> What did you have in mind?

ANG3L:

> Something... naughty

2HORNED:

> I have every confidence that you'd be able to take my mind off anything you wanted and put it ON anything you wanted

ANG3L:

> How about we focus it on you filling my pretty pussy with your cum. I want to feel you dripping out of me

2HORNED:

> Fuck. You already have me hard

ANG3L:

> Good

We chat for another hour. I like it, this powerplay we have between us, taking turns giving and taking. He details how he would bend me in half so I could watch his cock go in and out of me. How good he'd fill me up.

Then he says he'd flip me over while I was still panting and out of breath. Still dripping with him. And he'd fill my ass next.

That's a new thing. The idea of it lights a little flame of excitement in me I haven't felt in a while. I'll have to add that to the list of things I'm apparently into.

I'm tempted to join him tonight. I almost do.

I've never climaxed with a client before, though I hate thinking of him as a "client." He's my friend. And even if I didn't get the same sexual satisfaction out of our conversation as he did, it made me happy to help him out, to lighten his mood. It's going to be hard to tell him I'm done with this app. But I'm not telling him quite yet.

> 2HORNED:
>
> Goodnight, Angel. Thank you for this

> ANG3L:
>
> Goodnight. Sleep well

> 2HORNED:
>
> I'll try

It's after three by the time I fall asleep and, consequently, I sleep in late. It's a little after noon by the time I get up and dressed and go out to the kitchen the next day.

Wood is nowhere to be seen, but Noah is in the kitchen with bowls strewn across the counter, the egg carton open, fridge door ajar, and is concentrating on a notecard in his hand so intently he doesn't even notice me until I'm sitting directly in front of him at the counter.

He almost jumps when he sees me, dropping the recipe card.

"Sorry," I say, trying not to laugh too much, then realizing I was supposed to be mad at him. Shoot.

"It's okay." He picks the card up from the floor. "I thought I would try and make you waffles."

My stomach rumbles loudly right at that moment.

"I'll take that as a yes?" he asks.

"Waffles sound great."

"I have to warn you, I've never made them before. They won't be as good as Wood's."

"I'm sure they'll be great. Can I help?"

He smiles slowly, his chiseled features mirroring the skull tattooed on his throat. Haunting yet beautiful. "I'd love that."

I come around to his side and pick up the recipe. "How about you do the dry ingredients and I'll mix up the wet?"

"Okay." He nods. He gets out the flour and measuring cups and spoons while I get out the milk.

"Sorry I was such an asshole last night," he says, flour on his chin. I can't help but smile.

"You were."

His expression falls. I nudge him with my elbow and wink, and he smiles, too. As we work, he starts in with all these random facts about Monet and Manet, and I have no idea where this came from but he's adorable trying to remember dates and the names of paintings while also leveling out a teaspoon of baking soda.

By the end, batter is in drips all around the waffle iron, spent eggshells litter the counter, and I'm sticky with syrup.

The waffles were not as good as Wood's—I don't think I beat the egg whites enough—but I don't care. My stomach is full, and my cheeks hurt from smiling.

"Oh! I got something for you," Noah says as he's washing the dishes.

"You did? You didn't have to do that. When did you even have time?"

"When you were sleeping this morning, silly."

I swivel around in my seat looking for anything wrapped or

new sitting around. "What did you get? Where is it?" Too eager. That was way too eager.

He chuckles. "I'll show you after I finish with the dishes. If Wood comes home and his kitchen is a mess, I'll never hear the end of it."

I hop off the stool and go to his side. "You wash and I'll dry?"

"Okay. I'll pretend you're offering to help from the goodness of your heart and not because you want your present sooner."

"Obviously. I only ever have pure intentions." I smile big as I dry the giant mixing bowl.

"It's up in the loft," Noah says after the dishes are done and put away. "Wood helped me set it up this morning."

Set it up? I scurry to the steps leading up to the loft, mind racing.

"Close your eyes. No peeking. It's a surprise," Noah calls after me.

I close my eyes as his steps come light right up behind me. I clasp the railing, glancing down through my lashes as I take the stairs slowly.

"Hey, I said no peeking!"

"I need to see the steps. I don't want to fall."

"Here. I've got you." He's right behind me now and he puts his hand over my eyes, his fingers warm and just a little calloused from where he holds his tattoo gun.

We walk up the stairs in tandem, his chest brushing against my back, wrapping me in the scent of his day-old cologne.

"This is the last step," he says softly against my ear. "Ready?"

CHAPTER 10

NOAH

"**R**eady," she says.

I uncover her eyes and step aside. My hands are sweaty. I stuff them in my pockets.

Her jaw drops as she looks at the large easel now prominently in the center of the loft.

"This is for me?"

"Yeah."

She blinks a couple times, mouth still hanging open while my ears become hotter.

"I knew you were only able to get clothes and a few bathroom things from the apartment, and I wanted you to be able to draw and paint while you're here. If you want."

Is it too much? It's too much. I knew it. Maybe it's the wrong kind. It's bigger than her other easel. She hates it.

"I can't believe you did this. I love it." She walks over to it and touches the wood frame.

"You do?"

"Yes." She beams at me, her smile radiant.

Relief washes through me like an exhale of cool air. "I also got you these." I show her the box of stuff behind the easel. A few blank canvases, a new sketchbook, pencils, charcoals, a fresh set of oil paints, some new brushes, and a full can of mineral spirits.

A knowing look passes between us.

"Maybe no candles up here, yeah?" she says, forcing back a grin.

"Agreed." I refrain from commenting that we'll be safe as long as she doesn't flash me what's between her legs again. And now I'm thinking about that pretty...pink...

Fuck.

I shake my head and try to distract myself from my growing erection.

"I tried to get you all the same things you had before, but I couldn't remember all the exact brands, I hope I did okay."

"You did more than okay. This is great. Truly, I think this is the nicest thing anyone has ever done for me."

I smile at her, and her eyes are getting shiny, and I'm not sure what to do so I just keep talking. "We set it up here, so it'd be kind of private. I know you don't like people looking at your works in progress, but if you want it somewhere else, I can move it. Maybe down by the windows or—"

She jumps up and flings her arms around my neck. Startled, I instinctively wrap my arms around her waist. Her toes are barely touching the floor and I'm holding her up while all the softest parts of her are pressed against me.

"It's perfect," she whispers against my neck. "Thank you."

Her hugs always feel so wonderful, so genuine, so perfect. So...right.

I exhale all the tension and squeeze her a little tighter. She buries her face into my shoulder, and we linger in the embrace a few moments longer. Neither of us says a thing.

She thanks me again as she pulls away, and I realize I'm reluctant to let go.

I follow her down the stairs and we settle on the couch. She puts that silly show on. I check emails on my phone and shoot some texts out to clients checking on how their new tattoos are healing and reminding others of upcoming appointments.

"I thought Zeke was into Camber." I glance casually up from my phone.

"No, she's hooking up with Braxton."

"But weren't they kissing last episode?"

"That was three episodes ago. He's trying to start something with Ainsley."

"That's never going to happen. She's been eyeing Josiah since day one."

Livvy quirks an eyebrow at me. "I thought you weren't interested in this show."

"I'm not." I just happen to be in the living room whenever she's watched it this week, that's all.

She laughs. Still smiling, she starts typing on her phone. Probably texting someone.

Probably Anthony.

I don't know why that idea irks me so much.

So I go back to my phone, too, Braxton whining to producers about how girls don't like nice guys nowadays in the background.

I sent Angel a message when I first got up, but she hadn't replied by the time I started the waffles. I open the app to see if she's responded yet and there she is. Three tiny dots pop up as she types. My chest tightens as my heart does a stupid little leap.

2HORNED:

Good morning, beautiful

ANG3L:

You're "good morning, beautiful"-ing me?

2HORNED:

Too much?

ANG3L:

I mean, you don't even know what I look like, it's very presumptuous of you

2HORNED:

I know you're beautiful on the inside, that counts. And I have a feeling you are on the outside too

ANG3L:

You do?

2HORNED:

Yes. I'm very good at guessing these things

You know, there is a way to settle this. Just send me a picture

She doesn't reply right away. Finally sending me an eyebrow raised emoji.

No pictures is one of her rules. I shouldn't have suggested it. I know that.

2HORNED:

What about no face? A body shot.

Men are very visual. It'd give me something to look at or imagine next time I get off for you

She hasn't replied in a minute and I'm starting to panic. My attempts to backtrack are somehow simultaneously doubling down and making it worse. I decide to go light, play it off as a joke.

2HORNED:

What about just a shoulder? Chin? Foot?

ANG3L:

I didn't know you were into feet

I'll make a note of that

2HORNED:

I'm not. But I don't know.

Maybe I'd be into yours

ANG3L:

> I'll think about it

She'll think about it? That's what moms say when they don't want to say no but the answer is unequivocally no.

I need to change the subject. Fast.

The whole exchanging pictures conversation is dangerous, anyway. What if Wood is right and she's not who she says she is, or I'm just not attracted to her at all? The illusion shattered. The soulmate on the other side of the screen who I can talk about anything with, gone.

That would be devastating.

I look up, Livvy is across from me, looking at her screen, worrying her lower lip. Talk about cute. She's adorable. And that lip. Her fucking perfect plump lip. I throw a pillow at her.

She looks up when it bounces off her shoulder. "Hey!"

"You're missing your show."

"I'm listening to it."

"Mhm."

2HORNED:

> Oh hey, so thank you for your advice last night. The present was a great idea

ANG3L:

> So things are all good between you now?

2HORNED:

> I think so

ANG3L:

> Oh good! And, you're welcome

2HORNED:

> I appreciate you letting me bug you with my problems last night, I know it was late. It was like 2am for me

ANG3L:

You never bug me! Yeah, it was 2am for me too

2HORNED:

Oh shit

Wait

Did we just establish that we live in the same time zone?

ANG3L:

I guess we did. It's okay, it's a big time zone

2HORNED:

Let me guess, you're in California

ANG3L:

I'm not! I was going to school in Oregon but I just moved back home to Washington

I don't know why I'm telling you this

2HORNED:

Wow. I'm in Washington, too

ANG3L:

Really?

2HORNED:

Yeah. But it's a big state. I mean, I live in a city with a metro population of 3.5 million, it's not like we're going run into each other on the street tomorrow

ANG3L:

You live in the Seattle area?

2HORNED:

Yes

ANG3L:

Me too

Fuck.

Holy fucking shit.

2HORNED:

> Oh. I take back what I said, then

My pulse is racing. What if this is it? What if it's a sign from the universe or something? The push I've needed. What if it's her? What if she really is my soulmate?

2HORNED:

> We should meet

Why the fuck did I just say that?

I shouldn't have said that.

She hasn't replied.

It's been minutes.

The little dots appear.

Then they disappear.

I've freaked her out.

I've freaked out my soulmate and now nothing will ever happen beyond our phones.

That was stupid. I've ruined it.

Worse, what if she agrees to meet and she's not even close to my soulmate? What if we have nothing in common and give each other the ick and then this friendship is ruined?

Fuck.

I'm overthinking.

She still hasn't replied.

I need to put my phone down before I get too in my head over it.

But then the dots pop up again. She's typing.

I hold my breath as I clutch my phone.

ANG3L:

> I don't think I'm up for meeting right now

That awful sinking feeling trickles down my spine, cold, and lands in a heavy heap in my stomach.

I knew it. I knew the moment I said it, it was a mistake.

I'm disappointed. I'm relieved. I have no idea how to feel or what to say back. Everything I think to reply sounds wrong. I should shut up before I make it worse.

I toss my phone onto the coffee table, telling myself I'll respond in a little bit when I can figure out the right thing to say, and look over to Livvy.

She's staring at her phone, her eyebrows knitted and nose crinkled in the cutest way.

"Are you okay?" I ask.

Livvy lifts her eyes from her phone as she lays it face down on the couch next to her. "I'm fine." She smiles then turns to the TV.

Camber just walked in on Braxton canoodling with Sierra in the hot tub. I never even used the word 'canoodling' until this show.

Livvy and I groan simultaneously as the episode ends and we'll have to wait to see the aftermath until next week.

She turns it off, the little crease between her brows still there as she chews her bottom lip some more.

"You sure you're okay?"

She releases her lip from her teeth. "Yeah. I've just got stuff on my mind."

"Me, too. Let's distract each other."

"How—"

I grab her foot by the ankle and extend her leg toward me. She squeals and pulls it back.

"What are you doing?"

"Give me your foot."

"Don't tickle it. I'm super ticklish."

I wasn't planning on tickling her, but now... "You shouldn't have told me that."

She yelps when I touch her foot again.

"I won't tickle you."

"Promise?"

"I promise. Just give me your foot."

She stretches it toward my lap slowly, eyeing me the whole time. I pick up the permanent marker from the coffee table as I steady her foot on my thigh. It's a pretty foot. I'm not into feet, and I've never thought they were pretty, but hers are. That's a weird thought. I try to push my conversation with Angel out of my head.

"What should I draw?" I ask as I take the lid off with my teeth.

"Hm. You pick."

I grin, looking at her from under my lashes. "Okay."

She giggles when the felt tip touches the top of her foot and tries to wiggle away from me as I draw the first line. I shoot her a look.

"Hold still for me. Can you do that?"

She nods.

"Good girl."

She bites that fucking bottom lip again when I say it. But she holds still as I start to draw again. *Don't think too much about how well she responded to being called "good girl," Noah.*

She wants to laugh and squirm but after a few minutes she relaxes. Fifteen minutes later I'm happy with the little design.

"All done."

Livvy sits up and looks at the "tattoo" I gave her.

"Going biblical, huh?" She chuckles.

It's a snake twisting around an apple with rippling scales, its fangs piercing the flesh of the fruit. I'm proud of it for a quick piece.

"I like it," she says, taking the marker from my fingers. "My turn."

"I don't think there's anywhere for you to draw except for my face. Unless you want me to take off my clothes."

Her eyes widen and her cheeks darken. I probably shouldn't

have said it. I gave myself a half-chub. But she cools her expression and tugs my hand to her, turning it over to my bare palm.

"Unless you'd *rather* I draw on your ass?" she says, extra sassy.

My turn to try not to blush. "Next time."

She pulls my hand closer. I scoot along with it to accommodate her, sitting very close now by her side. She rests it on her knee and starts drawing.

"Don't look," she says, shooting me a glare.

I chuckle. "Fine." I look around the room and out the windows, her fingers soft as she holds my hand in place.

I don't know how long it took me before I came back around, my gaze falling on her and staying there, but they haven't left. Nothing else is as interesting as watching her eyelashes flutter against her cheeks or the way the tiniest tip of her tongue is sticking out from between her lips.

"All right. I'm done. You can look now." She lifts her face to the light, a golden glow about her. "What do you think?"

I look at my palm. She's drawn a scorpion with detailed legs and pinchers, the tail starting to curl up my thumb.

"That's a rad drawing. Did you choose it because I'm a Scorpio?"

She smiles, nodding as she tucks some hair behind her ear. I lean down and pull the pant leg of my sweats up to reveal the scorpion tattoo I have on the back of my calf.

"Did you design that one?" she asks.

"No. But now I'm wishing you had. I like your drawing better." I drop my pant leg and sit back.

"Really?"

"Seriously. You're so talented. What is it you want to do? With your art, I mean?"

She looks past me, then down at her hands. "I don't know. I'm supposed to have figured that out by now, right?"

I shrug. "Not necessarily."

She looks up. "All I know is I want to see my art hanging. I want other people to see it. To be moved by it. To want to buy it. To like it enough to come see it in a gallery. Maybe to have a permanent place in a gallery. I don't know..." she trails off and I want to hug her. Touch her.

"Well, while you're working on getting there, if you want to learn to tattoo, I'd be happy to take you on as an apprentice. You'd make more money than the front desk. It's not a paint brush, but it is an art."

"It is." She nods, her eyes trailing slowly over the tattoo sleeves on my arms and it's like I can almost feel the touch of her gaze, warm and curious, on my skin.

"Or," I say, swallowing, "you could do piercing if you wanted. That's what Taryn decided to do on the side, and now she's by far the best piercer in the shop."

"So, if I wanted my nipples pierced, *you* wouldn't do it?"

I choke. On nothing. My spit, maybe air.

"Do...do you want your nipples pierced?" I manage to get out. I can still picture her breasts and those perky pink nipples of hers. Just that split second image has me hard as fuck.

Fuck.

"Um, no. I don't think so." She laughs and it's a beautiful sound, light and airy and joyous and open. And when she stops, breathing heavily, it's just us, sitting on this couch, so close her knee is brushing my thigh.

"For the record," I say, "Taryn is a better piercer than I am, and I would refer anyone to her. But I *would* pierce your nipples if you wanted me to." I meant it to come out like a playful offer, but it came out like an oath.

"You would?" she whispers.

I nod. And I am *not* thinking about how soft and round her breasts are and wanting to know what her skin feels like there and how that pretty pink nipple would pebble under my touch. And I'm not noticing how her hip is pressed against mine and every-thing is quiet except for our breathing. And how the little vein in her neck is pulsing fast and how her pupils are dilated. Or that she's looking up at me, her face closer. Or how I seem to have leaned in as well.

The door to the apartment rattles and opens with high-pitched laughter and the jarring, clacking of footsteps on the concrete as Bex and Macy walk in the door, arms full of shopping bags.

CHAPTER 11
LIVVY

Noah immediately bolts up from the couch, stuffing his hands in his pockets and muttering something about needing to get ready to head into the shop. It's hard to hear him over Bex and Macy's conversation.

"You need to wear the red dress," Bex says.

"I don't look good in red. It clashes with my hair."

"Redheads can wear red. That's a myth."

"How about black?"

"Black is boring. You're going to be posting pictures from tonight, and everyone is going to see you. You need to look fabulous."

"What's happening tonight?" I ask.

"Spencer and I are going out to dinner to celebrate our anniversary. Six years."

"Girl. He is definitely going to propose to you tonight," Bex adds.

"Do you think?" Macy beams.

"He's taking you to the fanciest restaurant downtown. He has to be. He'd be an idiot not to."

"Who's an idiot?" Wood walks in the front door in a loose-fitting tank, gym bag over his shoulder.

"Hopefully not Spencer," Bex says.

Wood grunts.

"I can't wait to see the ring!" Bex says and she and Macy both squeal. "Hey, Wood, keep us company while we get Macy ready for her big date!"

"Oh, no. I've got to go shower and get ready for a date myself." He starts to head toward his room when Macy says his name and he stops in his tracks.

"I needed to ask you something," she says. "It's about the trip to your lake house over the fourth. Spencer and I were wondering if his brother could come along, as well? He just moved back after finishing med school at Stanford and doesn't have any plans for the holiday."

"Oh, I didn't realize Spencer was able to come, too. He's so busy being a surgeon, and all," Wood says flatly.

"He was able to make it work," Macy says, smiling.

"That's great. Sure, his brother can come. Why not. The more the merrier."

"Wood, hold up!" Bex calls as he turns again. "Real fast, we need a guy's perspective." She takes out two dresses from the bags on the floor. "Should she wear the red one or black one?"

"Green," he says. "Macy's color is green." His gaze lingers on Macy for a second then he disappears down the hall.

"Well, that was no help," Bex says, rolling her eyes.

❤ ❤ ❤

"Hold still."

"It tickles." Macy scrunches up her face as Bex applies some concealer under her eyes.

We've moved to the bathroom, all three of us crowded in here, Bex's makeup bag exploded all over the counter.

It reminds me of when Bex and I were little, twelve and eight, and she would pull me into her closet, dress me up in her clothes, and put tons of makeup on my face. I loved her giving me all that attention. I always looked up to her and thought she was so cool.

It wasn't until years later, after our parents' divorce, that I put together she only did it when they were screaming at each other downstairs.

"Stop being a baby. I'm only using a little bit." Bex tilts Macy's chin side to side, looking at her work. "See, great. I'm not even going to use foundation because your skin is flawless, and I don't want to cover up any of those freckles."

I stand to the side, eating chips, having been designated Bex's assistant, or "brush bitch" as I've decided is more accurate.

"I need that big angled one for the blush."

I hand Bex the biggest angled brush.

"This one is for bronzer."

"Oh. Oops." I trade it for another, slightly smaller angled brush.

"Thanks."

Clearly, she should have said second biggest angled brush.

"You look so pretty. Spencer is going to fall over himself when he sees you." Bex smiles at Macy, who looks on the verge of tearing up.

Bex finishes Macy's makeup while I finish this bag of chips. Macy normally doesn't wear more than mascara and Chapstick. It's strange seeing her all done up, but she really does look beautiful.

She has on the black dress and a pair of Bex's heels. Then she starts to take her curlers out.

"Oh no. Bex, oh no."

"What?" Bex goes over and helps take out the back ones.

Macy's normally curly hair has a more blown-out look and is sticking straight up from her head.

"My hair! It looks terrible. Holy crap!" She glances at me. "Excuse my language." She looks back in the mirror. "Oh no, oh no, oh no. Spencer is going to be here any minute."

"It's fine," Bex assures her. "We can fix it. Don't cry—you'll ruin your makeup."

"Okay," Macy says, tearing up.

"Stop it!"

"Should I get the wine?" I ask.

"No," Macy says at the same time Bex says, "Yes."

Ten minutes and a glass of wine later, Macy has settled down enough her face barely looks splotchy anymore and Bex has managed to tame her hair into somewhat of a chignon.

We walk out to the living room at the same time Wood is leaving, dressed in a dark blue pair of jeans and a fitted black button-up shirt. He stops at the door, adjusting his watch, then catches a glimpse of us.

He pauses, fingers still on his watchband. "Wow. You are absolutely stunning, Mace."

"Thanks." Macy takes another shaky sip of her white wine.

"She does look great," Bex agrees. "See, tell her Spencer would have to be an idiot not to propose to her tonight after six years."

Wood's gaze lingers on Macy's face for several more beats. "A complete idiot." He shakes the daze off his face, his signature lopsided smile reappearing. "Have a nice night, ladies."

He leaves, and we wait.

Spencer knocks promptly at seven-fifteen.

"What did you do to your hair?" is the first thing he asks when Macy opens the door.

"Tried something different," Macy says, her smile faltering.

"Hm."

By all accounts, Spencer is handsome, but I can't for the life of me pinpoint why. He has very nondescript brown hair. His face is face-shaped. Straight nose. Brown eyes. Maybe it's that his face is very symmetrical? He's wearing navy dress pants and a white button-up shirt with a subtle blue stripe.

He clears his throat as he straightens his shirt cuffs. "Come on. I don't want to be late for our reservation."

♥ ♥ ♥

It's late. Almost midnight. Bex has been at the bar working since nine, Wood is still out on his date, and I haven't heard Noah come home yet, either.

I'm in bed. Correction, I'm in Noah's bed. It doesn't smell like him anymore.

I haven't heard back from 2Horned all day. That's unlike him. He always responds, even if it's just to tell me he can't talk because he's busy or working or something. He never leaves me on read.

I check the app again. Still no response. Just my last one telling him I didn't want to meet.

I probably hurt his feelings. Maybe he's mad. Maybe he feels rejected.

This sucks.

I knew this relationship, or whatever it is, between us would be ending. Soon, even. But not like this. Not with hurt feelings.

ANG3L:

Hey you. Are you around?

Half an hour later and still no reply from him.

When we'd realized today we both live in Seattle, I was shocked. What a fucking coincidence, right?

Bex doesn't believe in coincidences. She thinks everything is connected and mapped out in the stars.

Do I believe we're ruled by the planets and stuff? No. Not

really. But I have to admit it feels like more than a coincidence. Like something I shouldn't ignore.

I almost said yes.

But then I started to second guess. What if he doesn't like what he sees? I mean, I know I'm pretty—even though I sometimes forget I'm not that ugly duckling I used to be. But what if I'm not his type? What if I'm not what he's expecting?

He's expecting a confident, sexy woman. A woman who has done the activities we've talked about. What if I'm disappointing in real life? What if I'm not charming or funny without the security of the screen between us?

What if he finds out I'm a virgin? A fraud? What if he thinks I'm a liar?

I'm too in my head about this. I know I am.

I throw my head back into my pillow, exhaling hard, letting my phone drop and land with a plop onto my chest. He's my friend. He's told me about his family—something he says he never talks about with anyone—and I've told him things I haven't told anyone else, too. I told him about being terrified of ET, for god's sake! I need to fix this.

I want to make it up to him.

He *did* ask for a picture...

No.

Maybe.

The thought swirls around in my head as I lie here in the dark. I could take one little picture for him. A cute picture? A sexy picture? I've never even taken a sexy picture. Angel would send a sexy picture.

Fuck it.

I flip on the lamp and dig out the only cute bra and panty set I own. They're white lace, the fabric design *just* intricate enough to obscure the bits and pieces. I put them on.

Don't overthink it.

I lie down, turned so that my bruised side is hidden from the camera, knees together, arch my back, suck in the tummy, and take a few pictures.

I scroll through the pictures, face heating. To my surprise, I like them. I look good. Damn good. Fuck, I'm really doing this.

I pick the one I like the best and attach it to a message to 2Horned. At the last second, I go back and crop out my face.

Then I hit send.

That's it. It's done. I can't take it back now.

My heart is racing.

Did I just send a semi-nude? I haven't felt a rush like this since...since I posed nude for Noah.

I change back into my pajamas then check my phone.

Nothing. No response.

What if he just doesn't say anything? Or what if he comes back with the driest reaction? What would be worse?

I stare at my phone for what seems like minutes, but in actuality, I can't look at the sent picture with no reply for longer than thirty seconds, so I throw my phone down on the bed and pace for a bit.

There will be no sleeping. I need something to take my mind off it before I freak out.

Noah had said I could go up to the loft and draw or paint any time I wanted, and I never heard him come back. He must be doing a long tattoo tonight. I'll go paint.

Good. Great. Excellent idea, even. Good thinking, Livvy.

I step out into the dark hallway and through the living room. The entire apartment is still and quiet. The only light is what's shining in from the city lights in the distance out the large windows. The moon is obscured by dark clouds. Rain patters lightly against the glass.

I tiptoe slowly up the steps to the loft. But when I get to the top, hand on the light switch, I'm not alone up here.

Noah is lying on the couch, shirtless. Pants and boxers pushed down around his thighs. Phone in one hand, his cock in the other.

His large, hard, cock.

He's stroking it. Squeezing it at the base, his tattooed hand making a fist. And I am frozen in place. Paralyzed. In shock and awe.

Then our eyes meet. "Fuck!" He sits up.

Fuck!

Knocked out of my daze, I turn away with a screech. "I'm so sorry! Oh, my god." And I run down the stairs, skidding across the floors to Noah's room where I close the door and jump into bed, burying my head under a pillow.

Holy fucking shit, I can't believe I just saw Noah jerking off. And I just stood there, gaping at him.

I'm panting. Sweating. Out of breath.

My whole body is on fire.

I don't know what to do with myself. So I check my phone, naturally.

He's replied to my picture.

2HORNED:

> Holy fuck. You're gorgeous. So sexy. And the white? You have me hard as fuck

He sent a picture, too. It's cropped in tight of his crotch, wearing black boxer briefs, with a clearly defined bulge of a big, hard cock, straining under the fabric.

2HORNED:

> I'm stroking myself to your picture

ANG3L:

> Are you still touching yourself?

2HORNED:

> Yes

ANG3L:

> I am, too

I say it out of habit. But I'm warm all over, my skin tingling. I don't know if it's from his picture or his words or seeing Noah with his...

Breathing hard, I slip between the sheets and shimmy down my shorts. I'm already throbbing between my legs when I slide my fingers there. Ready and needy.

2HORNED:

Do you want it gentle or hard tonight?

ANG3L:

Hard

2HORNED:

I can do that

ANG3L:

I know you can

2HORNED:

Should I pin you down?

ANG3L:

Please

2HORNED:

Are you going to be my good little slut tonight?

ANG3L:

Yes

2HORNED:

Good girl. Spread your legs for me, Angel

Show me that pretty little pussy

ANG3L:

It's all yours

2HORNED:

I can't wait to taste you. But I'll take my time. I'll kiss and lick you nice and slow.

ANG3L:

Fuck. I want that

2HORNED:

I'll go down on you until you are writhing under me. Until you beg me to make you come

ANG3L:

I want you to make me come

I want to come for you

And I do, I want to, *need to*, satiate this ache. My fingers are slippery as I touch and play, getting wetter by the second.

2HORNED:

Good girl. I won't stop until you do. Until you can't form words and your legs are shaking and my face is covered in you

ANG3L:

Jesus Christ

2HORNED:

No. I'm quite the opposite

I'd beg to differ. The way he can stoke my libido with his words and have me panting through my screen is godly. He tells me how beautiful I am, laid out before him and how perfect my moans are. And even though it's all imaginary, it feels real. My reaction is real. I feel beautiful. Powerful. Sexy.

I moan for him, not even trying to be quiet. I wonder if Noah is still touching himself upstairs while I'm bringing myself close to climax. Did I ruin his fun, or did he like it? Is he thinking about me as he strokes himself now? If I moan loud enough, can he hear me?

The little devil in my phone pushes me farther, urging me to come for him, telling me how much he wants to come, but he won't let himself until I do first.

I imagine him between my legs, my faceless devil. But it's Noah's face. It's always been Noah's face. And now it's Noah's cock, too. I'll never be able to picture anything but his...perfectly thick and smooth...

Fuck. I'm so close.

I picture Noah up there, coming in spurts across his chest and abs while listening to me masturbate, and it pushes me over the edge. I fall into an abyss. Dark and weightless. I am not a body, only pure sensation and joy. Stars sparkle around the edges of my vision as I come back to myself, heavy and panting on the mattress.

CHAPTER 12

NOAH

My wakeup call is Wood singing "Driver's License" by Olivia Rodrigo down in the kitchen—if one could call that singing, it's more like wailing.

With one eye open, I check my phone. It's almost nine in the morning. And I have a message from Angel, from only a few minutes ago. I grin.

ANG3L:

Maybe...we should meet?

Holy shit.

2HORNED:

Tell me when

I can't tell if the speed of my pulse is from excitement or anxiety at the thought. The three little black dots pop up.

ANG3L:

I'll be out of town next week over the Fourth of July weekend (it's also my birthday) so maybe after that?

2HORNED:

I'm going out of town next weekend, too

so that works for me

Also, happy birthday! 22, right?

It's kind of a crazy coincidence, Livvy's birthday is over that weekend as well. It's on *the* fourth, actually. That's probably not a very common birthday. I ignore the urge to ask Angel which day is hers—I don't want to push for too many specifics too soon.

ANG3L:

Yes! Thank you

I walk downstairs to the scent of bread filling the apartment. Wood is in full-apron mode, oven mitts on both hands as he pulls two loaves of bread out of the oven to join the—Jesus Christ—five other loaves on the counter.

"That's a lot of bread."

Wood smiles, wiping some flour off his forehead with the back of his arm. "I've been baking since five-thirty. It relaxes me. There's sourdough, wheat, rye, banana bread, banana bread with chocolate chips, zucchini bread, and a cinnamon swirl loaf. Be careful, that one's hot."

"Wow, it smells so good out here." Livvy comes out, a sleepy look still in her eyes, her light brown hair tousled, barefaced, the tiny freckles across her nose more visible than usual.

She's wearing my T-shirt again.

"Thanks." Wood beams. "I just got the urge. Takes my mind off stuff."

"What kind of stuff?"

Wood looks at her with his lopsided grin but his eyes dodgy. "Um...just stuff and things. Here, let me get you some."

As he's slicing each loaf of bread, Livvy and my eyes meet.

She instantly flushes and my cheeks start burning as well as memories of last night come flooding back. Not only because of what she saw me doing last night in the loft, but also because of what I did after.

I got off with Angel, that wasn't new, and the picture she'd sent had me going immediately. It was hot, it was perfect, just like I knew she would be.

But then I'd found myself thinking about Livvy. How she looks in her little white shorts and tank top. How the tips of her nipples clearly strain against the thin fabric when they're hard. How her pouty lips were parted, and she let out a little gasp when she saw me with my cock in my hand.

My cock had throbbed when I saw her watching me. Looking at me, looking at it. I'd wanted her to stay. The words were dancing around my tongue. *Don't go. Come here.*

Of course, I didn't say that. And after she'd left, I'd tried to focus on Angel. On her words. On her picture. But since I don't know what her face looks like, my brain kept filling in the gaps—with Livvy. Livvy's face was on that body. And then it was Livvy's naked body under mine. Her scent. Her moans.

I came harder than I have in a long time. Maybe ever.

And it was all Livvy.

Livvy's eyes are wide when Wood hands her a plate piled high with warm slices of bread.

"I made some honey butter, too, if you want."

"Oh, yes, please. Thank you." Livvy takes the heaping plate of bread and sits down.

I sit next to her with my coffee, and she mouths *help me*. I chuckle and take the piece of zucchini bread, devouring it before Wood has a chance to sit down.

Bex saunters out to the kitchen, yawning in an off-the-shoulder sweatshirt and little athletic shorts, just as Wood sits down with us.

"Have some bread," Wood says.

"Wood made bread," Livvy says, biting her lip and smirking.

"A lot of bread," I add.

"Holy shit." Bex gets the blender out and sets it by the sink along with ingredients to make a smoothie.

"So..." Wood says casually while slathering honey butter on his banana bread. "What happened last night?"

"What do you mean?" I ask at the same time that Livvy says, "Nothing."

Bex starts the blender, and it whirls to life in all its deafening glory, crushing up the fruit and ice, the sound of it vibrating off all the hard surfaces in the kitchen.

Livvy and I exchange a glance, her pretty blush returning to her cheeks and ears.

She's thinking about last night again. I know it. And so am I.

The blender stops. Wood's mouth is full of banana bread.

"I mean," he says, chewing, "does anyone have any news to share? Any new developments?"

I shoot a look to Livvy again. He's not talking about what she saw me doing last night. There's no way he'd know about that.

Then why are your hands sweaty?

He's getting at something else, but I don't know what it is.

"Ugh." Bex walks around the counter with her giant purple smoothie. "I have some news." She plops down next to Livvy and takes a sip of her smoothie. It's thick. It takes forever to inch up the straw.

She finally gets some to her lips.

Wood's knee is bouncing, eyes on her. "What is it? What's the news?"

She swallows. "Oh, so get this. Last night at their anniversary dinner Spencer told Macy that since he's going out of town this week for a work conference, and his brother is living there right now, too, he doesn't think it's"—she uses air quotes and rolls her eyes—"*appropriate* for her to stay there alone with his brother."

"That's an icky thing to say," Livvy says, scrunching up her face.

"Right? He actually wanted her to find somewhere else to stay this week. So fucked up."

Wood is unusually quiet, buttering more bread.

"So, anyway," Bex continues, "I'm going to be staying over at Spencer's place with Macy and his brother this week."

Wood looks up from his bread. "Did he propose last night?"

"Oh! And that!" Bex takes a long pull from her smoothie again, Wood biting the inside of his cheek, adding impossibly more honey butter to his already slathered bread.

"Nope," Bex finally says. "He didn't propose. Macy was disappointed." She slurps her smoothie some more.

I'd have thought he'd be happy she didn't get engaged last night. But he's not.

Wood's mouth is set in a hard line, his jaw clenched as he tosses his bread to his plate. "He's an idiot." His chair screeches across the floor as he gets up and leaves.

Bex nudges Livvy, her straw between her teeth. "Looks like we need to get on that apartment hunting sooner than later."

Livvy nods.

My chest tightens. A pang—unexpected, unwelcome—hits me at the thought of her not being around. I was just getting used to having her here. Eating together, her silly reality show on in the background, watching over her...

♥ ♥ ♥

She's a natural.

It's been less than a week of training her as an apprentice and she's already taking the tattoo gun apart and cleaning it exactly like I showed her. Her soft, delicate fingers handling the machinery like a pro.

I don't need to sit here and watch her—she's doing a great job.

Her attention to detail is impressive. But I don't feel like doing anything else. Being anywhere else.

She sat with me all day today, while I did a six-hour piece. Right next to me. The scent of her hair—strawberries and something else—affected my thoughts all day.

I realize I'm sitting too close, leaning in more than necessary. Trying to get a hint of that scent again. *What is the something else?* I can't place it.

"The piece you did today was beautiful," she says, handing me the cleaned parts to put away.

"Thanks."

She sweeps her hair away from her face, tucking it behind her ear, exposing the side of her neck. Her skin is so smooth. Flawless. That little spot, where neck meets shoulder—the perfect place to nuzzle and kiss...

"Noah?"

I tear my eyes off that spot and up to her eyes. "Huh? Sorry, I was spacing out. What were you saying?"

"I can tell." She laughs, lightly touching my arm. "It's okay, that was a long session. I'm sure you're tired. I was asking how long until you think I'll be starting to tattoo on real skin."

"That won't be for quite a while. Unless you want to start practicing on yourself."

She tilts her head to the left, the corners of her mouth turning up into a devilish little smirk. "Can I practice on you?"

"Me?"

She nods. "Yeah. Why not?"

I smile. "I'm about out of real estate. Where are you suggesting, exactly?"

"From what I could see the other night, your butt looked pretty bare. No one would see it."

I thought we were doing the whole, "pretend it never happened" approach to our little accidental encounter the other night. But here she is, bringing it up.

My cock twitches.

"You want to tattoo my ass?"

"Were you saving it for something special?"

I laugh. Harder than I have in a while.

"No, I guess not."

She quirks an eyebrow at me and I'm going to be letting her tattoo my ass, aren't I?

"I'll get you some pig skin soon," I say.

But I'm smiling at how much I don't hate the thought of her tattooing my ass when Anthony strolls up. Sidling up next to where Livvy is sitting, leaning against the wall, flexing his arms, cocky grin.

"'Sup." He winks at her.

His face is extremely punch-able.

She stands, smiling at him. A big, breathtaking smile that's all teeth and peachy cheeks and red lips...

"Oh hey, Anthony."

I don't want her smiling like that at him. I want her to smile like that for me.

Only me.

"So, uh—" His gaze lazily slides from her face down to her chest.

I have to physically unclench my jaw.

"I didn't get the chance to ask after our last date—" He glances at me as he clears his throat.

The image of his arms around her, her hands on his waist, his lips on hers clouds my vision. My hand aches. I put down the tattoo gun grip I've been holding—or squeezing.

"—but I wanted to ask you, in person, if you wanted to go out with me again some time."

No.

No.

Say no.

Her smile widens and she nods. "Yes, I'd love to go out again!"

I don't know where this voice in my head is coming from, but it's screaming. *No. Mine. Don't go out with him. Go out with me.*

And there it is.

Fuck.

It's not protectiveness. It's jealousy.

I want Livvy.

♥ ♥ ♥

I'm in a foul mood all evening. Livvy and I eat in silence in the dark apartment, a single light on in the kitchen. It's storming outside, wind and thunder at the windows while rain pelts against the glass.

She keeps looking at me with her big eyes.

I don't know what to say or how to act. I'm an asshole. I'm supposed to be her friend. Roommate. Boss. I've known her since she was little. I'm not supposed to be pining for her. Thinking about her perfect curves. Jerking off to her. Wondering what her lips taste like. Or pissed off that Anthony knows that answer.

I rinse the dishes and she loads them into the dishwasher. We don't say anything.

Normally we'd be talking. Laughing. She'd put on her ridiculous show, and I'd pretend I wasn't just as invested as her to see who Ainsley is hooking up with now and who's talking behind Braxton's back.

She puts the last glass on the rack then turns toward me. "Are you mad at me? Did I do something?"

Shit. "No, Liv. No, you didn't, I'm sorry. It's me, I'm just in my head tonight is all. Thinking about stuff."

She steps closer, her arm brushing my elbow. "Is something bothering you? Do you want to talk about it?"

I shake my head. No, I don't want to talk about how badly I

want to kiss her and how I want her to tell Anthony to fuck off and spend time with me, instead. Only me.

Mine.

"No," I say. "I'm fine. I'm sorry I've been in a bad mood. And I'm sorry about the other night, too."

"You were in a bad mood the other night, too?" She scrunches her face up in the most adorable way and it makes me smile.

"No, I mean when you saw me, um...upstairs."

"Oh!" She turns red and I regret saying anything.

I want to make her feel many things—happy, safe, content, aroused...but not embarrassed. Never embarrassed.

"I'm the one who should be saying sorry about that," she says, not looking me in the eyes. "I mean, this is your place and I just wandered up there in the middle of the night. Next time, I'll make sure to announce myself. Loudly."

She looks up and smiles at me and it warms me from the inside.

"Honestly, I didn't think you were home, and on the off chance you were, it was so quiet and dark I didn't want to wake you if you were sleeping—"

She's cute when she rambles.

"You don't need to worry about that. I hardly ever sleep."

"You don't sleep?"

"Not much. Insomnia."

She grimaces. "That sucks. I have a friend who has a hard time sleeping, too. I can't even imagine."

"Yeah. It's even worse on the couch."

"Oh my god." She takes a step back, her eyes widening, mouth dropping in horror, hand going to her chest. "And I've taken your bed."

Fuck. "No, no, no. Don't worry about it."

"No, we need to switch. I'll take the couch. Bex is with Macy tonight, so it works out."

"Absolutely not. You get the bed."

She crosses her arms over her chest, narrows her eyes, and purses her lips. "I'm not going to let this go."

"It's nonnegotiable. I won't let you sleep on the couch while you're staying here."

"Fine," she says, lifting her chin.

"Good. We're in agreement."

"We'll just both sleep in the bed, then."

It takes me a second to register her words. I must not have heard correctly. "What?"

"You won't let me sleep on the couch and I won't be the reason you can't get better sleep in your bed. So, us both sleeping in it seems to be the only solution to me."

"I don't think that would be a good idea."

"Why not?"

Because I want to fuck you.

"Um." Shit.

"I promise I don't have cooties. It's just sleeping on the same mattress. Is it that big of deal?"

Yes. "No, I guess not. Are you sure?"

She laughs and reaches out, touching my arm lightly. "Yes, I'm sure it's no big deal."

So now we're brushing our teeth, in tandem, in front of the mirror in my bathroom. Her in her thin white tank top that rides up, showing a strip of bare stomach and the shorts that barely cover her ass.

And I have to stand here pretending I don't know exactly what she looks like under those clothes. That I don't know how smooth her skin is over her hip bones. The color of her nipples.

Don't get a boner while brushing your teeth, Jesus Christ.

Even the way she spits out her toothpaste is fucking cute. *What is happening to me?*

We pad down the hall to my room in darkness and quiet—except for the storm. Wind howling. The rain, a constant thrum.

The sliver of moon shining through the curtains puts her in

silhouette, the lavender light a crescent around the curves of her hips and breasts, her hair glowing in the hazy darkness.

She slips into my bed, and I follow, like a puppy, hopelessly lost.

My heart thrashes against my chest as I lie next to her.

A rustle of sheets. She shifts, the mattress dips. Quiet breaths. Her scent is all over my pillow, entwined in the sheets and filling up the room. The heat of her body radiates toward me.

She's everywhere. In my head. In my bed. Inches away. And yet, I can't touch her.

The wind is a low hum, the rain a tinkling spatter against the windows.

Livvy sighs.

A soothing symphony of sounds. A safeness. Lulling me away, pulling me further into a dark space where I can float into nothingness.

"Noah," Livvy whispers.

I open my eyes.

"Are you awake?"

"Yes," I whisper back.

"What do you want tattooed on your ass?"

I let out a hard laugh. "I don't know. Can I think about it?"

"Hm. Yes."

"What would you pick?"

"Wait—for your ass or mine?"

"I didn't know yours was on the table." *Stop picturing her ass.*

"It's not—I don't think."

"Well, if you do ever want your ass tattooed, you've got to let me be the one to do it."

"Deal," she says softly.

I roll onto my back, listening to the storm and the way her breaths slow and even out until, finally, I can't hear them anymore at all.

"Livvy," I whisper. "Are you awake?"

She doesn't answer.

I exhale, staring at the ceiling, preparing for the unending thoughts to start worming their way in. The memories that keep me awake. The conversations never had. Everything that's been nagging at my brain, any worry that's been creeping around the edges of my mind, are all about to flood to the surface now.

Livvy lets out a sweet sigh and rolls toward me, pressing the side of her body against me. And now all I can think about is her. Next to me, touching me. Her warmth. Her scent.

I close my eyes to the sound of the rain.

I don't wake up until the sun is streaking through the curtains. Livvy is next to me, unmoving. Soft, rhythmic breaths. Her feet have tangled with mine in the night, but I won't move and risk waking her.

I slept all night. For the first time in years. Since I was a teenager. Since before.

Livvy's dark lashes are fanned across her cheeks, hair sparkling golden in the morning sunshine. The light dances around her, warming her skin. So much skin. Her bare arms and delicate shoulders, her slender neck, across her collarbone, and down to the soft flesh of her breasts, which are trying to free themselves from her tank top.

Ignoring how just the tiniest peek of a single pink nipple has my cock throbbing, I tug on the strap of her tank top, twisting and pulling it up to cover her.

A hard knock rattles the door and vibrates through the room.

"Livvy," Wood calls from the other side.

Her eyes open, my fingers still intertwined in the strap of her shirt.

Shit.

CHAPTER 13

LIVVY

Noah snatches his hand away from me.

"I was adjusting, uh..." He gestures toward my top, looking comically distressed.

For a moment we're still. His eyes locked on mine. Dark gray blue. He's so close his breath tickles my skin. Holding my breath, I slide my foot against his. He closes his eyes and lets out a little sigh that almost sounds like a whimper.

A knock comes again. Wood. Fuck. Noah throws the covers off and pads to the door.

Wood's voice is muffled through the door. "Sorry to wake you. Do you know where Noah is? I can't find him—"

Noah opens the door, Wood is standing there, fist in the air as if he's about to knock again, mouth open.

"I'm right here," Noah growls.

Wood blinks, his eye shifting to me lying in Noah's bed.

"It's not what it looks like," I say.

Wood puts both palms up and takes a step back. "None of my business. I won't say anything."

"There's nothing going on." Noah's morning voice is husky and rough.

"Exactly." Wood does an exaggerated wink.

Noah sighs.

Wood claps his hands, smiling. He's wearing swim trunks and a white T-shirt, his blond hair poking out of a backward baseball cap. "Well, now that you're no longer missing. It's time to start packing up so we can hit the road. I got snacks!"

♥ ♥ ♥

Wood's family lake house is on the south side of Lake Chelan. Noah and I ride with Wood while Bex and Macy follow behind with Spencer and his brother.

It's a three-hour drive on twisting highways along riverways surrounded by thickening forests and misty mountains in the distance.

Wood sings his heart out the whole drive.

We turn off the main highway to a dirt road hidden past a moss-covered pine tree. It winds through trees so tall and dense the sun can barely poke through the canopy.

Then the trees clear and Wood turns onto a large, circular paved drive and up to the house. I guess I was expecting a smallish cabin tucked away somewhere. Not this.

It's a three-story mansion with giant stone steps, a wraparound porch, arched windows, and large eaves. The east side is dripping with purple wisteria, and the cedar shingles are grayed and weathered, adding texture and character.

We hop out of Wood's black SUV. It's humid and warm, the cloud cover threatening rain. Noah carries my bag as well as his own and we walk up the stone walkway lined with white hydrangea bushes to the house.

Noah holds the door for me as I step inside the wide, tiled entry with an elegant staircase with carved wooden spindles. A family portrait with a young Wood, even more blond and tan than now, hangs on the wall.

"Make yourself at home," Wood says as he passes with the cooler. I follow him to the kitchen where he starts unloading beers into the fridge. "The bedroom down that hall is my parents' but you can choose from any of the other seven rooms."

"Seven?"

He nods, popping open a bottle. "You get first pick 'cause you're the coolest."

I barely have time to marvel at the crisp white kitchen with a marble island large enough to sleep four before I look out past the family room. The entire back of the house is a wall of windows, and the view is spectacular.

Eagerly, I go to the glass. Past the expansive wood deck are steps down to a sandy beach with a massive fire pit surrounded by Adirondack chairs and a private dock jutting out into the lake. The water is sapphire blue and smooth, stretching to the horizon. We appear to be tucked into a little cove of the lake, surrounded by woods and mountains without another house in sight.

"Hey." Noah's voice catches me off guard, and I almost yelp at his sudden presence by my side. "The best view is from one of the bedrooms on the third floor. Come up with me."

He directs me to go up first, following closely behind, one tattooed hand on the railing, the other softly at my back.

"That one," he says when we reach the landing.

The room is large and bright with white walls, buttery wood floors and a plush, ornate rug. In the center there's a four-poster bed with a fluffy cream duvet and a light blue quilt. The ceiling slopes down toward the floor on one side with a dormer of arched windows across from the bed. The view stretches for miles, the clouds starting to break to show bright blue sky and streaks of sunlight hitting the trees and sparkling on the lake.

"This is beautiful," I say.

Noah is next to me. He looks out of place in this pretty room —dressed all in black, skin covered in ink.

"You take this room. I'll stay in the one next door."

"Okay. Thank you." I nudge his arm with my elbow. But I don't step away after. I let it linger there, our arms brushing. He doesn't move away to break the contact either.

I want this. I want him. I've wanted him for so long, and it always seemed impossible, a little girl's stupid dream. But not now. He's here and he's real and he's looking at me like he wants me, too.

And I try not to think about how last night we were in the same bed. Or how I dreamt about him all night. About us doing more than sleeping in that bed.

His gaze drops to my mouth for a second. Instinctually, I arch toward him.

For an instant, I think he's going to lean in, too.

"I'll go get our bags," he says as he steps back and turns to leave.

After taking in the view for a few more minutes, I head back downstairs, too, right as the others are pulling up to the house in Spencer's fancy car. Spencer steps out in Dockers and a Polo shirt, Rayban sunglasses on his head.

Macy gets out of the car in a yellow sundress, followed closely by Bex, her blonde hair flowing in the breeze. She's wearing cutoff jean shorts and a loose tank top, her red string bikini showing underneath. "I need to pee and then a margarita, stat."

Spencer squints up at the house. "My parents' place is much nicer than this. It's not too late to go back. We can drink champagne while we have the perfect view of the fireworks over Puget Sound."

"It'll be nice to do something different this year," Macy says.

Spencer hmphs.

I can only assume the man who steps out of the passenger seat in shorts and boat shoes is his brother, Jake. He looks just like

Spencer, but a little younger with broader shoulders and a squarer jaw.

"Howdy!" Wood calls out from the open double doors. "Margaritas are mixed up and the hot tub is ready," he says as Bex and Macy run inside with flushed cheeks.

"Woodall," Spencer says, opening the trunk.

Wood tips his beer to him. "Hayes."

"Still have a talent for drinking at noon, I see."

"I have many talents. Just ask your mom." Wood gives him a big smile with lots of white teeth.

"Charming."

"She thinks so."

"Livvy!" Bex squeezes me around the middle, sandals clacking on the tile. "Happy birthday weekend! Woo! Booze and bathing suits for the next three days, let's go!"

Macy leans in and whispers, "She already started the booze part. She had three spiked lemonades on the way here."

With the party underway, I change into my bathing suit in my room. It's a black one piece that's backless with a low-cut scoop neck in front. Out the window, Wood and Noah are taking turns jumping off the dock. Macy is sitting on the side with her feet in the water, lathering sunscreen on her pale skin, wearing a giant, floppy hat. Bex is laid out next to her in the sun, all tan skin under her barely-there bikini.

I opt to keep my jean shorts on over my swimsuit and head out to join them.

Spencer and Jake are debating something as I pass them on the patio and stroll down the beach. Wood rushes out of the lake, water droplets coming off his hair and beading on his rippling chest. He looks every bit the all-American swimmer, polo-player, and rowing captain the trophies lining the shelves in the den have touted him to be.

Maybe Bex was right when she said I should consider Wood. But then Noah follows after, dark hair dripping, skin covered in ink, his trunks riding low on his hips, showing that delicious shelf of muscle shaped in a V leading right to his—

"Beer or margarita, girlfriend?" Wood asks.

"Oh! Margarita, please. But you don't have to serve me, I can get it."

"Nah, I was getting out anyway to fire up the grill."

He makes me a huge lime margarita with a salted rim, and the afternoon slips into evening before I know it.

Many margaritas and hot dogs later, we're sitting around the bonfire under a clear sky full of stars. There's a slight chill in the air, but the fire is hot, embers crackling in the night. It smells of woodsmoke and beer. There's conversation and laughter and Wood telling stories.

The night's a bit hazy after the fifth margarita.

I remember the fire and laughing and Noah taking my hand and leading me upstairs. I remember peeling off my swimsuit as soon as I got in my room and him putting me to bed. I remember asking him to stay with me. His warm body sliding in next to me. The scent of him. The soft sounds of breathing as we fell asleep.

♥ ♥ ♥

Waking up on my birthday with a hangover is less than ideal.

Rolling over to Noah lying next to me, shirtless, and realizing I'm not wearing any clothes is...interesting.

His eyes are open, and he's propped up on an elbow, but he hasn't noticed I'm awake yet.

I lick my lips, but just before sound comes out, he picks up his phone. I pause. He's texting someone. *Who would he be texting right now?*

My stomach drops. I know it's a girl, even though I have no evidence he's seeing anyone right now. Not even a mention of a situationship.

I shift to my side, and he immediately drops his phone face down on his chest, hiding his screen.

That confirms it.

"Morning. Happy birthday."

"Morning."

It doesn't matter that he's in bed with you half naked, he's not for you. He's your sister's ex. He's your boss. He's your friend. And most importantly—he doesn't see you like that, anyway. Move. The. Fuck. On.

He smiles and gets out of bed, careful to keep the covers in place. "I'll, uh, let you get dressed. See you downstairs."

I try not to stare at the conspicuous bulge in his black boxer briefs as he leaves. It's not like I had anything to do with it. It's probably morning wood. Or maybe whoever he was talking to gave it to him.

I glance at my phone before I get up. I wasn't expecting any messages since I'd told him I was going to be out of town this weekend, but there's a notification from the app.

2HORNED:

Hey, I need to talk

Seems ominous. Okay.

ANG3L:

Yeah, sure. What's up?

2HORNED:

So I know I was the one who originally brought up meeting, but I don't think we should anymore

Oh.

ANG3L:

Oh?

2HORNED:

> Yeah, I'm sorry. I met someone a little while ago and I've been thinking I want to try and start something with her, see how it goes. And I don't think it would be fair to her or a new relationship to meet each other

> ...considering what we've chatted about

ANG3L:

> That makes sense. I'm really happy for you

And I am. Really. I could always tell he was deeply lonely, and this is good. Good for him. Good for us. I wanted to make a clean break with this app anyway. This works out.

But then why am I so sad?

Happy fucking birthday to me.

2HORNED:

> But I'm still here for you. You've been an big part of my life the last year and I'd like to stay friends

ANG3L:

> Thank you. I really appreciate you being open and honest with me

2HORNED:

> I'll always be honest with you

I send him a heart emoji. I really do appreciate him and the honesty. But I can't come up with any more words right now.

I put my phone down, needing to be done with this conversation. It's my birthday. No sad feelings today.

I'm going to shower, and do my hair cute in loose waves, and put on mascara and my new sundress and enjoy my day. The dress is a pretty soft lilac with straps that tie in little bows. I can't wear a bra with it, but I've got a cute thong with tiny white flowers on it.

Looking in the mirror, I tell myself it's my sexy, confident, hot girl era—not my sad girl, pining over boys who aren't obsessed with me era. I am not sexting with them, and I am *definitely* not asking them to share a bed with me. That's over.

Done.

Everyone's already sitting around the breakfast table when I come downstairs. Sunlight glitters off the lake and reflects in through the windows.

"Perfect timing," Wood says, stacking three fluffy pancakes onto a plate. "They're blueberry." Then he ladles a heap of glossy strawberries over the stack before covering them with a swirl of fresh whipped cream. "Red, white, and blue pancakes." He smiles proudly. "Happy Fourth of July."

"Festive." I nod as I take the plate.

His eyes widen. "Oh, hold on." He stoops down below the counter then pops back up and places two white candles in my pancakes with one hand and lights them with a lighter in the other. "Also, happy birthday!"

"Thanks."

"Make a wish!" Macy calls from the table.

Fuck. Can I just wish for my headache to go away? I close my eyes and blow out the candles.

Noah catches my eye as I walk up to the breakfast table. There's an empty seat next to him and one other one next to Bex. The corner of his mouth turns up, his lips parting just enough to see the edges of his teeth.

Hot girl era, not lead yourself on and hurt your own feelings era.

I sit next to Bex.

Do I take pleasure when Noah's smile disappears almost instantly as I sit? No.

Okay, maybe a little.

"Coffee?" Bex asks.

"You're my favorite sister."

"Remember that when I'm pouring your birthday shots later." She smiles sweetly.

And my sister, the bartender, is, indeed, pouring shots by two in the afternoon.

We spend the day mostly lounging around in the sun on beach towels, snacking and chatting. We're perfumed by coconut sunscreen and pina coladas.

Spencer and Jake decide to take the kayaks out around the lake. Bex raises her bottle of vodka at them in salute as they go.

Wood entertains us by doing dives and cannon balls off the dock, splashing us every time he walks by.

Noah walks up the beach toward us after his swim, eyes on me. He grabs a towel and Bex offers him a beer. I look away.

Know your worth era.

He goes to sit under one of the patio umbrellas instead. Brooding in the shade alone.

By late afternoon, Macy has sunburnt shoulders, Bex is napping, her skin getting golden brown, and Wood decides to fire up the grill for burgers.

My buzz has mostly worn off by the time it's dark and we're sitting on blankets around the dying fire to watch the fireworks over the lake.

"Can I sit here?" Noah leans over, offering me a watermelon hard seltzer from the cooler.

"Sure." I take the drink and scoot over.

He sits closer than he needs to on the blanket. As I take my first sip, he looks over to where Bex and Macy are huddled on the other side of me. He leans in like he wants to say something without them hearing, but then the high-pitched scream of the first firework cuts through the quiet and he sits back.

Bright, shimmery streaks of gold shoot through the ink-colored sky then explode with a pop, flashing and sparkling, each one bigger and louder and more mesmerizing than the last.

After the last firework lights up the sky and finally fizzles out and dissolves into nothingness, Spencer stands and clears his throat, looking down at Macy.

"It's still early," she says.

He doesn't move, say anything, or change his expression.

She puts her half empty drink down and looks around at us, her mouth downturned. "Night, guys."

After they leave, Bex points her drink at Jake. "Question. Was your brother born with a stick up his ass or did he acquire it later?"

Jake, who had just taken a sip of his beer, almost spits it up, his coughs turning to laughter. He raises an eyebrow at my sister.

She shrugs. "It's a valid question. Maybe I'll ask Macy if she's ever seen it. It's got to be huge. Oh! I know what we should do!" Bex downs the rest of her drink then grins, the flickering flames of the fire reflecting in her eyes. "We should go skinny dipping."

What? My stomach plummets with that sickening sinking feeling.

"Let's go." Wood pumps his fist in the air, standing, already loosening his shorts.

Wait—

"I'm in," Jake says.

Bex jumps up and runs toward the lake. "Come on, Livvy!"

She leaves a trail of clothes along the dock—her white tank top and little cut off shorts, Jake and Wood close behind her, bare-assed in the moonlight. They disappear into the darkness and then there are screams and loud splashes.

Noah looks at me, the tip of his tongue running along his lower lip and stands. "Do you want to?" He holds his hand out to me. I take it and he helps me up.

"I don't know," I say.

"Okay." He pulls his shirt off and tosses it to the sand next to our blanket. Eyes still on me, he undoes the button of his shorts.

Oh.

Sexy, confident girl era, remember? What would Angel do? She'd have been the first one stripping down and jumping in.

"Okay," I say. I pull the ties on the straps of my dress, and it falls off, crumpling in a pile at my feet. I'm keenly aware my breasts are bare and nipples be nippling. I leave my thong on. "But I don't want to jump off the dock," I say. I don't know how deep the water is there.

"We'll just walk in, then." He drops his shorts. Boxers, too and I avert my eyes out to the water and then back to his face.

Don't look down.

We run toward the lake, through the sand and down to where it gets rocky near the water's edge. He takes my hand and holds me steady as I step over the larger stones and rounded pebbles shifting underfoot.

The water makes my toes curl. It's cold even though the temperature was almost a hundred degrees today. But Noah still has my hand, and he leads me farther in without slowing.

"Don't overthink it," he says.

So I go with him, the water prickling at my legs, and then it's up to my waist. Deeper. I step out until it's at my chest, the pressure of the water constricting my lungs.

Noah lies back, extending his arms and kicking out away from me. Farther.

I want to go out there, too. I want to join them and have fun, but I know the next step I take, the bottom will drop out from below me and I'll have to swim.

I *can* swim. Kind of.

It will be okay. It's a lake, not an ocean. There isn't a current that's going to pull me out or under. I'll be fine. It's like a big swimming pool. A big, dark, cold, scary swimming pool that I can't see the bottom of and is surely full of little creatures and slimy plants. It's cool. I'm fine.

I take the step out and suck in a breath, filling my chest with air and kicking my feet.

Keeping my arms moving, I wade out closer to Noah. The other three aren't much farther out, but their heads are barely visible above the water and only lit by the stars.

See, I can do this. I'm wading. I can tread water.

But I do wish they would come back in, just a little bit. There's really no reason to be out so far. How long does a skinny dip last, anyway? I mean, we've dipped.

Noah had been right by me, but now I'm not feeling the ripples from his kicks in the water anymore. I look around and go to call out his name, but the water at my chin is suddenly to my nose and when I open my mouth, I take it in.

I bob back up, spitting out water and getting a breath.

But now I've lost them. I can't see anyone.

I want to go back.

I turn to go back the way I came, but it's not right. The beach should be there. The fire. The lights from the back of the house—I don't see them. The moon has gone behind the clouds and all there is around me is darkness, water somehow turning into trees. There's no horizon. No beach. No land. No friends. No sister. No Noah.

I keep spinning around to see the house. I don't know which way is in or out. My arms are cold, and my legs are getting tired.

"Noah!"

"Livvy, over here!" He sounds far away.

I don't want to swim out there. I want to go back.

I open my mouth to call to him again, but I slip under for a second. Water fills my nose and my eyes. I come back up, coughing. My side has a cramp and my legs feel stiff.

I can't stay up.

I can't stay up.

Water overtakes me again.

I'm flailing.

I go under and I can't tell which direction is up.

Kicking with all the strength I have, I burst to the surface again, splashing and waving and I scream for help.

I inhale and water rushes in. I can't breathe.

And then I go under. Sinking. I kick. But I can't get back up.

CHAPTER 14

NOAH

The splashing stops just before I locate the disturbance in the water. And then it's gone. Livvy's gone. Nothing. She'd been right behind me.

The water is calm.

"Livvy!"

No call back.

The hairs on my neck prick up, all my senses going on alert as dread tightens in my chest.

I race to where I saw her last.

There's no trace of her. No waves. No air bubbles.

I dive down.

I can't see anything.

There's movement.

It's Wood. He brushes against me as he dives below me.

Then I see her, tiny air bubbles swirling around her hair like a halo.

She's not moving.

I swim faster than I ever have in my life, barely able to see in the dark water. Hooking her around the middle, I shoot to the surface.

As soon as I do, gasping for air, Wood takes her over his shoulder and swims back to the beach.

I don't like not having her in my arms. She's not okay. I need to make sure she's okay. But Wood is literally a champion swimmer. He can swim with her in one arm faster than I can with two.

He has her laid out on a blanket by the fire when I get out of the water. I snatch up two more blankets and cover her, dropping to my knees by her side.

"Call 911," I bark at him.

He runs for his phone.

Her lips are blue.

I don't think she's breathing.

I press my cheek to her face, hoping to hear her, to feel warm breath on my skin. But she's cold.

A blood-curdling scream breaks behind me. Frantic footsteps in the sand as Bex and Jake run up to us. Bex is yelling, "What's happening?" already crying.

"I know CPR." Jake kneels next to us, and I scramble away to make room.

Bex is hysterical, sobbing, crumpled on the other side of Livvy as Jake starts to administer CPR.

I can't do anything but watch.

Her body is so still.

I take her hand. Her fingers are freezing and limp. Minutes ago, they were wrapping around my hand so tight, warm, holding on to me. Trusting me.

I shouldn't have let her out of my sight. I should have stayed right next to her and made sure. Kept her safe. How did I let this happen?

My stomach is so tight it hurts.

He rips the blankets off her and places his hands between her breasts for chest compressions.

I want to vomit.

I don't know if I can watch.

I close my eyes, squeeze her hand, and prepare myself for the sickening cracking sound to come next.

There's a raspy gurgle. I open my eyes as Jake is turning Livvy onto her side. She heaves, water gushes out of her mouth and into the sand, and then she starts coughing and taking pained, wheezing breaths.

"Oh, my god!" Tears are streaming down Bex's cheeks.

Livvy looks so small. I want to go to her, cover her up, wrap her in the blankets and hold her close. But Bex throws herself over her and hugs her tight, rolling Livvy away from me. Her hand slips out of mine.

"Hey." A warm hand clasps my shoulder and I look up at Wood, his face pale, expression sober. "She's going to be okay. An ambulance is on the way. Are you okay?"

"I'm okay," I say, standing. The breeze is cool on my cheeks, and I realize they're wet with tears. I wipe them with my palms. I want to say *of course I'm okay, I'm just worried for Livvy*, but he knows.

He knows I'm not okay.

He knows what kind of thoughts are clawing around in my head right now.

"She's going to be okay," he reassures again.

I nod. I want it to be true. I want to believe him.

The paramedics arrive just as Macy runs out. She and Bex don't leave Livvy's side the entire time they attend to her, giving her oxygen and checking her vitals.

She's awake and talking.

I'm pacing along the beach, hands still shaking.

I can't stop replaying the moment I realized she'd gone under. What if I hadn't seen her? What if we couldn't find her? What if instead of sitting there on the beach, she was at the bottom of the lake—

And then I think about them. My family. The accident.

The water.

Cameron.

But that's not Livvy. They say her vitals are good, but they're going to take her to the ER and keep her overnight, just to monitor her and make sure she's safe.

They load her into the ambulance, Bex climbing in after her, holding her hand, her face tear streaked.

Just before they close the doors, Livvy's eyes meet mine—wide and watery and beautiful and it feels like I should be the one in the back of the ambulance with her, holding her hand and telling her that everything's fine.

It kills me that it's not me.

Wood and I follow with Macy and Jake in the backseat. Spencer decided to go back to bed.

They'll only allow family in her room after hours. So, I sit outside her room in a little chair with scratchy gray fabric and a worn-out seat cushion. I pace. I watch the clock. I sit back down.

Finally, Bex comes out of the room. I stand, straining to look into the room before the door closes behind her.

"She's sleeping," Bex says.

"We should go get some rest, too. We can come back in the morning," Macy says.

"I'm staying here," I say.

"Me, too," Bex adds.

"All right. We'll stay." Macy nods.

"I'll go find some coffee," Wood says. "Do you need anything, Mace? A snack?"

"I'm fine."

He tilts his head as he looks at her. "You haven't eaten in a while."

She nods. "Um, yeah." A bit frazzled, Macy looks around for her purse. "I should check my levels—"

Wood grabs her purse from the chair across from me and they head down the hall.

I sit back in the chair.

People walk by. Quiet conversations down the hall, the incessant little beeps and doors closing. I hate hospitals. They're depressing as fuck. I'm glad I didn't have to spend any time in the hospital after everything.

No, they all died on scene. Would have been nice to be able to say goodbye, though.

♥ ♥ ♥

I was the last one awake by five in the morning, but my body finally succumbed, and I passed out.

Now my neck is stiff, and my back protests as I unbend myself to get out of this chair. The morning sun shines in from somewhere around a corner and people are no longer speaking in hushed voices.

We get her checked out around eight and drive back to the house. She sits snug between Bex and Macy in the middle seat while I clench my jaw in the front seat, unaware I'm digging my fingers into my knee until we pull onto the circle drive.

As soon as Wood puts the car in park, I jump out and rip the back door open.

Bex hops out, looking confused.

"Come here," I say to Livvy, holding my arms out to her.

I don't care about the looks Bex and Macy give me when I scoop her up in my arms and carry her into the house. I don't stop. I carry her up both flights of stairs, her head on my shoulder.

Her breath is warm against my neck, and the simple realization that I can feel her breathing almost sends me to my knees like last night.

"I'm okay. I can walk," she whispers. Her voice is hoarse, and I clench my jaw, tightening my hold on her.

I take her up to her room, and I know I should put her down, let her get cleaned up, dressed, whatever. But I don't want to let go. I don't even want to let her out of my sight.

So I sit on the bed, cradling her in my arms. She puts her arms around my neck and looks up at me. A tear streaks down her cheek, and then another.

"I'm sorry," she says. "I shouldn't have gone out there. I should have told you I'm not a strong swimmer, I shouldn't—"

"Shh." I hug her to me and kiss her forehead, letting my lips linger there for a second, breathing her in. When I pull back, more tears have fallen, and I wipe them away with my thumb.

She looks up at me, and I can't imagine never having gotten to see those beautiful green eyes again, smell her hair, see her smile, hear her laugh. Her lips are parted, back to their pretty pink color, perfectly plump. It would be inappropriate to kiss her right now.

But god, I want to kiss her.

"I'm cold," she says, shifting on my lap.

My first instinct is to tear back the covers, put her in bed and climb in behind her, hold her tight to me. I'll hold her as long as she wants and keep her warm.

"I'm going to go take a hot shower. Get cleaned up and dressed."

Oh. Right, that makes sense. "Do you need help?"

She rolls her eyes and lets out one breathy laugh. "I'm not going to drown in the shower, Noah."

I don't think she realizes how her words rip through my gut like a serrated knife. "I know, I just—" Fuck. "I'll wait here."

She squeezes my hand and smiles. "Thank you." Then she goes into the bathroom, and I lie back on the bed, listening to the sound of the running water, trying not to see her disappearing in the lake again.

I'm trying not to picture her with blue lips and lifeless eyes and limp, cold fingers.

I'm trying not to think about them. Or him. Cameron.

"Where's my sister?"

I sit up, having not even heard Bex walk in. She's changed into sweats, her eyes red and puffy from almost as little sleep as me.

"She's in the shower."

"Okay. Thanks for bringing her up here. You can go now. I'm going to stay with her."

"I don't mind staying with her."

Bex scoffs. "You don't need to, I'm here. I'm her sister."

I unfurl my fists and exhale slowly. I already had to endure not being able to be next to her for the last eight hours. I left her side in the lake. This is my fault. I'm not leaving her again. "I said I'd do it," I say through my teeth, trying not to growl.

"You're being weird. Go away."

"Are you guys fighting?" Livvy comes out of the bathroom in a white robe, drying her hair with a towel.

"No," we say simultaneously.

"I'm going to stay in here with you," Bex says, grinning triumphantly then sticking her tongue out at me when Livvy's not looking.

"Is that necessary? I really feel okay. I think I'm just going to read, maybe take a nap."

"They said we need to keep an eye on you, and I'm your big sister. I'm staying."

My knuckles ache, my hands balled up at my sides, fingernails digging into my palms.

"Oh, okay."

"A nap sounds perfect." Bex pulls the covers back and gets in the bed. "I hardly slept. You should go sleep, too," she says to me. "You look awful."

"Thanks," I deadpan.

"Oh! Should we check for ET under the bed first?" Bex asks Livvy.

Livvy tosses the towel over a chair. "Haha. No, we don't need to check for ET under the bed." She shifts her eyes. "He's much more likely to be in the closet, anyway."

"ET?" I twist my face, trying to follow the conversation.

"Yeah," Bex laughs. "Livvy used to be terrified of ET when she was little."

"The little alien from the movie?"

Livvy nods, her cheeks a deep pink. "Shut up, Bex."

"It was cute," Bex insists.

ET? I have the strangest sense of déjà vu as soon as she mentions it. Like, I've had this exact conversation before, only with someone else.

And then it hits me. I have.

I stride to the door. "I'll just be in the room next door. Let me know if you need anything." I make eye contact with Livvy before I leave, hand on the knob. "Anything. I mean it."

I can't shake the feeling nagging at me when I get into my room.

There's no way.

No fucking way.

It's just a coincidence that Angel told me she used to be afraid of ET as a kid. That's probably a pretty common and not at all unusual thing. Right? Right.

There's no way.

But the feeling picks at the base of my skull and everything else starts clicking into place. Like a puzzle I didn't even realize was in front of me the whole time. All the things I hadn't given much thought to before. They're the same age, their birthdays are both this weekend, they both just graduated college and moved back to Washington.

The odds of them being—no, it's too far-fetched.

But still, I take my phone out as soon as I close the door behind me. Frantically thumbing to the app and back through our messages, back to the picture she sent me.

God, she's beautiful. Perfect. Familiar.

I was more than a bit preoccupied with other thoughts when she sent it. Not to mention all the blood going to one extremity in particular. Maybe that's why I didn't see it. It didn't even cross my mind. From the curve of her hips to the size of her breasts, the amount of softness in her belly and thighs—Livvy.

I zoom in on the picture, focusing on the hips. The spot is covered by her white panties, but I keep zooming until I can't anymore.

And there it is. Right above the waistband—the tiniest sliver of a curved black line inked into her skin. It's nothing, really. There's no way to tell what the tattoo is or if there is a matching one on the other side because of how her body is turned.

Anyone looking at the photo would say it's proof of nothing—and I would agree—if I weren't the one who'd done the tattoo myself.

CHAPTER 15

LIVVY

Bex has already dozed off. It only took minutes, every once in a while letting out a soft snore.

I'm glad she's resting. I know I'm the one who almost drowned, but she went through it, too. She cried the whole time the paramedics were checking me out. Her eyes were still red and swollen at the hospital. She was exhausted.

She's always been my protector, getting in trouble multiple times for punching kids on the playground. Our parents labeled her the troublemaker, the hellion, the difficult one from an early age. She allowed me to be the sweet one, the quiet one, the perfect daughter. An angel.

But what my parents never knew—or, rather, never cared to know—is that she only ever punched kids who were bullying me. She might have been a little liberal in her definition of *bullying*, but she's always looked after me. It's been her and me, together, always.

Especially after the divorce.

She's really the angel here. My guardian angel.

I let her sleep and grab my book to read, sliding in next to her.

A hard knock comes at the door.

Bex groans.

"Livvy, can I come in?" Noah says from the other side.

"No. Go away," Bex yells. "We're sleeping."

"I really need to talk to you, Liv. Like, now."

"It can wait," Bex says, before I'm able to speak up.

There's silence from behind the door, and then he says, "No."

Tension twists between my shoulder blades.

"You can come in," I say.

"Ugh." Bex shoves her pillow over her face as he opens the door.

He clears his throat, filling up the doorway. "I need to talk to you. Alone."

"Fuck off," Bex says, muffled under the pillow.

He glares at her, an unmoving lump in the bed, then looks at me with an intensity that makes it hard to breathe.

"We'll talk. Soon," he says, jaw clenched, then shuts the door.

He looks at me with the same hard look all throughout dinner, chewing his steak like he has a personal vendetta against this cow.

Everyone else talks around us but he's silent. Eyes on me. Drilling into my skull and making the hairs on the back of my neck stand up. I look away, try to focus on anyone else, anything else. But I still feel his eyes. And when I glance back, he hasn't moved.

Most everyone seems content to stay up and drink, Wood offers to start another fire on the beach. I excuse myself to bed and quietly go up the stairs.

I hear him behind me, half a flight down.

Heart racing, I grip the handrail. His footsteps on the wood treads echo mine as he follows me up to the third floor in darkness.

I don't dare turn around and look at him until I get to the landing. When I do, he's only a few steps down, in shadow. *Why isn't he saying anything.*

For some reason I don't want to turn my back to him again, so I step backward, slowly, toward my room as he comes up the stairs. We never break eye contact. As he steps into the hall, I have to tilt my head to look at him. Heart thumping. His tattooed throat bobs.

I back into my darkened room, and he follows me. The light from the moon casts a cold, blue light onto the angles of his face. He looks...different. His eyes have a certain wildness in them that I haven't seen since...since I walked in on him stroking himself. Heat rises in my cheeks.

Noah shuts the door behind us, and now we're alone.

And then he looks at me. Silently we make eye contact, and I have no idea what's going on here. My heart thuds loudly.

He steps toward me, not breaking his stare, not blinking. I stagger back and run into the bed. Caught off guard, I fall backward onto the mattress.

Noah keeps moving forward and sits on the bed next to me. Not a new thing, but the air is entirely different. The mattress sinks under his weight and pulls me to him. My knee presses against his thigh.

"What—"

"I know who you are," he whispers.

I tilt my head. Huh?

"You're nothing like I thought you'd be," he continues. "You're so much more and so much better than I could have even dreamed."

"Noah, I have no idea what you're talking about."

"Do you know who I am?" He turns over his wrist and shows me a small tattoo of a devil face with two large horns.

"You're Noah Dixon. What do you mean *do I know who you are?* Is there something else I'm supposed to know about you?"

"You said you wanted to meet. Here I am, Angel." He tilts his head, the light catching his dark blue eyes.

"What did you say?"

"You heard me."

My stomach drops. He grins wickedly, the sharp cut of his bicuspid contrasting against his soft lower lip. My heart is racing, having put the pieces together before my brain can comprehend it.

Bex barges in, banging the door against the frame, a fluffy pillow under her arm.

She throws the pillow at Noah with a grunt. "I'm sleeping in here tonight. Go away, Noah, she needs to rest."

"We were talking." He glares at her.

My mind is still spinning, heat erupting from my chest to my ears.

"Time's up." She picks her pillow up from the floor and flings herself on the bed. "You can talk tomorrow." She pulls the covers over her as she rolls to her side, huffing.

Noah looks at me, that smirk still on his lips. "Yes. Yes, we will."

♥ ♥ ♥

"She's not going."

"She says she feels fine."

Bex glares at Wood over her waffles and eggs.

"Maybe it would be better for her to stay and rest," Wood concedes.

"I really am feeling perfectly fine," I say.

"You're not going on a six-mile hike after almost drowning." Bex takes an aggressively large bite of waffle.

"This is probably the only time I'll ever say I agree with Bex," Spencer says over his earl gray tea.

"An abomination that will certainly never happen again," Bex says. "So, that settles it. You are staying here, and I will stay with you."

"I can stay back, too. You know, just in case you need someone with medical training," Jake chimes in.

"That's so sweet of you." Bex smiles at him.

He smiles back.

"Oh crud. Jake, I know you were really looking forward to the hike, I can stay back in that case. I *am* a nurse," Macy says.

Spencer puts his hand over hers. "This is your vacation, too. The fresh air and exercise will be good for you."

She nods, blinking up at him. "Yes, you're right."

"Cool. So, it's just me, Macy, and Spencer. Cool, cool," Wood says, chuckling as he shoves an entire strip of bacon in his mouth.

Noah's tall figure darkens the stairwell as he ambles down the steps in black joggers. His dark hair is messy, circles under his eyes. Eyes that find me as soon as he saunters into the kitchen. My pulse quickens.

"Noah! You're coming on the hike today, right?"

Noah chuckles while filling a mug with coffee. "No."

Wood's shoulders droop.

"This is ridiculous. I don't want anyone missing out on a good time because of me." I look at Bex, trying not to make eye contact with Noah again. "I will go lie down. I'll stay in bed the rest of the day and just rest and read my book. I promise. No one needs to stay and look after me."

"Are you sure?" she asks.

"Yes!"

"Okay." She looks at Jake and then Wood. "Looks like we're coming after all."

"Oh good!" Macy bounces in her seat.

"Thank fuck," Wood mutters under his breath.

Noah sits in the open seat directly across from me, his dark gaze is thick on my skin, heavy, impossible to ignore.

I pause, about to take a bite of waffle, fork midair. A heavy bead of syrup drips from my bite, slow and stringy down to my plate.

He bites his lip. "I'd like some of your syrup."

I don't move. I don't blink. I'm not certain I'm breathing. Is he brazenly flirting with me at the breakfast table in front of everyone?

"Livvy," he says.

My fork goes clattering to my plate. Oh, fuck. "Huh?"

"Will you pass me the syrup? Please." He gestures to the bottle of syrup directly next to me, a dark chuckle in his voice.

Right, right. I pass him the syrup and he leans over to take the bottle from my hands, his fingers grazing over mine as he takes it, lingering there for a second. Skin on skin.

He flashes me the little devil tattoo on his wrist.

It's him. It really is him. I laid awake for hours last night trying to convince myself that it wasn't true, that I'd misread what he had said. He isn't 2Horned and he doesn't know about my extra-curricular activities as Angel. He doesn't know.

Everything I know about 2Horned and Noah runs through my mind like a slideshow.

Noah is busy running his shop. He's successful. But he doesn't go out. No women in his life that I know of. He doesn't sleep well. He never talks about his family, except for Wood.

2Horned is lonely, doesn't do much other than work. He's suffered from depression on and off and has had insomnia since he lost his family—his father, mother, and brother all died in a car accident several years ago.

Fuck.

What if it is true? What if it's him? The man I've crushed on, lusted over, dreamt of, for the last eight years, is the man I've been sexting with for the last eight months?

The things we've talked about doing with each other—doing *to* each other. Blood throbs in my veins, heating my cheeks and warming me all over.

He looks up at me from under his thick lashes. He knows. He knows what I'm thinking. He can read my mind and every naughty thought that's running through it about him, about us.

"We better get going before it gets too hot." Wood stands,

starting to clear the table. "Are you sure you won't join us?" He's looking at Noah, but Noah doesn't take his eyes off me.

Noah grins slowly. "Not a chance."

♥ ♥ ♥

I snuck away upstairs while everyone was running around getting their hiking boots (Jake) and sunscreen (Macy) and grabbing snacks (Wood) and filling water bottles (Spencer) and flasks (Bex).

They all left toward the trailhead half an hour ago in Wood's SUV, and I've been lying on my bed pretending to read ever since, heart pounding, sweating. The look in Noah's deep blue eyes consuming every thought.

"Can I come in?" he says from the hall. No knock.

I take a deep breath. "Yes." My voice sounds weird. *Why does my voice sound weird?*

I sit up as he walks in. It feels like I'm watching him in slow motion, or from outside of my body. It doesn't seem real. The way he's looking at me, like I'm prey. Like he's about ready to pounce. To devour me.

He gently takes the book I forgot I'm holding out of my hand and sets it on the bedside table and then sits next to me.

"Livvy."

"Noah."

There's silence. Nothing but the invisible buzzing electricity in the air between us.

"It's you," I say.

He nods.

I take his face in my hands, looking back and forth between his eyes. Knowing. I know him. I know this man. And he knows more about me than probably anyone else.

He closes his eyes, letting out an exhale and lets me hold the weight of his head before turning and nuzzling into my hand, kissing my palm with the softest touch.

He looks back up at me and it's like all the sorrow in his eyes, I finally understand.

"I know," I say. "I know."

He smiles just before his expression breaks and then his hands are cupping my face, too.

"It's a relief that you know. That you know everything. I'm so glad it's you, Livvy."

"You are?" I think I already know, but I need to ask anyway. "And the girl you met you wanted to try and start something with?"

He moves in, dropping his hands to press into the mattress on either side of my hips. "I was talking about you, Liv."

"Oh."

Heat radiates from his skin. His scent fills my lungs. He's so close, it'd only take a second to close the gap between us. Feel his lips on mine.

His fingertips graze up the side of my wrist.

"Do you want this?" he whispers.

I want to say *yes*, but I can't speak. I'm frozen.

He runs one knuckle along my jaw, raising goosebumps on my neck that tingle down my side.

"What am I going to do with you...my angel?"

I let out a shaky breath. "I'm not Angel."

He raises an eyebrow.

"I mean, she's sexy and confident and in control. I'm none of those things—"

He scoffs. "Of course you are—"

"No. I misled you. I deceived you."

"What are you talking about—"

"I'm a virgin," I blurt.

He pulls back and sits, expression unreadable.

I straighten. "I'm sorry. I'm a fraud."

"Liv," he says, his voice low and stern. "You are not a fraud. You are smart and funny and gorgeous. And when you dropped your robe to pose nude for me, you were the epitome of sexy and confident."

"I was terrified."

He slides nearer to me on the bed. "Fooled me."

"I haven't done any of the things we talked about."

"I don't care." He leans in closer.

"You don't?"

He shakes his head. "Liv, do you want to do all those things we talked about? In our scenarios?"

"Yes," I exhale.

"With me?" His hand finds mine, our fingers interlocking over the blankets. "Because I want to do them. With you."

I nod. "Please." But the word comes out on a quivering breath.

He smiles as his fingers tighten around mine. "We'll go slow," he whispers.

My throat tightens. "Slow is good."

He grins. Then his gaze drops to my mouth. "Do you know how long I've wanted to kiss you?"

"No." My chest heaves with quickening breaths as he leans in.

"Too fucking long."

Noah comes closer, the tip of his nose touching mine. His thumb on my cheek brushes the corner of my mouth.

His pupils are blown out, his eyes look almost black. My heart is racing. His lips are so close, the heat from his breath makes me shiver.

"I'm going to kiss you," he says.

He is?

The sharp intake of air through my lips is audible.

He's staring at my mouth, one of his hands slides around into my hair, but he doesn't move in or pull me closer. It's like he's waiting for something.

I breathe out the word, "Yes," so soft I'm not sure if it wasn't just in my head.

But he must have heard because he doesn't hesitate another second. He makes eye contact, his stare hot, needy, and pulls the back of my neck toward him at the same time he tilts his head, eyelids heavy, and lowers his mouth to mine.

His lips are soft, gentle. I don't want him soft. I need him as greedy for me as I am for him, as I've been for years.

I twist my hands into his shirt, urging him further.

I am consumed by him. There is nothing but him and me.

His hand at my lower back pulls me in closer, his other hand in my hair tightens around the back of my neck.

I whimper as I part my lips.

His tongue touches mine, sweet with a hint of maple syrup.

He lets out a sigh and then he's holding my head, hard-pressed to him as he goes deeper. Heavy breathing. Heart pounding. Devouring me and all my heady moans. Tongues slick. A gasp for air. Arms around me tighter. Closer. Not close enough.

I lean back and he follows me down easily, laying me down on the pillow. Pressing his weight on top of me. Kissing. Panting. I dig my fingers into his back as he sucks my lip between his teeth.

I can barely breathe. I don't want to breathe if it means we stop kissing.

He presses me harder into the mattress as he trails his fingers up the side of my ribs. His hand is warm and soft as it moves up, grazing the side of my breast.

I hum into his mouth and arch against him. He slows the kiss, his lips soft yet demanding. He sweeps his tongue against mine without hesitation, but yields to my movements, letting me set the pace. The heat of his hand cradles my breast, and he applies gentle pressure.

More. I want more. More of this. More of him. More of everything I've never had before.

He rubs the pad of his thumb over my nipple, and it hardens

under his touch. He groans, and the sound turns me liquid, warm and melting under him into a puddle of carnal need and desire.

Noah slides his hand down, my body thrumming with each stroke. Down to the hem of my shirt where he plays his fingertips over the bare skin there, just above the waistband of my shorts. It lights me up.

Then, with the lowest rumble from his chest and firm hand, he grips my hip and grinds against me. His erection is hard, the length of it rubbing against the inside of my thigh.

I whimper at the sensation, heat flooding between my legs, the need—the ache—growing by the second.

He breaks the kiss, our noses still touching, our hard, quick breaths filling the inch of space between us. "Is this too much?"

"No," I say, but it comes out too high pitched and more like a question.

Noah kisses my nose, then pulls back a little, his eyes never leaving mine as he sweeps a strand of hair off my face, a faint smile playing at his lips. "Sorry, I said we'd go slow and I'm already all over you."

"It's okay. I want it." I tug on his shirt, urging him back down to me.

"Yeah?" He tilts his head, pupils dilating as he comes closer. "What do you want?"

"I—" I swallow, my heart pounding harder than can surely be healthy. I don't know.

We lie in silence for a minute, chest against chest, his breath warm against my lips as he plays with my hair.

"I don't know what I want. But I know I want it with you," I finally whisper.

"Good," he says low. He licks his lips as he shifts on top of me. He's still hard against my lower abdomen. "Can I ask you something?"

"Okay."

"All those times you told me you came when we were chatting, did you actually get yourself off?"

I'm quiet for a heartbeat. Two. Three beats.

"Once," I say, heat surging in my chest.

One side of his mouth turns up. "When?"

I swallow. "The last time."

He looks off to the left then back to me, his expression turning slightly sinister. "After you walked in on me...and saw my—"

"Yes." I squirm under him, the cock in question getting impossibly harder, growing bigger across my hip as I wiggle.

He growls as his devilish grin grows. "Show me."

"Huh?"

"Show me how you touched yourself. Show me how you like it."

"You want to watch?"

"Yes."

Oh.

"Tell me"—his voice is like velvet—"were you dressed when you got yourself off?"

I shake my head. "I was naked."

He smiles.

"In your bed," I add.

His eyes roll back as he presses his lips between his teeth. "Can I see?" He sits back on his heels, hot, dark gaze on me.

I sit up. It's like slow motion. I undress silently as he watches me. I pull my tank top off, my bare breasts jiggling slightly as I toss it aside.

After hooking my thumbs into the band of my shorts, I lift my hips then slide them down my thighs and off. I'm left sitting here in my peach cotton panties.

Noah looks up and down my body. My nipples tighten as his gaze passes over them.

I've always thought my breasts were a bit small, not even a

handful, but they're perky and firm and oh god, he's licking his lips.

I hold my breath to keep him from noticing how shallow my breathing has become.

"You're fucking perfect," he whispers. "So beautiful."

I let out a breath and try to smile through quivering lips.

"Show me what you do next," he says.

I spread my legs apart.

"Good girl," he rasps. Warmth ripples down my spine and settles in my core, tinged with nerves and excitement.

His eyes follow my hand as I slide it down my stomach and over my panties. Down to where I'm heated and achy, to where the cotton is already damp. I rub my fingers over the fabric, the light pressure against the pulsing between my legs is barely enough to soothe the ache. The need. The hollow, empty feeling.

He presses his palm to his groin, his erection straining under his pants.

I curl two fingers along the side of my panties and move them over, exposing my most sensitive, pink skin to Noah's eyes.

"Fuck," he growls.

I stroke my fingers between my folds where it's hot, my finger-tips already wet and slippery. Teasing them up slowly until they brush the underside of my throbbing clit.

A moan escapes my lips, unbidden.

"Talk to me. Tell me what you're doing and how it feels," Noah says.

My cheeks burn.

He looks up from where my hand is pressed between my legs to my face. "I know you can do it. I know how naughty you are, my angel."

I nod. Heart racing, I push my panties down my hips.

"May I?" His eyes are burning.

"Yes," I breathe.

He inches closer, fingertips barely brushing my thighs as he loops them into my underwear and pulls them down my legs.

I lean back against the pillow and resume stroking circles around my clit.

"Does it feel good?" he asks.

"Yes. It feels so good. I'm so wet, Noah."

"I can see how wet that pretty little pussy is for me."

My breath hitches. "Do you like it?"

He nods. "I like it. I like you—spread out, wet, and eager for me."

Oh. Oh fuck. I drag my soaked fingers down and back up through my pussy. Slow strokes then faster circles over my swollen clit.

"Fuck. My cock is so hard for you. Can I take it out?"

"Yes. Please." My words are stilted.

He groans and I pant. In a lust-filled haze, I feel bold.

"Stroke it for me," I say. "I want to see you, too. I want to know it's because of me."

"It's always because of you." He reaches over the back of his head and pulls his shirt off in one fluid motion. He shoves his pants and boxers down, his cock springing forward, smooth and thick.

Taking it in his hand, he squeezes it at the base then glides his hand up the shaft.

I watch him stroke himself, mesmerized as I continue to coax my own pleasure.

The morning sunlight has broken through the clouds, bathing the room in white light and warming my skin. Sweat beads between my breasts.

Soft moaning fills the room and I realize it's me.

Noah is still watching me, thick-thighed, the muscles in his forearms flexing, abs tensing as he strokes his cock with one hand and pulls his balls with the other.

Pressure builds low in my stomach. My moaning has turned

desperate, the tension coiling just under the surface, the need for release intensifying.

"I'm so close. Almost there."

"Can I—can I finish you off." His voice is hoarse, breathing heavy.

I nod.

He gently encircles my wrist and lifts it away, but then he brings my hand to his lips. He kisses my fingertips then sucks the two fingers I've been using into his mouth. And now he knows how I taste. He licks them clean, not breaking eye contact.

"Fuck," I breathe.

"You taste so good. I knew you would."

He smirks and dips down, lips brushing my thighs just long enough to make my skin prickle and then his mouth is on me. Wet and warm, his tongue slipping between my folds, making me gasp.

He licks my clit and I cry out, feral. His tattooed fingers dig into my thighs. The little slurping and swallowing noises he's making fill my head as my clit pulsates under his tongue.

Ecstasy vibrates under my skin, coming in waves and echoing out to my extremities. I'm moaning and sighing and cussing under my breath.

I can't help but roll my eyes back with each current of pleasure. But I keep looking back, because watching him is hotter than I could have imagined. His beautiful face between my legs, the broad side of his tongue as he licks me, his lips shiny as he kisses me there. My pussy lips spread and dark pink as he sucks on my pulsing clit.

"Oh fuck."

He sucks harder.

One of his hands leaves my thigh and I glance down to see it gripped around his cock, jacking himself off as he goes down on me. The sight of the red, stretched head of his cock slipping in and out from his fist, his neck flexing, the humming in his throat from his own pleasure as he's coaxing mine to the surface—it undoes me.

My climax breaks without warning and I cry out, louder than I expect. It crashes through my body hard and hot, intense, pure bliss, then fizzles out slow, staying shimmery along the edges.

Still shaky, my lips tingling, I open my eyes and he's there, erection jutting out in front of his stomach, thick, skin pulled taut, fisting himself faster, grunting, gasping. His whole body locks up as he shudders, then groans, emptying himself into his discarded boxers.

CHAPTER 16
NOAH

The light is orange behind my eyelids. My cheek is on something soft and warm. Sweet smelling. It rises and falls softly with each of her quiet breaths.

Livvy.

I open my eyes. We're cuddled up under the covers, my head on her chest, her fingers combing lazily through my hair, her head turned from me, reading her book.

Her thick eyelashes flutter in the light and I follow the curve in her pert nose down to her pouty lips, then further to her bare chest, breasts out of the blankets, a perfectly pink nipple inches from my mouth.

I haven't had the chance to properly explore and touch and kiss and lick every inch of her body yet. It's a crime.

I stir against her, tightening my arm around her waist.

She puts her book down. "Morning, you."

"How long was I out?"

With a little smile and a hum, she glances at her phone. "Almost three hours."

"Wow. Guess I needed it. I hardly slept last night."

"What kept you up?"

"You."

"Yeah?"

I nod. A much better reason than what normally keeps me up. She peers down at me, a little crease between her eyebrows, her green eyes golden in the light, her mouth slightly downturned.

She knows. She knows what keeps me up at night. She knows about the accident. My family. So few people in my life know about it—because that's how I want it—but the fact that she knows fills my chest with a lightness I can't describe.

That sinking rock in my gut, a feeling I've become so accustomed to, isn't there. It's gone. No longer weighing me down. No secrets.

She knows, and it's overwhelming and freeing and terrifying and wonderful at the same time.

"Can I stay here with you tonight?" I ask.

"Yes."

I grin, noticing the pulse in her neck speeding up. I kiss her right there, at her pulse point. The prettiest sigh escapes her lips.

She smells like strawberries, and I want to taste her again.

Ignoring my throbbing cock, I nuzzle down, brushing my lips along her jaw.

I press light kisses down to her collarbone. She whimpers, and tiny goosebumps rise on her skin in a trail behind me. I keep kissing as I go. Lower.

Just as I reach the top swells of her breasts, her breaths becoming more rapid, I look up at her.

Her cheeks are flushed.

"Is this okay?" I ask, my voice coming out more strained than I expect.

She nods.

I watch her eyes roll back as my mouth meets that soft skin. I kiss her breast and move down to lick her hardened nipple. She trembles beneath me as I suck tenderly on it.

At the same time, I trace my hand over her hip bone and down her leg, feeling the goosebumps on her skin in my wake. I slide my hand up, fingertips light on her skin, between her thighs.

She gasps when my middle finger slips between her lips. She's warm and soft, already wet and pliable for me.

A vehicle rolling up the driveway, gravel grinding under the tires, breaks this little light-filled bubble we're in.

"Shit." She throws her head back against the headboard.

I let her nipple slip out between my lips, glistening and now dark pink.

"Do you think they'll wonder where we are?" I ask.

"I think my sister will come barging in here first thing to make sure I'm still breathing." Her tummy and breasts bounce a little as she lets out a light laugh.

"Guess we better get dressed, then. I'm not in the mood to get punched in the face today."

I sit up and stretch my neck. But I don't want to leave her bed. I don't want to get dressed.

Part of me wants her to shrug and say, *eh, let Bex see us* and then assure me Bex won't punch me in the face for corrupting her little sister (she will).

But Livvy smiles and nods. "Yeah, that'd probably be best. I mean, with you being exes, it could get...complicated. It might be better if I talk to her on my own."

"Right, yeah, of course." *Complicated.*

Obviously, I know Bex and I dated. I haven't forgotten about that—but it was so long ago, I don't really think about it. I wasn't thinking it'd be that complicated, but maybe she's right. I don't want to cause a strain in their relationship, especially for something that is so brand new. Too new to even call it a *thing*.

Maybe Livvy doesn't want this to be anything more than casual fun. After all, she's young. She's been dating and exploring her options. I've been pining over her through my phone screen for months, but as far as I know, her feelings for me could be only weeks or days or hours old.

And didn't she tell me she's been trying to get over a crush she's had for years? I irrationally hate that guy. No, this thing between us is new for her.

I clear my throat. "You don't have to tell her anything right away. There's not much to even tell her yet, right? We can wait until we see what this is between us." I nod reassuringly, trying to keep my smile from falling.

She blinks, then nods, too. "Right."

"Right." I keep nodding.

Right. Good.

♥ ♥ ♥

An entire day of shared glances and secret touches and looking for every opportunity to steal her away into a corner or hallway or closet and kiss her senseless. Even if it's only for half a minute. Those seconds are giving me life.

We're sitting around the fire again on the beach, though conversation is a bit more subdued. It's the last night here.

I sip my beer as the flames dance, flicker, and crackle against the black sky. The fire is warm, but the breeze coming off the lake is cool.

In my periphery, I see Livvy shivering and rubbing her arms. I have nothing to offer her, and it's killing me I can't just slide up close to her and put my arm around her.

I've never envied people in relationships, but I find myself irrationally furious with Spencer and how he has his girlfriend sitting right next to him and yet he doesn't put his arm around her. He doesn't hold her hand or squeeze her thigh or give her forehead kisses.

Forehead kisses?

I don't even know who I am anymore. I'm never like this. I'm always the one to be a little at a distance. Don't fall too hard. Don't fall too far. Don't lose anyone else. Don't get hurt.

But I want to give Liv forehead kisses. And hold her hand. And fall at her feet and give her anything and everything she wants.

I push the intrusive thought of her lying only a few feet away with blue lips out of my mind and lean over toward her.

"Do you want to go inside?"

Livvy turns to me, eyes bright, with a small smile, the fire glowing warm on her face.

Anything for her.

She nods. "Yeah, I think I do want to go in."

"We're turning in, too." Spencer stands. "I want to get in an early morning run before the drive tomorrow. Jake, if you're running with me, it might be a good idea to stop drinking and turn in, too."

Jake raises his beer bottle to his brother with a smirk. "Nah, I'm on vacation. I'll be sleeping at five o'clock, but you enjoy your run."

Spencer purses his lips and looks at Macy until she stands, then walks off.

Macy waves at us with a tight-lipped smile and then scurries to catch up with Spencer already well on his way to the house.

"I'll come with you," Bex says, holding her bottle of beer up to the light. It's over halfway full still.

"Oh, no. No, really you don't have to. I'm fine, I promise. Stay and have fun." Livvy glances at me then back to her sister.

"Are you sure?" Bex's gaze flicks quickly toward Jake.

"I'm sure."

"Okay. Let me know if you need anything." Bex tips back her beer and I grab Livvy's hand just as she stands, brushing sand off her legs.

"Meet me at the hot tub?" I whisper.

She bites her lip and nods quickly before retreating into the house.

I wait a few minutes before I get up as well.

"Bro, it's still early. Come on!" Wood tries to hand me another beer, but I shake him off.

I'm already wearing my swim shorts, so I go around to the hot tub. It's down a cobblestone path along the side of the house, surrounded by thick greenery and evergreen trees. Through the bushes on one side is the light from the kitchen, and through the trees on the other side are hints from the fire on the beach. Otherwise, it's completely private.

I take off my shirt and get in the hot water, looking up at the stars while I wait.

"Hi." Her voice is soft. She's standing on the path in her black bathing suit, hair tied up, towel over her arm, biting her bottom lip.

"Hey," I say. The sight of her kills all thoughts in my brain. There is only her. Standing in front of me.

She steps down into the tub across from me and sits in the water. "I didn't know if I should wear my suit or...not." She looks up at me from under her lashes.

The idea makes my pulse quicken. She has an exhibitionist side. The second she posed nude for me I should have known.

"You like my eyes on you?"

"Yes," she says.

"It turned you on, when you posed nude for me."

"Yes."

I love the idea that her little pink pussy was wet for me the whole time I was drawing her and struggling with my own hard-on.

"You like the idea of being watched? The risk? The possibility of being caught?"

Her throat bobs, and she licks her lips, parting them, her breathing becoming rapid and shallow. She nods. "Yes."

"You want me to pull down the straps of your swimsuit and

for someone to see your perfect tits bouncing while I fuck you here in this hot tub."

Her mouth opens in a perfect little 'O' shape, her cheeks darkening. "You think my tits are perfect?"

I let out a hard laugh. "Yes. They are."

She smiles, but then she's worrying that bottom lip again.

"Don't worry, Liv, I said I'd take it slow." I won't fuck her. Yet. "Come here." I reach for her, and she comes to me, wrapping her arms around my neck. I encircle her waist and kiss her lips.

Her soft, little hums as I suck on her lips and stroke her tongue with mine make my cock swell. Needy bastard.

I break the kiss and she whimpers in protest, her eyes half-lidded, lips swollen.

Taking her face in my hands, I kiss her nose and then her forehead. "Turn around, sit on my lap."

She leans her back against my chest, wiggling her perfect ass against my erection.

"Careful," I say in a low tone.

"I'm not doing anything," she says in a light voice.

"Mmhmm."

She smirks, looking at me over her shoulder.

"I've been thinking about you all day. Wanting you, all day," I whisper into her ear.

She hums as I squeeze her tighter to me.

"Wanting to make you come again. You come so pretty, Liv. And the sounds you make—"

"The sounds I make? Are they okay?"

"They're perfect," I say.

I press my lips to the spot on her neck behind her jaw. She leans back against my shoulder, giving me more access to trail kisses down to her collarbone. Relaxed.

Under the water I rub her thighs, slowly making my way up. She spreads her legs as I slide my hands between them, and just that small move makes my cock pulse.

I rub over her bathing suit first, until she's squirming on my lap and breathing heavily.

My cock between her ass cheeks is almost painfully hard and throbbing as she arches against it.

But her pleasure comes first. Always.

I slip two fingers under her suit. She's lush and warm. Soft. She purrs against me as I touch her. Slow, long strokes at first, side to side, just like she touched herself earlier. Every time I touch that spot, I elicit pretty little moans from her lips.

Dipping lower, I press my fingertip just inside her opening. She stills. Her heavy breathing stops.

"You okay?"

"Yes," she says, breathing again.

"Is this okay?" I push my finger inside a little more, wondering if anyone has ever touched her here.

She nods again, gripping my thigh.

"Am I hurting you?"

"No."

"More?" I ask.

"Yes."

I slide my finger in to the knuckle, massaging circles over her clit with my thumb.

"Oh," she gasps, closing her eyes.

I kiss her cheek while I continue the slow thrusting and rubbing. Her pussy clenches around me, pulling me in deeper. My needy girl wants more.

"Two fingers?"

"Mmhmm." She breathes.

She stretches easily around my two fingers as I circle her clit. I keep the pace steady until she's pushing back on my hand, grinding against it, urging for more pressure. And I give it to her. She's writhing.

"My greedy girl wants to come?"

"Yes," she pants. "Please, Noah."

She throws her head back, completely open to me, trusting that I'll take care of her. And I will. I've got her. She's safe anchored against me. Safe to focus only on the pleasure I'm giving her. She knows I'll read every little moan and change in breath, arch in her back and thrust against my palm.

She knows I'll make it good for her, and I won't let up until she reaches that peak and spills over the edge. I whisper in her ear how beautiful she is, how perfect, how she's my good girl.

Her hard little clit pulses under my finger and with an exhale she cries out and shudders in my arms, contracting on my fingers inside her. I hold her while she falls apart, out of breath, spasms coursing through her body.

After a moment, her rising chest eases. I kiss her temple and she lets out a quiet, contented sigh before she twists around and kisses me hard on the mouth.

She pulls back, eyes lust-filled, pupils dilated.

"Can I?" She grips my thigh under the water before sliding her hand along the length of my erection. She smirks as she moves her hand up, up, and then down into my swim trunks.

The instant she touches my cock all thoughts leave my body. I am nothing in this moment but hers. All hers. I nod dumbly.

I stand and she tugs on my shorts, pulling them half-way down my thighs. My cock springs out, jutting straight at her and the little gasp she makes at the sight of it makes it jump and my balls tighten.

She looks up at me and licks her lips. Fuck.

"Tell me... Tell me how you like it."

I groan. "Fuck. Anything you do will be perfect. Trust me, I'll like it."

She moves in tentatively and presses her soft lips to the tip of me. Then she kisses it again, this time with an open mouth, her tongue snaking out to lick the underside of my shaft. She looks up, as if asking for approval.

"Perfect," I say. She's perfect.

Her tongue is warm as she licks the length of me. Fuck. Her hands soft as she holds onto my thighs to steady herself. She sucks in the head. Jesus. Then takes me all the way in. My eyes roll back. I'm dizzy. Overcome.

"Go slow," I say, already knowing I'm not going to last long.

Not only has it been a while since I've gotten head, but the way she's looking up at me, with those big eyes, all innocent and beautiful, with my cock in her mouth—the sight is sending me. It's too much.

I can't look away. She moves up and down on me, pausing to lick or kiss before sucking again, harder then softer, gauging my reactions.

"Good girl. Good fucking girl."

Looking at her, thinking about her, I'm already tensing all over, my cock pulsing with the need to climax between her perfect lips. I could hold it off by thinking about something else. But I don't want to think about anything else, picture anything else but her.

She closes her eyes and squeezes me at the base, humming when I hit the back of her throat. I grunt, white-knuckling the sides of the hot tub, trying to hold still, to hold back.

But I can't help it. She has me moaning. I thrust my hips in rhythm with her and she starts to bob faster.

"Fuck. Liv, I can't—I'm going to—if you don't want it—" Shit.

She locks her eyes on mine and sucks harder, no intention of letting me finish anywhere else.

It unravels me.

I erupt instantly.

Her eyes are on me as I convulse into the whimpering, vulnerable, shivering mess she's made me. She doesn't shy away, milking every last drop I have to offer.

There's a rustle from the pathway. A scraping of branches. The thwap of sandals on cobblestones.

Livvy pulls back, scampering to the other side of the hot tub while I hastily pull my shorts up just as Wood emerges from around a bush, towel over his shoulder, beer in hand.

"Oh, hey, guys! I didn't know you were in here. Sweet." He hangs his towel and climbs in with a smile and a sigh as he sinks into the hot water.

He takes a sip of beer then looks around. At me then her. And back. His eyes shifting. It's quiet.

I keep my expression cool, but I shoot him a look when his lopsided smile starts to appear, a look that says *don't fucking say it.*

"Well..." Livvy's smile is unnaturally cheery. "I'm pretty warm. And tired. I think I'm going to head in now. Night."

"Night," Wood says, waving as she grabs her towel and dashes away. He turns back to me, tilting his chin, biting back a grin.

"Don't say it."

He holds his hand up and shrugs. "I'm not saying anything."

"You look like you want to say something."

"Nope. Not me."

"Right."

Wood starts to tell me how they saw a bear in the woods on their hike today and how I should have been there. He already told the story around the fire when we were eating dinner.

"Anyway, you should have been there, bro."

I grunt.

"I know, I know. You're not into hiking. And the bear definitely wasn't as pretty as Livvy."

"Careful."

"Hey, I'm the one always telling you to go meet people, make connections, find your person. I'm happy for you."

"But you're not saying anything."

"Nope."

I was going to wait longer to follow Livvy up, but fuck that. "I'm heading in."

"Have fun," Wood says with a wink.

"It's not like that."

"Mmhmm." He smiles as he brings the beer bottle to his lips. I check him with my shoulder on my way out.

I go up to my room and change, then pad down the hall to Livvy's. There's no answer when I knock softly on her door.

I turn the knob slowly then crack the door open. "Liv?"

Silence.

I peek in. She's curled on her side under the covers, the moon-light caressing her figure.

After closing the door and locking it behind me, I go to her. Quietly, I lift back the blanket and slide in behind her. I tuck my legs into the crook of hers and wrap my arm around her middle.

She wiggles back against me and entwines her arm with mine, clasping it to her chest with a contented sigh.

I press my lips to her shoulder, inhaling her scent. "Go back to sleep."

♥ ♥ ♥

It's weird, waking up when the sun's already out and realizing I slept more than a few hours uninterrupted. I reach over to Liv, my hand skimming over the soft sheets. She's not there but her spot is still warm.

Birds flit past the window, chirping.

Hard banging on the door jolts me upright.

"Get up, Sleeping Beauty! We leave in twenty minutes!" Wood's voice booms through the door.

"Fuck off."

He chuckles. "Knew you were in there."

Shit.

Livvy's scent lingers on the sheets and in the room, but she and her stuff are all gone. So I drag my ass out of bed and pack up my stuff in my room.

Wood and Livvy are already at his SUV, the back hatch open, loading up as I carry my bag down the front porch steps.

Livvy glances at me over her shoulder. She smiles at me, rivaling the sun. Her eyes brighten, color coming to her cheeks. Just the sight of her and my heart picks up speed, and a rush of euphoria washes over me. I could float off the ground like a hot air balloon with a goofy-ass smile on its face.

I'm in fucking trouble.

Macy rushes up to me, grimacing with a deep crease between her brows.

"Did you see Bex in there?"

I shake my head. "Nope. Sorry."

"Son of a biscuit!" She runs past me into the house.

On the other side of the driveway, Spencer is standing next to his car in his loafers and Oxford shirt, one hand on his hip, glaring at his Rolex watch on the other.

Oh, shit! I left my watch by the hot tub last night.

"Ayo! Let's hit the road." Wood grabs my bag and throws it in the back.

I hold the car door open for Livvy and help her in, not passing up the opportunity to hold her hand and give it a little squeeze as I do.

I'm giddy over holding this girl's hand. *The fuck is wrong with me?*

"I'll be right back. I forgot something," I say, backpedaling and then jogging around the side of the house along the cobblestone path.

It should be right around—

I round a bush toward the hot tub. There's a gasping sound and a grunt and thump. But my feet are moving faster than my brain can comprehend the noises.

Bex is bent over the side of the hot tub, tits spilling out of her dress, nipple piercings on display, her skirt flipped up while Jake pounds into her from behind. The slap of skin on skin echoes around the alcove.

"Shit!" Jake stumbles backward, pulling up his pants and fumbling with his belt.

"Fuck." Bex stands up, fixing her dress and smoothing down her hair.

And now we're all standing here, completely normal, like nothing was just happening and two of us aren't sweaty and out of breath.

"Sorry, guys. I just came to get"—I point over to where my watch is sitting on the edge of the tub—"that."

"Oh yeah, no problem." Jake hands me my watch with a jovial smile.

"Thanks. They're, uh, looking for you."

They nod and I turn to leave.

"Hey, Noah?" Bex blinks up at me with her sweet blue eyes. "Will you not tell anyone about this?"

Right.

What's another secret?

CHAPTER 17

LIVVY

"**O**kay, open your eyes."

Noah removes his hands from over my face, and I am standing in front of one of the black walls in the tattoo shop.

We're over by Noah's station in the back, his elaborate white chalk drawing covers several feet of wall behind his tattoo chair.

"What am I looking at?" I ask.

"This!" He's so excited I don't know how to tell him I still don't know what this is about. "This is your spot."

"My spot?"

"Yeah. You can put up whatever you want. It's your spot."

And then I see it. Black wall. Chalk free. He cleared a space for me.

"I can draw whatever I want?"

He smiles, biting his lip as he nudges me with his arm, letting the touch linger there for a moment. "I know whatever you do will be amazing. I can't wait to see it."

I beam back at him. I love it.

"I know it's not like a real art gallery, but—"

I cut him off, reaching up to touch his face. "I love it."

I want to pull him down and kiss him, but I stop just short, remembering we're at work. His gaze is on my mouth, too.

Licking his lips, he leans in bit. "Fuck," he says under his breath. He brushes his thumb along my chin for the briefest second before making a fist and stuffing his hands in his pockets. "I have some paperwork to do in my office. Will you let me know when my next appointment comes in?"

I nod. He hesitates, the tip of his tongue on the edge of his teeth. But then he turns and goes to his office, looking over his shoulder with the cutest little grin before disappearing.

I turn back to the wall.

Now all I have to do is come up with something amazing to draw. No pressure.

Taryn walks up behind me, assessing the blank space on the wall with her arms crossed. "He's giving you a spot on the wall. Right next to his. And you've barely started apprenticing. Wow."

I nod and smile. "Yep. He has a lot of faith in me. It's nice. Don't you think?"

She steps into my space, her silver piercings catching the light as she arches a brow. "I know you're enjoying being his favorite right now, but don't get used to it."

I step back, crossing my arms.

"I've been working for him for three years, and I knew him before that. He doesn't date. At least, he doesn't do the whole boyfriend-girlfriend thing. He goes out with someone three, four dates, tops, before he loses interest and moves on."

"I don't know why you're telling me this."

She huffs out a laugh, looking me up and down. "I just thought you should know what you're getting into, and that fucking the boss doesn't make you special. You're not the only one, sis."

Her words are a sucker punch to the gut. "I'm not... I mean, we haven't—"

"Interesting." She pauses, like she's assessing and scrutinizing my entire being. "My advice…" Taryn leans in and lowers her voice. "Get it while you can. Enjoy it. Before he gets bored of you. But be prepared for the fallout. Protect yourself. Don't let yourself get hurt. And if he does hurt you—don't let it show."

She purses her lips at the wall behind me then saunters away.

I'm dizzy. Nauseous.

I sit at the front desk the rest of the evening while Noah finishes up his tattoo session. It's almost midnight when he's done with his client. It's only me and him left in the shop, and I help him close up like we've done a dozen times before.

Taryn's words keep circling back in my mind. *No. Don't let her get to you, Livvy.* She doesn't know about what we have or anything about our relationship. Not that we're officially in a relationship or anything.

"Are you okay?" Noah asks when we get into the elevator to go up to the apartment.

"I'm fine."

He studies my face for a moment, narrowing his eyes. I lift my chin, keeping my eyes bright, and hope my smile is convincing. He takes my hand and gives it a squeeze.

See, nothing to worry about.

But I can't help thinking about the type of women he's been with as we ride up to the top floor. Bex and Taryn. They're both beautiful, exciting, outspoken, outgoing. They're not quiet or shy. Or boring.

The ding of the elevator pulls me out of my head, and Noah waits for me to step out. He puts his hand on the small of my back and walks me to the door. We fling our stuff down once we get in the door. Noah rolls his head, stretching his neck as he opens the fridge.

He gets stiff after a long day of tattooing. Maybe I should offer him a massage. Maybe I should offer him sex.

Get it while you can.

"Should we order something in?" he asks, still staring into the open refrigerator.

"Do you want to do something, I don't know, more exciting? Like go out for dinner or drinks? We could hit up the bar, go dancing."

He shrugs. "Nah. Wood's usually the one dragging me out to do that kind of stuff." He looks at me and tilts his head, that look he gave me in the elevator returning. "Do you want to go out? I'll take you out if that's what you want. I just want to be wherever you are."

Enjoy it. Before he gets bored of you.

I swallow. "You sure?"

"Yeah." He walks over to me, backing me up to the counter and wrapping his arms around my middle. He kisses my forehead. "Didn't the finale of your show come out the other day?"

"I can watch it another time. You don't have to watch it with me. I know you think it's silly."

He looks off, scratching the back of his neck. "If you want to put it on, that would be fine. I know it's kind of a big deal or whatever."

"Do you *want* to watch it with me?"

He shrugs again. "I mean, I wouldn't mind hanging out with you while *you* watch it."

"Are you sure?"

"Yeah, like, the last episode did leave off on a bit of a cliffhanger, so..."

The way he's being intentionally casual and avoiding eye contact makes me smile. "Okay. Chinese and the finale. I think there's a reunion special to watch after, too."

His eyes light up.

♥ ♥ ♥

"I can't believe Braxton said that about Camber. It's like they forget they are being filmed." Noah grabs the last wonton and shakes his head at the screen. "And are they even going to acknowledge what Zeke did in the last episode?"

He's pacing between the living room and the kitchen by the end of the reunion special.

I turn it off and offer him that massage I was thinking about earlier.

It takes him a few minutes into the neck and shoulder rub to relax, finally close his eyes, lean his head back, and hum softly.

"If you're just doing this to get into my pants, it won't work," he says, peeking one eye open.

"It won't?"

He cracks a smile. "No, yeah. It will totally work."

I giggle as he crawls up my body. He presses me onto the couch and covers my mouth with his, kissing me slow at first. Deep, gentle strokes of the tongue turn greedier and more impatient as we go on. Hands roam over clothes and up shirts. He urges his thigh between my legs, and I rut against it. Needy. Achy. Panting.

Noah pulls back, both of us out of breath, flushed, hot.

He kisses the tip of my nose. "There's something I want to do with you tomorrow before we head into the shop. So, we need to get up a little early."

"Oh?" *What does he want to do?* "I guess we should go to bed, then. I'm tired."

"Me, too." He sweeps hair off my forehead, his eyes searching mine. "I wish I could sleep with you every night."

And I know he means sleep when he says it. I see the sadness in his eyes. The exhaustion.

I wish I knew when Bex was going to be home. She's not working tonight, just out. I have no idea when she'll come walking through the door.

The jingle of keys in the door handle alerts us and I sit up as

Noah hurries off me and to the other side of the couch. He adjusts himself and it brings a smile to my lips.

"Wow, your place is so nice!" an unfamiliar female voice says. A tall brunette walks in, followed by Wood.

"Oh, hey guys." He glances between us. Noah's lip is a little red from where I bit it and I'm still breathless. "Don't mind us. We'll be out of your hair. Go back to what...ever you were doing."

"We were just watching TV," I say.

He looks at the black screen. "Mmhmm. You two have fun." He winks, guiding the girl past us and to his room.

♥ ♥ ♥

My eight o'clock alarm goes off far too early. It actually goes off at precisely eight o'clock, but that's beside the point. We're heading into work at noon, and Noah said the thing he has planned for us will take a couple hours, so here we are.

I turn the alarm off quickly to not wake up Bex—

There is no Bex.

The bed is empty.

That's weird. She always comes home, even if it isn't until three or four in the morning.

ME:

> Hey, noticed you didn't come home last night, just checking in

I get up and as I'm walking to the bathroom, Noah and Wood are in the kitchen.

"Okay, so whipping the egg whites is the secret to light and fluffy waffles. You just want to beat them until they reach soft peaks." Wood hands Noah the hand mixer.

"Soft peaks?"

"Yeah, so not hard peaks like in a meringue, soft peaks."

"I don't know what any of that means."

I let them be and continue to the bathroom. When I come back out, the soft peak egg white situation must have been figured out because Noah is ladling batter into the waffle iron. Wood is humming "Party in the USA" by Miley Cyrus, slicing up an orange he adds to a plate that's already loaded with bacon and a waffle covered in melted butter.

"Where's your lady friend?" I ask as I sit opposite him at the counter.

"She's in bed, sleeping. I hope."

Noah comes around behind me and almost knocks the air out of me as he wraps his arms around me tightly from behind.

His lips brush along my ear. "Morning," he whispers.

Wood smirks at us. He puts the plate on a tray along with a small carafe of syrup and a glass of orange juice and carries it away to his room without another word.

I squeeze Noah's tattooed arms to my chest and tilt my head, giving him more access. He kisses along my jaw and down my neck, making me grin.

"How long has Wood known?"

"Since the morning we left for the lake house."

"That tracks."

The green light flashes on the waffle maker and Noah rushes back to the kitchen.

"Wood helped me, so they should be better this time." He plates me a giant waffle.

"They were great last time," I assure him.

His dark blue eyes brighten, and I have half a mind to throw the waffle aside and kiss and taste him instead. But I don't.

The waffle *is* better this time.

My phone dings in my pocket and I check my notification.

BEX:

Yeah I stayed with a friend last night,

sorry to worry you!

A "friend."

Interesting.

"Bex didn't come home last night," I say, casually. "I think she might be seeing someone."

"Hm." Noah takes a giant bite of waffle, syrup dripping from his lip. He shrugs then starts tidying the mixing bowls and measuring cups, avoiding making eye contact.

"Do you know something?" I ask.

He looks up and says, "No," quickly. Too quickly.

"You know who she's seeing."

He shakes his head. "I don't care what Bex does or who she does it with—that's her business. I'm sure she'll tell us when there's something to tell."

I go to him and put my arms around his neck as he encircles my waist. "Okay."

He kisses my forehead.

"So, where are we going?"

He parts his lips just enough to show the edges of his teeth. "We have to get changed first."

♥ ♥ ♥

Wood's parents live in a gated community up in the hills overlooking Seattle and Puget Sound amongst other multi-million-dollar properties. Noah and Wood's mothers were sisters, and, from what I can tell, came from an average, middle-class background. But Wood's dad apparently comes from "old money."

"Don't worry, they're vacationing in Italy right now." Noah puts the car into park in front of a house with flat roof lines and endless planes of glass walls, half of it seeming to jut out over the hillside like it's floating.

He holds my hand as he keys in a code on their fancy security system and then walks me through the house and out to the back where a crystal blue pool stretches the length of the house, the far edge disappearing into nothing but air as the landscape drops off to the valley below.

"Ready?" Noah takes off his shirt and tosses it to one of the pool lounge chairs.

I nod.

The sun reflects off the pool water and onto his inked skin as he backs into the pool and beckons me to join him.

I take a deep breath and take off my cover-up then step into the pool. My heart picking up speed a little, remembering the last time I tried to swim.

Noah dunks his entire body in the water, coming up and shaking water from his hair before slicking it back.

Fuck, but he's gorgeous.

And he's with me.

At least for the moment.

Shaking that thought, I go to Noah's arms, standing where the water is at waist height. The water is cool but comfortable.

He looks down at me as he places his hands on my hips, sun blazing behind him, water dripping from his hair.

"I'm nervous," I whisper.

He tightens his fingers into my hips and kisses my forehead. "This is important. I've got you. I won't let anything happen. I need you to be safe."

"I trust you."

He gives me a tighter squeeze when I say it, his eyes saying even more.

"First, we're going to work on your back float," he says.
"I know how to float."
Sort of.
"Great. Show me."

CHAPTER 18
NOAH

"**D**on't let go." Livvy closes her eyes. The sun is golden on her skin, gleaming off the pool, water droplets sparkling on her body.

"I won't let go. I'm right here." I'm barely touching her back with my fingertips as she floats in front of me.

It took quite a few tries before she relaxed enough to do it.

I drop my fingers away.

"See, you're doing it! All by yourself."

Her eyes snap open and she sinks, splashing and thrashing under the water until she finds her bearings and pops back up.

"You let go!"

"You were doing great until I said something." I chuckle.

She wipes her face. "I hate getting water in my eyes."

I'm more concerned about water in her lungs. I kiss her forehead. "You're doing great. Come here."

I lean her back, head against my shoulder and glide us backward around the pool. She gets the rhythm of the kicks easily and I guide her arms up and around in correct form for a backstroke.

My fingers trace along the lines of her arms, her skin so soft.

She turns her head, pressing her lips lightly to the underside of my jaw. And just like that, the swimming lesson is over.

I should have known it would devolve into making out and rubbing each other's bodies in the pool before too long. But when Livvy dives her hand into my swim trunks to grip my extremely hard cock, I have to put a stop to it. No matter how needy I am for her, my aunt and uncle have a security system with cameras they check regularly while away.

So, I promise we'll continue this later.

My hand is on her thigh the whole drive home. But we have to go in to the shop. And then it's Bex's day off and she's around, the whole fucking night. I want to wrap my arm around Livvy, snuggle with her on the couch, kiss her freely—but I can't.

While Livvy's in the bathroom getting ready for bed I shoot Bex a look. "Hey, shouldn't you be off with lover boy tonight?" *Please leave.*

She pulls a beer out of the fridge, no signs of leaving or heading to bed any time soon. "He's working tonight. And keep your voice down." She shifts a glance over to the hallway. "I don't want anyone finding out. At least not yet," she says in a hushed tone.

Bex comes around the island to where I'm sitting, getting real close, and points her finger at me. "Noah," she says, somehow whispering and yelling my name at the same time. "Promise me you won't say anything! Even to Livvy. No one can know."

Before I can answer, the patter of footsteps sounds from our left and Bex and I scurry away from each other just as Livvy comes in.

"What's going on?" Livvy asks, a little crinkle in her nose.

"Nothing's going on. Want to watch a movie?" Bex says casually.

So, we watch a movie. Livvy's on the opposite side of the couch, already way too far away, and then Bex sits right between us.

The next day and night aren't much better.

It's been two days, and I haven't had the chance to get Livvy properly alone. I'm dying for her. She's all I think about.

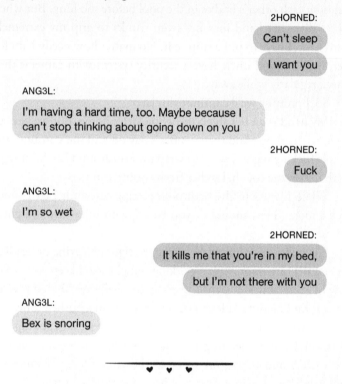

2HORNED:
Can't sleep

I want you

ANG3L:
I'm having a hard time, too. Maybe because I can't stop thinking about going down on you

2HORNED:
Fuck

ANG3L:
I'm so wet

2HORNED:
It kills me that you're in my bed,

but I'm not there with you

ANG3L:
Bex is snoring

♥   ♥   ♥

I lean over the railing in the loft, overlooking the living room and then out the large windows, the serene water and the skyline of downtown Seattle.

The sky is a hazy gray this morning. No one is up yet. I've been awake for hours.

Movement below catches my eye. I barely catch a glimpse of Livvy's ankle, a towel swishing over her arm as she disappears into the bathroom.

Water is running, steam beginning to fog the mirror when I slip inside and lock the door behind me. I whisper her name, not wanting to startle her and risk waking anyone else up. "Can I come in?"

"Noah?"

I peek my head inside the curtain, not being able to keep down my face-splitting grin at the sight of her. Rivulets of water stream down her body, her skin rosy from the hot water.

"Morning, you," I say, almost stepping in fully clothed.

She bites her lip as she runs a washcloth over her shoulders and across her chest, soapy bubbles sliding down her perfect tits and over her darkened nipples.

Fuck.

I undress in a frenzy, throwing clothes behind me carelessly, practically fumbling over myself to get in with her.

My hands are immediately around her face and in her hair. Pushing her up against the tile. My mouth on hers, devouring her strained gasp.

"Shh. We've got to be quiet." I pull away, rubbing my thumbs along that full lower lip of hers.

She nods.

"Good girl. Now, keep washing up. I'll just be down here."

I drop to my knees. My fingers dig into the soft flesh of her hips and thighs, spreading them just enough to get my face between them and my tongue where we both need it.

The thump of her hand smacking the wet tile along with a muffled moan comes when my tongue strokes her most sensitive spot, but otherwise, my girl is so good. So good and so quiet while I eat her out.

I close my eyes as the hot water streams down my face, concentrating only on how her clit is swelling against my tongue and holding her hips tight as her legs start to shake.

She grips my shoulder with one hand, panting above me. Her

other hand twists in my hair as she starts to rock against me, grinding her pussy against my face.

Good fucking girl.

There's a knock-knock at the door.

"Hngh," Livvy whimpers over me.

The knock is harder. "Livvy, you've been in there a long time, are you almost done? I really need to pee!" Bex yells.

Fuck!

"Shit. She's never up this early," Livvy says through heavy breaths.

I look up at Livvy, her lips dark and swollen, nipples hard, chest heaving.

"Almost finished!" She calls out to her sister.

Then she fists my hair. "Don't you dare stop." And yanks me back between her thighs.

Oh. My already hard cock jumps. Pulsing. It's the hottest thing any woman has ever done to me.

I lap her up, concentrating on her little throbbing clit. Her nails dig into my scalp, a rush of sweetness hits my tongue, and she goes limp.

Bex knocks again.

I've got her around the waist as I turn off the water and grab us towels. She's still coming down when I dry her off and wrap it around her. Her cheeks are flushed and she smiles dazedly up at me.

"Come on!"

Liv's eyes go wide. "Just a sec!" She hops out of the shower, right onto my sweats. "Shit," she says.

"Shit."

She scoops up my sweats from the floor, shirt from the counter, and boxers from the sink, stuffs them under her towel, then runs to the door.

I close the curtain and sit in the corner of the shower.

"Finally!" Bex's hurried footsteps hit the tile as she runs in, and I try to block out the sound while trying not to make any of my own.

I cannot block out the sound. It's awkward.

I stay in the shower for a few minutes after Bex leaves, finally poking my head out and wondering what to do next.

The door opens and I almost fall back into the shower.

"It's clear," Livvy whispers. "Bex went back to bed."

I go to her, and she turns, giggling. I follow her out into the hall, through the living room, and up the stairs to the loft, all while clutching this too-small towel together around my waist.

I reach for my clothes. "Can I get dressed now?"

She hugs them to her chest and smirks. "Or..."

Taking several steps toward me, that devilish grin growing, she sets my clothes down on the table. Then she comes to me and drags her fingertips down my chest, over my abs and down to the towel, which opens and falls to the floor with a simple touch.

I'm hard instantly.

Livvy presses both palms to my chest, looking up at me, angelic. Then she walks forward, pushing me back until my calves hit the couch.

"Sit," she says.

I sit.

She licks her lips.

My cock is standing at attention.

Then she turns my legs and lifts them up onto the couch.

"Bend this knee."

I do, still not sure what's going on.

Then she moves my right arm, laying it over my hip. "And this one here," she says as she adjusts my other hand. "And turn to look this way."

I turn my head.

"Perfect. Now, stay just like that." Livvy backs away from me until she's in the corner. At her easel. "Your turn," she says with a smile.

"Oh, really?" I throw my head back, laughing.

"No moving." She shakes her pencil at me, scowling. Cuter than ever.

"Sorry."

"If you're good, maybe you'll get a reward after I'm done." She smiles and I straighten, getting back into position.

Modeling is hard. I know that now.

My hip aches. I let out a little sigh. It feels like I've been in this position for hours.

"I'm almost done," she says. "It's only been thirty minutes."

After another hour, which, according to Livvy is only fifteen more minutes, she finally says she's done, and I can relax.

"You did a good job." Livvy walks over to me, biting her lip, a burning in her eyes.

"I did?"

"Mmhmm." She drops to her knees and my erection springs instantly to life.

As soon as her perfect lips close around the bulging head of my cock, I throw my head against the sofa, eyes rolling back.

"I'll pose for you any time you want," I pant.

She takes me in, to the back of her throat.

"Multiple times a day if you need me to."

♥ ♥ ♥

"So, can I see the drawing?" I ask as I pull my sweats back on.

Livvy wipes her mouth with the back of her hand, her cheeks still crimson, pupils dilated. Sexy as hell.

"Sure." She nods and I follow her over to the easel.

She's oddly quiet, biting her lip as I come around to look at it.

It's gorgeous.

It's a hell of a lot better than any of the drawings I did of her. I expected to see a drawing of me lying on the couch. But this—this is more of a study of light than anything. It captures the whole space. The feeling of the room, somehow. The large windows behind me are bright while my figure is mostly in shadow. My profile is outlined in a perfect glowing rim light. It's peaceful, contemplative. It feels warm.

It's how she sees me and at the same time, it's how she makes me feel.

The way Livvy talks about art, how a piece can have the power to evoke an emotion, to have a deeper meaning to the viewer—I've never experienced that before.

"Wow," is all I can say.

"Do you like it?" The tiny crease between her eyebrows vanishes as her smile grows. Her smile takes my breath away.

"I love it," I say.

A voice in the back of my head whispers, *you love her.* What the actual fuck? It's not my normal breed of morbid intrusive thought, but somehow, just as horrifying.

I shake it from my mind.

"You can have it."

"Really?"

"Yeah." She laughs. "I'll even sign it for you. I don't know if it's special enough to display or anything, but you can do what you want with it."

She's wrong there. It is beyond good enough to display and I already know what I want to do with it. "Do you know what you're going to put up on the wall in the shop?"

"Um, yes." She's gnawing on her lip again.

She takes out her sketchbook from behind the easel, wedged between a couple blank canvases.

We walk over to the couch, and she opens it to the right page for me, handing it to me as we sit down.

I recognize the reference of her sketch immediately. "It's The

Kiss."

The two figures are in the same position as the famous painting, bent over, embraced, him kissing her face. But these two
figures are an angel and a demon. Her wings are large and drape
around her, the tips touching the ground, while he has dark claws,
hooves, a tail, and two, very large, twisted horns.

"This is spectacular," I say.

"You think so?"

"Yes. This is amazing." I look at her. "*You* are amazing." I am in
awe of her.

You love her.

I clear my throat. "May I?" I hold up the page as if to turn it,
and she nods.

We look through her sketchbook in silence. She leans her head
against my shoulder, her body pressed against mine as I flip
through the pages. Every time I think I've found a favorite drawing, I turn the page and the next one is even better.

"Thank you." I hand the sketchbook back to her. "I know you
don't like people looking through your stuff. But these are
wonderful."

"I don't mind anyone seeing my finished pieces. I showed
pieces all the time in school. It's the unfinished and half-drawn,
and abandoned things I don't like to share."

"Those are my favorite ones!"

She pulls back, that crease forming above her nose again.
"Really?"

"Yes. I love the ones that are a bit messy, not finished and
polished and perfect. I like seeing your hand in it—all the strokes,
how your mind was working. They're the most free and expressive.
Besides, is anything ever finished?"

"In art? Some might say it's finished when the artist says it is."

"But we artists know the truth."

She nods. "We could go on tweaking a project for eternity and still see more that could be done, fixed, changed. It's never perfect."

"Exactly. We're all works in progress."

We lock eyes. My hand is on her knee, and she puts hers over it and gives it a squeeze.

"They'd be proud of you," she says, eyes glistening.

Fuck. My chest tightens and my eyelids start to burn. The sting of unshed tears becoming almost unbearable. But, while all these boiling emotions are churning inside me, she keeps my hand in hers. I am a storm, but she is calm. She is peace. She is warmth.

We don't need words.

♥ ♥ ♥

Livvy has been putting her drawing up on the back wall of the shop all shift. Her spot on the wall is right next to mine, right next to my station, and it's taken all I have not to keep putting my equipment down and watch her create.

"It looks so good," I tell her after my last client is finished up.

"Yeah?" She looks up at me with those green eyes and a smudge of white chalk across her forehead.

"I think it's the coolest one in the whole shop." I lean in. "Don't tell anyone I said that."

"Thanks." Her cheeks turn bright pink, and she wipes her forehead with the back of her arm, smearing more chalk. "I need to go clean up."

"I have to take care of a couple things in my office. Come find me when you're done."

I bend down and kiss her on the temple. I don't even think about it, showing her affection is as natural as breathing.

But as soon as I pull back and see her eyes are wide, I know I shouldn't have done it. I glance over my shoulder and around. I don't think anyone was looking or saw. Not that I would care if they had, but Livvy might. We should talk about it. Soon.

I go around the corner to my office and Taryn is blocking the door, standing with her arms crossed, a scowl, and her stare laser-focused on me. "We need to talk."

"Okay." I move past her and open the door, gesturing for her to go on.

She takes the same stance in front of my desk as in the hallway and as soon as I shut the door, she opens her mouth.

"Are you fucking the new girl?"

I blink in a stupor. It takes me a second to register her words. "That...is none of your business," I say.

"So, you are."

It's not a question. It's an accusation.

Livvy and I haven't had penetrative sex yet. I could probably say no and not be lying on a technicality. But that doesn't feel right. I can't say yes, either. I won't betray Livvy's confidence or right to privacy. We haven't talked about telling people—she hasn't even told her sister about us yet.

We haven't talked about what "we" are yet. I don't even know what we *would* tell people. Are we just having fun and hooking up? Are we dating? We haven't gone on any official dates. Are we in a relationship? It's to be determined.

"Listen," I say, in as casual a tone as I can manage, "I know you and I went out a couple times a few years ago, but we decided when you started working here that it wasn't a good fit. I thought we were way past this."

Taryn's scowl deepens. "*We* didn't decide anything. *You* decided that. And I *am* past it. I'm not asking because I'm jealous. I want to know because I don't like drama. I don't want it in my life or at my job, and if it's true, shit's about to get real messy in the shop."

"Anthony."

"Uh huh."

Fuck.

Just the reminder, the memory of him with his hands on Livvy, his lips on her, has me clenching my jaw.

"Seriously," Taryn says, "if this place gets uncomfortable, I'm out."

I take a measured breath, reminding myself I have to stay in calm boss-mode, not feral boyfriend-mode.

CHAPTER 19

LIVVY

"**N**othing is going to get out of hand."

My hand is on the office door, but the tone of Noah's voice from inside causes me to pause.

"Tell me you're fucking her."

Taryn?

"You don't need to worry about me and Livvy. I've got it under control. I promise, it's not that serious."

He and Taryn are talking about me? Not that serious?

I drop my hand from the doorknob and step away.

Right. I mean, he basically said he wanted to keep things casual at the lake house. I should have known. Silly me.

"Sup, girl!"

I look up to see Anthony smiling. My feet must have been moving of their own accord because I am suddenly out in the lobby of the shop.

"How you doin'?" he asks.

I put on a smile, but I can barely focus my eyes on him. "Good."

He rubs his hands together. "So, hey. I was just thinking about how you agreed we should go on another date, and I wanted to make a plan, see when you're available."

I'd totally forgotten I agreed to a second date.

Maybe this is a good thing. Maybe this is exactly what I need. What did Bex say? *Play the field. Have fun. You don't owe anybody anything.* Right.

"I'm free right now," I say.

Anthony raises his eyebrows. "Cool, yeah, sure. Let's do it." He scoops his arm around my shoulder and leads me to the door. The bell rattles when he pushes it open for me.

"What are you doing?" Noah's dark voice hits me from behind.

We turn to see him standing there chest out, arms at his sides, somehow filling the entire space.

"We're going out, boss. Catch you later." Anthony smiles and winks as he turns back toward the door. But I can't pry my eyes away from his glare.

"Liv. I need to talk to you. Now." The angle of Noah's jaw gets sharper as his dark brows narrow.

"Can it wait—"

"No," he barks.

I mouth "sorry" to Anthony then follow Noah.

When I enter his office, he's standing in the middle of the room, back to his desk.

"What's going on?" he asks. His voice is controlled, but there's an edge to it I haven't heard before.

"He asked me on another date after our first one, I figured tonight was as good a time as any." It takes every ounce of will in my body to not let my voice waver on my words.

"I'm confused." He tilts his head, shadows exaggerating the depth of his eyes and cheekbones.

"About what?" I don't manage to hide the shake that time.

"*About what?* Why are you going on a date with him? I thought—" He clenches his jaw, nostrils flared.

"Am I not allowed to? We're not *that* serious, right? We haven't agreed to be exclusive."

He leans back against his desk, arms crossed, brows lowered. "No. We haven't."

Say you want to be. Say it. Please.

But he doesn't say it. He's unmoving, expressionless, unblinking.

"Okay then, glad we're on the same page. I'll be home later, don't wait up for me." I turn toward the door and then the desk screeches across the floor.

When I look back, Noah has closed the distance between us, looming over me. "You're not going out with him tonight. You're taken." His chest is heaving. He lowers his face closer to mine. "And if anyone's going to fuck you tonight, it's going to be me." His tone is low, menacing. Thick and velvety, seeping its way under my skin and twisting itself around my bones.

I love it. His is the only voice I want to hear whispered in my ear.

"Don't tell me what to do," I say. "You don't own me."

"Of course I don't own you. That doesn't mean you're not mine."

"I'm *not* yours."

"Yes you are. You're mine. Just like I'm yours."

I stare dumbly up at him. My breathing is too loud.

He touches my wrist.

I pull it away from him and square my shoulders. "Then why did you tell Taryn not to worry about me, that it's not that serious?"

"Is that what this is about?" He furrows a brow.

I don't say anything, steadying my expression, wanting to go off but afraid I'll burst into tears instead.

He softens his gaze and reaches for my hand, his fingertips grazing my palm as he lowers his head and quiets his voice. "She was concerned about our relationship causing drama. *That's* what

I was telling her not to worry about. *That's* what I was saying wasn't that serious. I am serious about you."

"You are?"

"Yes. I just—I didn't know how serious you wanted it to be. You're young and having fun. I thought you wanted to keep things casual—"

"No."

"No?" There's a hint of a smile on his lips.

"No." I shake my head and his smile grows.

He kisses me roughly, greedily, lips parting just enough so that the tip of my tongue tastes a hint of mint from his. Pulling away he takes my hand, interlacing our fingers, and we walk back out to the shop.

"Everyone," he says loudly, "listen up."

Everyone in the shop turns to look at us, those not with clients walk toward us. My hand burns, still interlocked with his.

Anthony's face is red.

"I wanted you all to know, so there's no questioning, Livvy and I are together." Noah looks at me, the grin on his lips soft, but his eyes sparkling. "I'm crazy about her. And it's *not* casual."

"This is some fucking bullshit." Anthony pushes out the door, the metal of the bell banging against glass.

"Here we go." Taryn rolls her eyes and walks off, her black boots thudding heavily against the floor.

Noah bends down to me. "Don't worry. I'll talk with Anthony."

"I guess it's time for me to tell Bex about us, then, too."

He nods, but says, "When you're ready. No rush."

But he is in a rush to get me upstairs, taking me by the hand to the elevators and kissing me the whole ride up. I breathe in his scent, the warmth of his skin under his clothes, the feel of his hands on me, his hard chest, his soft lips.

He said he's mine.

He's mine and I'm his and though I've imagined this scenario in my head hundreds of times, it was never this good, this right, this perfect.

His arm is around my waist as he shoves the door to the apartment open.

Wood is sitting at the kitchen counter with a bowl of cereal, spoon mid-air, milk dripping from between the honey nut O's.

"Don't you have somewhere to be?" Noah asks him, his grip on me tightening.

"Nah, bro. I'm just hanging at home tonight."

"You have somewhere to be," Noah insists.

Wood's face brightens. "Oh! Right, yeah. I do." He gets up and drinks the rest of the milk from his bowl and tosses it in the sink. "Thanks for the reminder." Wood flashes us a smile, sticks his tongue out, and claps Noah on the shoulder as he passes us on the way out the door.

And now we're alone.

Noah glances at his phone. "We've got a few hours until Bex's shift is over."

"She texted me earlier that she's staying somewhere else tonight. She didn't want me to worry. So, we have all night to..."

Noah raises his eyebrows. "Oh." He steps closer, his pelvis pressed against my lower belly. "To what? What do you want to do, Livvy?"

"You said, uh..." I pause, heart beating hard.

He tilts his head, running the edges of his teeth along his full lower lip. Waiting.

"You said you were going to...fuck me."

His eyes darken. "Is that what you want?"

I nod.

"I need you to say it, angel. Say you want me to fuck you."

I swallow, my throat dry. "I want you to fuck me, Noah."

He curls his tattooed hand around mine and, walking backward, pulls me into his darkened room. Everything is drenched in inky blue, the moon shining silver out the window.

"Come here," he whispers.

Cool air makes my skin prickle as he lifts my shirt up and off. In the quiet, he gives my hand a reassuring squeeze and kisses my temple. As he undoes my bra, he kisses my neck, right at the pulse point. He must feel it. He must know how fast my blood is pumping right now.

His fingers graze my sides as he slips my bra off, then they move up to cup my breasts. He rubs his thumbs over my hardened nipples, and I let out a whimper.

"You know I'm going to take care of you, right?" he asks as he slides his hands down to my pants. "You trust me?" He deftly unbuttons my jeans.

"Yes," I breathe.

"Good." He pushes my jeans and panties down at the same time. "Now, be a good girl and go lie down on the bed for me."

Scooting backward toward the pillow, I watch him loom over me, shadowed in darkness. He strips off his shirt and pants, standing there in only his black boxer briefs. He's tall and lanky. Black tattoos cover every inch, wrapping around each bulge and ripple of his muscles.

He pushes the boxers down next. He's already hard. And large. And holy fuck, he's going to put it inside me. Heat blooms all over my body, skin on fire, my center molten.

The mattress dips as he crawls to me, slowly, a hunter stalking his prey.

He comes up and kisses my forehead, then the tip of my nose. So soft, so gently I wasn't expecting it. Running a knuckle from my temple to my chin, he gazes into my eyes reverently, lips parted. Every part of me yearns for this man. I've never wanted anyone like I want him. Need him.

He's about to say something but I'm already grabbing his face and pulling him to me. Our lips come together, warm and soft. We move together perfectly. The rhythm of our breaths, mouths opening, tongues sliding in unison.

I squeeze his hips with my thighs. The pulsing between my legs is almost as distracting as the way his hard cock presses into my belly.

His hands roam my body. Electricity buzzes under my skin.

I can't help but rock my hips, needing more friction as our kisses go deeper, harder. He growls as he hikes his hard thigh up between my legs, and I rut up against him, both of us wet with my juices now.

"Fuck," he whispers between kisses. "You need more?" He reaches down and presses fingers to my clit, right where I'm throbbing for him.

"Yes," I pant.

I feel out of control. My body wants. Wants.

"Noah, please."

"I've got you." He kisses down my throat then moves to each breast, licking and sucking my nipples, making my back arch.

He kisses and licks down my sternum and down my trembling tummy as he goes between my legs. He nuzzles his cheek along the inside of my thigh, laying kisses, moving closer to where I'm empty and aching for him.

He dips his head down, kissing me there, too. I watch up on my elbows, holding my breath as he looks up at me with a wicked glint in his eyes, light catching the sharp point of his white teeth.

"Just like that," he says. "Watch me eat you."

As soon as his tongue slicks between my folds, I throw my head back. "Shit—" The word dissolves into a groan as my eyes roll back.

"What did I just say?"

"Sorry," I pant, trying to focus back on him.

He licks again, this time sliding a finger inside me.

"Oh."

"That okay?"

"Yes. More."

And he gives me more. He gives me everything, slurping and

licking long and slow, bringing me to the precipice and keeping me there until I'm a shaking, panting, mess. And then he sucks my clit between his lips until I shatter into a catatonic state of bliss.

I come back from the orgasm, catching my breath, light-headed, to him sitting back on his haunches, smirking at me. He wipes his mouth with his forearm.

"Noah," I breathe, reaching for him.

He comes to me, pressing his forehead to mine and kisses my lips. Soft.

I'm still shaking. Overheated. Skin slick all over.

He kisses me again. Rougher. But I devour it, digging my fingers into his shoulder blades. Needing more. I bite his lip harder than I mean to. He growls, gripping both my thighs and pressing his cock between them, running the length of it along my wetness.

Oh fuck. Fuck. "Fuck me," I gasp out as he's sucking my lip between his teeth and dragging the ridge of his cockhead over my too sensitive clit.

I watch, heart racing, licking my puffy lips as he gets the condom. He makes quick work of putting it on, though his hand shakes slightly as he rolls it down his length.

He lowers himself over me, hips snug between my thighs. My stomach quivers as the heat and hardness of his erection presses against me.

Noah locks his eyes on mine, and everything fades away. Everything is quiet except for our breaths and skin brushing against skin and blood pulsing in my ears.

"Are you ready? Are you sure?" he asks, one hand wrapped around the base of his sheathed cock, swollen and shiny, the other light on my hip, gently rubbing circles over my tattoo.

I nod.

"I need to hear it."

"Yes. I'm sure, Noah."

He guides his cock down, dragging the tip of it through my folds, up to my clit and down toward my entrance.

I shiver.

"Does that feel good?"

"Yes," I whisper.

He does it again. A zing of electricity makes me jolt when it grazes my still over-sensitive clit. He rubs a few more times, the head of his cock shiny and wet with my juices. I let out an exhale, my legs falling to the mattress, enjoying the sensation of it. But this time when he goes down to my entrance, he pushes it in, just the tip. He watches for my reaction as he does it.

"Oh," I moan.

"You okay?"

I nod.

He keeps eye contact as he pushes in farther. Another inch. Two. Stretching me as he fills me. It's weird. Different. Big. But while it feels wholly strange, it also feels right. More right than anything—him inside me. Us, as one.

He stills, lying over me, caging me with his arms.

I'm hot and wet and throbbing around him, and he's barely satiating the ache.

He kisses my nose then my lips. "I'll go slow," he says. "Tell me if you need me to stop."

I nod, swallowing, but inside I'm screaming for him to keep going. I want more of him. All of him.

He tilts his hips, pushing inside another inch.

"Fuck. You're so wet, Liv. It's hard to go slow."

"Don't go slow, then," I whisper.

He lowers his mouth to mine, kissing me deeply. Needy. I moan and suck on his tongue as he thrusts to the hilt.

I gasp.

"I'm all the way in. Still okay?"

"Yes." I'm breathing heavy, thankful he's not moving so I can get used to him.

He smiles, but his neck is tensed. He's straining holding himself back from me, about to break into a sweat.

"More," I say.

Leaning on one elbow, he grabs my hip with his other hand and squeezes my backside. Then he slides his hand down my thigh and lifts my leg, spreading me wider. He slips in even deeper.

"Oh, shit."

"Did that hurt?"

I shake my head. "Keep going."

"Wrap your leg around me."

I hook my leg around his back, and he eases out of me, never breaking eye contact.

"Keep breathing, there you go." He thrusts again, nice and slow. In and out. "Fuck. You're taking me so good, Livvy. Look how you're taking me, angel."

I look down, see the shaft of his cock disappearing inside me, making me feel exquisitely full, then pulling out, wet and covered in me.

"So fucking good for me," he coos.

I wrap my arms around him, pulling him close. We're nose-to-nose, and he kisses me again. Harder. We're skin-to-skin, our bodies entwined as he moves inside me. Frenzied breaths in the absence of space between us.

"You feel so good," he growls against my lips.

"Yes," I pant.

But then he pulls out, slipping away from me. I clutch at his forearm. "What—"

"Shh." He slides down my body, down between my legs and kisses me there.

Oh.

"Your just-fucked cunt is so pretty, Liv. Red and puffy." He spreads my lips with his fingers and laps at my clit until I'm wild. Bucking under him, grinding against his face. I've never been this wanton.

I moan and cry out, cursing his name under my breath desperately trying to get air.

"Please. Noah. Please."

He looks up at me, sucking hard on my clit. "Please what? What do you need?"

I'm trembling. On the edge again. "You. I need you. Please."

"You want me to fuck you some more?"

"Yes."

"Well, I have to give my girl what she needs." He crawls back over me, his cock hard and nudging at me.

I dig my fingernails into his shoulder blades as he slides all the way back in.

"You still good?" he whispers against my neck and kissing me there.

"More than good."

He pulls back so we're face-to-face. We undulate, our bodies in sync, my hips meeting his thrusts in a steady rhythm.

Little gasps. Eye contact. Nose kisses.

I cling to him.

"I've got you," he says.

And everything else melts away. We move together, skin slick, his grunts low, my moans high and soft. Each stroke more intense, heightening every sense. The scent of him, the sounds of each breath, the taste of his lips laced with me. Everything in this moment is perfect.

"You're perfect," he says, voice strained and shaky. He dips his hand between us, the pad of his thumb slippery, circling my tender clit. "You going to come on my cock, angel?"

I've been dangling on the verge of another climax, about to go over at any moment.

"Yes." It's more of a plea.

"Good girl." He applies a little more pressure to my clit, while he pumps in and out of me slow. Slow and steady and deep. So deep.

All the sensations are overwhelming. His cock inside me, filling me, pulsing. His touch, his words, the way he's watching me as I come again. I clench around his cock as my climax hits, squeezing his hips with my legs and pulling him in. Closer. Deeper.

He leans in, wrapping his hand around the back of my neck, barely containing his strength. He drags his thumb over my jaw and around my throat as he dips down to touch his lips to mine.

"Tell me you're mine," he says, just above a growl, applying pressure to the sides of my neck.

He thrusts into me harder, his expression primal.

"I'm yours," I say.

"Mine."

Almost instantly, he's shuddering over me as he comes, his body tensing and flexing, emptying himself inside me.

He kisses me with trembling lips, our breathing both shaky and broken, our bodies still connected.

I comb my fingers through his hair and then to the sides of his face, holding it and looking into his eyes as the last few tremors of his climax roll through him.

We're still and quiet. Just us and the moonlight, and I want this moment to never end.

He kisses the tip of my nose, a sheen of sweat on his forehead, and slowly pulls away, sliding out of me.

It's tender there, and as he leaves my body, I try not to wince.

"Shit, did I hurt you?" His face falls, cold panic in his eyes.

"No." I shake my head, but his expression doesn't change.

He gets up and disposes of the condom. "I'll be right back. Don't move."

After a moment, there's the rush of running water then he returns with a damp washcloth and kneels next to me on the bed.

"Spread your legs for me," he says gently.

He presses it between my legs, gingerly cleaning my inner thighs then higher. The washcloth is warm, the fabric a little prickly. It feels raw against me, and I whimper as he rubs it over my sensitive flesh.

"Fuck," he says under his breath. "I'm sorry if I was too rough with you, at the end. I was trying to be gentle and make your first time good, but I got carried away. It's hard to hold back, in that state."

"You weren't too rough," I say, but his mouth stays in a hard line. "It was perfect."

He lies down next to me, still pressing the cloth between my legs. After a few minutes he tosses the cloth to a nightstand and pulls the covers up over us. I settle on his chest, and he wraps his arm around me while stroking his fingers through my hair.

I close my eyes, listening to his heartbeat.

"I think I'll actually sleep tonight," he says, the timbre of his voice making his chest vibrate under my cheek.

I look up at him, but he's staring off, a million miles away. He told me months ago about how it's worse at night. That's always when the bad thoughts seep back into the foreground and keep him awake.

"Will you tell me what happened? I know about the accident, but not the details. Let me carry some of it for you."

He tightens his arm around me.

"I don't tell anyone about it. Obviously, my family knows. Wood. But that's it. I don't bring it up. Bex doesn't even know. It happened after we'd already broken up, and my parents and brother had moved a couple towns over, so it wasn't on the local news where you were."

He swallows hard, his pulse quickening. I give him a squeeze, staying quiet, giving him time.

His words come slow and soft. "Cam—Cameron, he was an amazing pianist. Like, genius-level. My parents wanted to put him in a fancy performing arts school when he reached high school, but me, being an asshole eighteen-year-old, didn't want to move right before my senior year. So, they let me stay with Wood's parents, and they went.

"It happened the fall after I graduated, right before my nineteenth birthday. They were coming back from a concert. It was raining. They were going over a bridge, and there was a large truck going the other way. It's unclear which vehicle crossed over the center line, but one of them did and they hit head-on. Their car went off the bridge and into the water. They all died."

He's quiet for a minute, his chest bobbing under me.

"The coroner's report found no water in my parents' lungs— they died in the impact. But my brother, in the back seat, he drowned."

An ice-cold sinking feeling slithers through my veins as my stomach drops. His insisting on giving me swimming lessons makes even more sense now. What I put him through at the lake—

"Noah." I wrap myself around him as much as I can, not knowing what else to do or say.

He's not looking at me, but out the window. I tuck my head under his chin.

"He was fifteen," he whispers. "They all tried to reassure me that he was probably unconscious from the accident when they went under, but there's no way to know for sure. That's the worst part. Knowing he was alone. Wondering if he was scared. If he watched the water come in. Wondering if it would've been different if I had gone with them—"

"Come here," I whisper, sliding up to hold his head to my chest.

He nuzzles down against me and wraps his body around mine. And I hold him. There's nothing I can say to make it better. Nothing he hasn't already heard, doesn't already know. He knows it's not his fault. That if he'd been in the car, it doesn't mean he would have been able to save them. Most likely he'd be gone too.

I hold him tighter, so thankful he wasn't with them, that he's here with me instead. And we stay like this, in the quiet, with the understanding I'll hold him for as long as he needs.

CHAPTER 20
NOAH

Livvy stretches, letting out the softest sigh, shifting the covers so they slip down, revealing her bare skin. The morning light kisses the curves of her body. Shapely shoulder, slim neck, plump breasts, hard nipples. Soft stomach, flared hips, rounded thighs.

I am as hard as a steel rod. Pulsing for her.

She yawns, blinking sleepily, and props herself up. "Hey."

"Hi, you."

"Were you watching me sleep?"

"Maybe."

She smiles. "Creepy."

I chuckle, running my finger over the curve of her hip. "How are you feeling? Sore?"

"Maybe a little."

I trace over the lines of the wing on her hip. "When I was tattooing these, I thought they were perfect for you—sweet and innocent. Now I know what they really mean." I look up at her face.

Her smile grows as her cheeks darken. "Since I was done with school, I was going to be done with the app—I *am* done with the app—but I wanted to keep a piece of Angel with me. As a reminder of the woman I want to be. Sexy. Confident."

"But you already are those things."

She shakes her head. "Not really."

I grab her hips and pull her down the bed onto her back as she yelps and laughs.

"I'll just have to show you," I say as I slip her panties off.

She bites her lip and spreads her legs, watching as I bury my face.

♥ ♥ ♥

"You're good, right? I'm sure we could make room for you at Spencer's place." Bex hoists her duffle bag over her shoulder as Livvy follows her out of my room into the living room.

She catches my gaze, making eye contact for a second, the pulse in her neck visible. "No, I'll be fine here."

"Okay, well Spencer's conference is all week. I told Macy that since we finally got everything figured out and our lease ended with our old apartment, we can start looking for a new place now, for the three of us." She gives Livvy a hug.

"Yeah, that will be great." Livvy smiles and nods and my chest tightens at the thought of her moving out.

"It will be! I'm sorry it has taken so long. Macy's been dragging her feet about apartment hunting. She keeps hoping Spencer will ask her to just stay there and move in with him, but he hasn't."

Wood mumbles something in the kitchen, scrambling his eggs more forcefully than necessary. I sip my coffee.

"I'll let you know about apartment hunting. Text me." Bex and Liv hug again before Bex leaves.

"Eggs?" Wood asks.

Livvy shakes her head. "No thanks, I'm going to go take a shower and get ready for work." She disappears down the hall.

"Noah?"

"I'm good," I say, wondering if I should make a show of waiting before I follow her into the bathroom or just go now. I've already forgotten what she tastes like, and that won't do.

Wood comes to the table with way too many fluffy eggs on his plate. "You can just ask her to stay, bro."

"What do you mean?"

"Like, if you were worried about my reaction or wanted my input before asking her, I'm cool with it. I think you should."

"I wasn't thinking about asking her to stay."

"I saw the way your face changed as soon as she and Bex were talking about apartment hunting. It's like you're under your own little storm cloud. Her being here makes you happy. Just ask."

"I can't do that. It's too soon."

"Too soon according to who? Society? Fuck that and what anyone else thinks."

I chuckle. "I didn't realize you were such a romantic."

He scoffs. "Did you forget that I'm a product of love at first sight? At least, it was for my dad. He knew the moment he met my mom she was it for him. And three months later they were married."

I raise an eyebrow. "And six months later, you were born."

"That had nothing to do with it. Twenty-seven years later and they're still together. My point is, it's your life and I haven't seen you truly happy like this since...since before."

The knot that is always somewhere in my gut twists and aches. "I'll think about it," I say.

Wood smiles.

"There is something, actually, that I want to do for her I was hoping you could help me with."

Wood leans forward, resting his chin in his hands. "I'm listening."

♥   ♥   ♥

The best part of the day is waking up with her in my arms, tangled in my sheets, skin on skin, soft breaths in the dewy morning light. Just the fact that I wake up—that I slept—she's my angel.

Every day gets better. She is sunshine. She paints and does little dances in the kitchen. She sits with me at work, watching, learning, an eager student.

And with every kiss, every touch, every time I look into her eyes as I slide inside her, with every gasp I draw from her lips, with every thrust, she is more mine and I am more hers.

Did I say the morning was my favorite part of the day? I lied. It's the night. It's the way she looks at me like I'm her last meal. It's the way she drops to her knees for me and how she always brings me to mine. It's the way our bodies move together and after we've given and taken each other's pleasure, she holds me.

She holds me and the overwhelming urge to tell her I love her slams into my chest. My throat is tight as I swallow the words. It's too soon. Sometimes we lie there in silence and sometimes we talk, and I wrap myself around her and caress her skin until I sleep.

I can't get enough of her. The everyday, mundane things—all magical when they're with her. Like lying here in bed, listening to the sound of the rain outside while she brushes her teeth. I make out the shape of her through the crack in the door in her little sleep tank and shorts. She doesn't wear a bra or panties under them, and I'm already hard thinking about it.

She turns the lights off and comes out, a silver-blue light on her skin. The rain beats hard against the window.

Mine.

That's all I can think as she walks toward me. Toward our bed. She's mine.

Livvy crawls over to me and I reach for her, greedily, wrapping my arms around her as she lies on my chest. I kiss the top of her head, breathing her in.

Wind whips outside.

"I'm sorry," she says softly. "About Anthony quitting. It's my fault."

I sigh. "No. It's mine. But don't worry about it. He'll find a spot at another shop, and I'll find another artist. It happens. Everything will be fine."

"I know, but I still feel bad—"

I pick her up by the hips and move her over so she's straddling me.

"Oh." She smirks as she sits on my lap, my erection pressed firmly between her legs. "Are you trying to distract me?"

"Maybe." I hold her hips firmly as I rock them back and forth on my cock. "Is it working?"

"Let's see." She lifts her thin tank top off and tosses it to the floor.

God, her tits are flawless, and I can't help but slide my hands up her body to touch them. They fit perfectly in my palms, her pretty pink nipples hardening when I circle them with the pads of my thumbs.

She grinds against me, and we both moan at the sensation.

"I think it's working," I rasp.

Thunder booms in the distance as the rain pelts against the glass.

"Mm," she hums as she slides away, pulling my boxers down with her.

She slips her shorts down her smooth legs and the sight of her bare hips, just the flash of the softness between her legs, has my cock bobbing against my stomach.

"Come here," I growl, reaching for her and pulling her in by the back of the neck. I need to taste her lips now.

Our mouths mold together. She always opens for me at the perfect time. So sweet. Her tongue is needy for mine, licking and sucking. We exchange heated breaths and groan against each other as she presses her body against mine.

She's hot between her legs, rubbing herself on my cock, making the tip of me wet. Fuck. She's ready for me.

"Good girl," I snarl against her mouth.

She sits up, the head of my dick slippery between her pussy lips.

"I like being good for you," she says.

"Show me."

My chest heaves and abs tighten as she kneels above me, taking me in her hand. Her pale skin, clear and smooth looks heavenly against all my black ink. She's an angel. Too pure for me.

It makes watching her impale herself on my hard cock that much more carnal. She lowers herself onto me, taking me inside her. I watch it disappear at the same time her heat envelopes me until she's fully seated on me, her perfect ass clapping against my thighs.

Holy shit.

"Good fucking girl."

Her cunt gushes around my cock at my words.

She smiles and eases up onto her knees until only the tip of me is inside of her then sinks back down. I dig my fingertips into the fleshy part of her, where thighs meet hip.

She strokes my cock with her body, up and down, slow and sensual. Every time she takes me fully in, it sucks the air out of me. The way her breasts bounce and the softness of her stomach make me want to touch and love every inch of her. At the same time, I want to hold her hips down and fuck up into her, hard.

"Fuck."

"Do you like this?" she asks, too innocently for the way she's riding my cock, milking it just right, thrusting her hips.

"Yes, angel." I slide my hand to her lower belly and slip my thumb down her slit to rub her as she rides me.

I'm rewarded by an instant moan and shudder from her. I

watch her face as I circle her clit. It swells beneath my finger, hard and hot. She closes her eyes, thick lashes dark against her cheeks, lips parted and panting. She arches back, doing her best to keep fucking herself on my cock as I demand her pleasure.

I want her to come for me, to feel her tighten and pulse around my cock as she screams my name. As I distract her, she overwhelms me with her beauty, her sent, her noises.

I'm already getting close, and the sight of my thick shaft, covered and glistening in her juices as she eases me out of her, about pushes me over.

"Fuck," I say.

She goes harder. Her juices...on my cock.

"Oh shit. Liv, stop."

She stills, snapping her head to me with big, doe eyes. "What's the matter?"

"No condom."

Her jaw drops. "Oh fuck." She scrambles off me, crab crawling to the edge of the mattress. "I'm so sorry, I wasn't—"

"You never have to be sorry with me, angel."

I take her hand and she comes to me, then I hook her around the ribs and toss her to the bed onto her back. She lands with a bounce and a squeal.

"Show me," I say.

She tucks her legs up and spreads her knees for me, showing me her beautiful body. Her inner thighs are shiny and slick, and I need to taste her.

She cries out as soon as my tongue licks between her lips and finds her most sensitive spot. Her hands immediately clamp to the back of my head. She fists my hair as I bring her to the edge, over and over, her legs quiver, her breathing heavier, moans louder, and then I pull back just to hear her whimper with need.

"Please," she whispers. "Please, I need you."

My cock pulses. I need the relief as much as she does. "I know. I've got you."

I sit back on my heels and open the bedside table to get the condom. She watches me slide it on as she lies there, legs spread, panting and flushed. The sight alone is enough to make me lose it.

As I lower myself back over her, I lift her arms over her head on the pillow. Both of her small wrists fit in my hand with ease, and I pin them down while I kiss her. Her lips are swollen and soft. She sucks on my tongue and pulls at my lips with her teeth.

She's needy for me. Greedy. Feral.

Such a good girl. I guide myself into her and she thrusts her hips up to take me deeper, faster.

Fuck.

I press my forehead to hers as we move together, her rolling hips meeting my thrusts. Skin slapping on skin. Breaths and gasps swallowed by kisses.

I sit up on my haunches, releasing her wrists.

"Keep your hands where they are."

She hums and whines desperately as I hold her hips and fuck into her. But she obeys, keeping her hands above her head. Such a good girl, my Liv.

I splay my hand over her stomach, my thumb dipping down as my cock pushes in and out of her. As I strum and circle her clit, I'm mesmerized by her face—thrown back in rapture, barely able to keep her eyes open, biting her bottom lip.

"Say my name. Say it when you come for me."

She tries to focus on me, out of breath, body rocking. "Yes."

"Good girl."

Her eyes roll back, and I change the direction of my circles, not too fast, not too hard. My thumb is soaked, my cock throbbing, my entire being aching to release.

But her first. Always her first.

I know when her breath starts to catch, the tempo of it. I know as her thighs tighten and she twists her hands in the pillowcase. She's there.

She bears down on my cock and grits between her teeth, "No —oh, oh fuck."

"There you go. Let go."

She comes hard around me, shattering and crying out beneath me. Breaking beautifully.

It feels too damn good. She brings me to the brink too fucking fast. She makes me lose control and I hate it. And I love it. And I love her.

I love her.

"I love you," I breathe, no power left in my lungs, plunging into her, looking into her eyes.

She doesn't say anything. She's still shaking, panting and coming down from her climax, glassy-eyed. After a moment she focuses back on me, the slightest curve to her lips.

I don't think she heard me.

It's for the better. It was dumb of me to say it while I'm inside her.

But I do. I love her.

She smiles and my heart lurches. I kiss her, hard. She wraps her arms around me, and I don't care that she forgot about keeping them over her head. I need her. I need her around me and to bury myself so deep I can't ever escape her.

My release comes, and she kisses me hard and doesn't let go, even after my body is done wracking.

She holds me until I'm quiet while I bury my face into the crook of her neck. I kiss her there, taste her sweat, while she trails her fingertips up and down my back.

It's here I am the most at peace, the most safe and loved I've ever felt.

It's also where I am the most terrified. Scared shitless that it's going to go away. That she'll go away. That I'll lose her.

I roll over and close my eyes. It's with her that I can sleep. Finally.

But the dreams haven't stopped.

Tonight, the water overtakes me. It surrounds me, closing in from every side. I can't breathe and I am sucked down deeper. Cold, dark, alone. Helpless.

Cameron reaches for me in the darkness, calling my name, saying *help, help me, Noah*. But then it's not him, it's Livvy in the water. She's blue and limp and sinking, farther and farther away until she disappears.

I try to get to her. I can't reach her.

I call her name but water fills my lungs.

I'm alone. Drowning. Panicking. Desperately clawing to get back up to the surface.

I wake up in a cold sweat, heart racing, gasping for air.

Dreaming about water and drowning—not new.

Dreams about not being able to save Cameron—I don't think they'll ever stop.

But dreaming about losing Livvy—it's a new torture that I don't want. A torture I don't know if I can endure, because every time I wake up and see her there, peaceful, the sinking feeling doesn't leave. Knowing that this nightmare can still come true is like a slow wrenching of my insides.

❤ ❤ ❤

Livvy is in the shower and I'm watching Wood sing "The Sign" by Ace of Base while making himself an omelet.

"So, what are you and Livvy doing on your day off, today?" he asks.

"She's going to go look at apartments with Bex and Macy."

He scowls as he sprinkles freshly grated cheddar cheese into the pan. "I thought you were going to ask her to stay."

I drag my hand through my hair and rub the base of my neck. "I decided not to."

"Why?" He brings his knife down hard on a bunch of spinach.

Because I'm already so far gone for her that it's just a matter of time she rips my heart out and I'm terrified.

"It's just too much, too soon. We already spend all our time together, living and working together. I was barely able to sneak away the other day. I think her moving out will be good for us. Give each other a little space, you know? Maybe I should step back a little, slow things down."

"So, you're going through all the trouble of sneaking around for this secret, and you're not even going to take the relationship forward. You're taking a step back? Do you really think this is a good idea?"

"It's probably a terrible idea."

Wood looks up and I'm braced for his look of disappointment. But he looks behind me instead, his face going pale, expression falling.

I look over my shoulder to where Livvy is standing, emerged from the bathroom, eyes round, pouty lips downturned. I don't have to read the hurt in her eyes to know she heard every word I just said.

CHAPTER 21
LIVVY

I wasn't supposed to hear that, obviously, by the look of panic on Noah's face.

I knew things were going too well between us. It's been... perfect. Magical. I've been subconsciously on edge waiting for the other shoe to drop.

And there it is.

He wants to pull away. Tired of me already.

Taryn's words seep into my brain, digging their jagged edges into every crevice.

And he's keeping something else from me? Sneaking behind my back? I have no idea what Wood meant. Like Noah said, we spend all our time together.

I can't make sense of it.

Noah's chair skids across the floor as he stands. "I thought you were in the shower."

"I decided to skip it and just put my hair up since I'm already running late."

He stutters, flustered. "Liv, that wasn't what it sounded like. Let me explain."

I shift on my feet. "Okay. Explain."

Wood shuffles out of the kitchen, eyes averted, then slips away.

Noah is still standing there at the table, mouth open, not saying anything. "Shit," he finally exhales.

"So, it was what it sounded like?" I turn toward the door.

"I guess it was, partly, but it came out worse than I meant it. And the secret thing I can explain, just not yet—"

He steps toward me, but I hold up my hand. "No, you're right. We do spend all our time together. It's a lot. I get it."

"Liv—"

"I don't have time right now. I have to go. We can talk about this later. Hopefully we'll find our new apartment today, and then I can be out of your hair altogether. I'll see you later." I hurry to the door.

He follows me out into the hall. "Livvy, wait. You're upset, don't leave like this."

"I really do have to leave. I'm already late to meet Bex and Macy," I say, stepping into the elevator.

"Please." He stands there, as the elevator doors close, the sharp angles of his face softening, his expression melting like hot candle wax.

The elevator goes down. Down. My phone pings and I glance at it. A text from Noah, saying sorry and he wants to talk.

But I don't know what to say to him right now. What can I say? He said he doesn't want me there with him. He's happy I'm moving out. He wants space, to take a step back from us, and to do whatever else it is he's been apparently doing behind my back.

My stomach rolls.

I'm still standing, staring at the phone in my hand when the elevator dings and the doors open on the ground floor.

I silence it and drop it in my bag. I'll talk to him later, when I've calmed down. I just need a little time. And I really am already late.

♥ ♥ ♥

"Bex, your sister's here! Come on, we're late," Macy shouts as she opens the door. She turns back to me smiling, though her hair is frazzled, brown eyes are wide, silently pleading for help. "We're supposed to be at the first showing in"—she looks at her phone—"twenty minutes." She lets out a high-pitched little laugh.

"Hey." I smile nervously as she ushers me in. "Sorry I'm late."

"It's okay, Bex is still in the bathroom. I don't even know if she's dressed." Macy throws up her hands and heads for the bathroom.

I sit on the couch, looking around Spencer's apartment. It's a white couch. White walls. Glass kitchen table and hard, black chairs. There are a few framed pieces of art on the walls—mostly of sailboats. His family is, apparently, really into sailing—in an attempt to personalize the space, but it all feels very clinical. I guess that's fitting for a surgeon.

Macy knocks on the bathroom door, and Bex calls back that she'll be out in a minute.

Light catches my eye. Bex's phone screen lights up on the floor, half hidden under the corner of the couch. It's weird she doesn't have it with her.

I pick it up to set it on the coffee table, but the words on the screen catch my eye.

New text message from **Noah (Dick)xon**.

Bringing the phone closer, the preview of the text reads: is Liv there with you?

But then the phone unlocks.

All. By. Itself.

Bex and I look too similar, the facial recognition must have done it. And it automatically pulls up the string of text messages between her and Noah.

This is an accident, I'm not trying to read them, but their last

few texts are right in front of me on the screen and my eyes just...
absorb the words.

BEX:

Promise you won't tell anyone about it?

NOAH (DICK)XON:

I won't mention what happened at the lake
house

BEX:

Thank you

My mind is spinning.
What happened at the lake house?
It could be nothing.
But what if it's something?
Those weird little moments between Noah and Bex after the
lake trip creep to the front of my brain, like they've been there all
along, waiting for this.

I don't know what's going on, but I'll talk to him when I get
home. I'm sure there's an innocent explanation.

Still, my body knows something isn't right. I push down the
churning feeling in my stomach.

I trust Noah. I do.

Nonetheless, the gnawing curiosity in my brain wins, and I
find myself swiping my thumb on the screen to scroll up and read
their earlier text messages.

"What are you doing!" Macy's raised voice startles me, and I
drop—no, throw—Bex's phone onto the coffee table before I can
read anything else.

But she's not talking to me. I look over to where she's standing
in the open doorway of the bathroom.

"Nothing," Bex says in a definitely-not-nothing tone.

I come up behind them and Bex is sitting there, wide-eyed and frozen, a little white pregnancy test with a pink cap clasped in her hand.

"Is that a pregnancy test?" Macy gasps.

"No," Bex says, hiding it behind her back.

"It is!"

"Uh-uh." Bex shakes her head.

Macy barges in and pries it out of Bex's grasp. "You're pregnant?" Macy's voice has gone up at least two octaves and a full decibel.

Holy shit.

"I don't know, I was just a few days late, so I got a test—"

"And you didn't tell me!" Macy has forgotten how to not shout at this point.

Bex looks at me from between Macy's flailing arms with a grimace.

"I didn't even know you were sleeping with anyone right now. I can't believe you didn't tell me. You tell me everything." Macy is beside herself.

"I'm sorry, Mace." Bex shifts her eyes back and forth, worrying her bottom lip.

"Who are you sleeping with? How long has it been going on? Is it still going on?"

Bex is silent. She doesn't want to say and now I'm counting back. The lake house trip was two and a half weeks ago. If she's a few days late that puts conception right around that time. There's a lump in my throat, my mouth suddenly too dry to swallow it down.

"I didn't tell you because it wasn't a big deal." Bex insists.

"Not a big deal? Who is it? Who's the father?"

Bex doesn't say anything.

"Do I know who the person is?" Macy asks. "Do *you* know who it is?"

Bex stands. "Of course *I* know who it is, Mace!"

"Then tell us."

"No."

"Why not?" Macy is red in the face.

"Because it's Noah!" Bex blurts.

I stagger back. It's like the wind is knocked out of me at the same time I take a blow to the head, and nothing makes sense. My ears are ringing. I can barely keep my balance.

Macy is saying something about how backsliding with an ex is embarrassing but understandable and I am clutching my stomach. I think I might vomit.

"Are you okay, Livvy?" Bex asks, tilting her head.

"Yeah, you look really pale. Do you need something to eat? I have a granola bar." Macy pulls a granola bar out of her pocket. Chocolate chip.

I'm definitely going to throw up.

"Oh, thank fuck!" Bex lets out a whooshing exhale, a brilliant white smile taking over her face, making the dimple in her left cheek deepen. "It's negative."

"Whew." Macy puts her hand to her chest.

Bex throws the pregnancy test in the trash can. With a dreamy smile, she checks her hair in the mirror and reapplies her lip gloss. "All right, let's go look at some apartments."

CHAPTER 22

NOAH

This doesn't look right.

Wood said it would be easy. Chicken marsala, his go-to dish to make when he really wants to impress a date. Delicious and *easy*, he said.

Yeah-fucking-right.

The mushrooms are supposed to be browning, but they just look sort of gray and wet? I've pounded the chicken, but fuck, I don't think I did it right. Scratch that, I know I didn't. There are parts that won't flatten and others I can see through. And I'm supposed to dredge the chicken in flour? What the fuck does that even mean? Dredge. Jesus fuck.

I just wanted to make a nice dinner for Livvy so we can talk and I can apologize for what happened this morning. What I said was shitty and not even true. We don't spend too much time together. I love that I get to see her all the time. She's my favorite person, and all I want to do is spend time with her.

And I'm going to ask her to stay. To move in with me. For good.

Fuck, this chicken really doesn't look right.

The front door bursts open, making me drop Wood's little recipe card.

I knew she was upset when she left. I knew she was still upset since she hasn't responded to my texts over the last several hours.

But I didn't expect this.

Livvy keeps her head down as she walks directly toward the bedroom, avoiding eye contact. Not acknowledging me at all.

"Liv, hey." I round the island, moving briskly to intercept her and reach for her hand.

She pulls it away.

When she looks up at me, her face is puffy. Her eyes are rimmed in red, still shiny.

Fuck.

I can't breathe. It feels like my ribcage is compressing in on me.

"Liv, angel, no. Come here." I go to her, opening my arms. I just need to hold her and fix this. Make it better.

She steps back, hardening her gaze and puffing up her chest. "I'm just here to get my things. I'm going to be staying at Spencer's place with Bex and Macy."

"What? No. You don't need to do that. I don't want you to do that. I know what I said this morning was—"

"I'm not doing it because you want me to. *I* want to."

Turning quickly, she goes to the bedroom. She's trying to get away from me. She doesn't want to talk to me, and I can't get my bearings on the situation.

I know I fucked up, but I didn't think it was this bad.

Her duffle bag is already laid out on the bed and she's throwing clothes in haphazardly. She wipes her face forcefully with her palm and stuffs a pair of shoes down the side.

My heart's racing. Sinking. I don't know what to say or do.

"I didn't mean what I said to Wood. I was making us a nice dinner so we could sit and talk, and I was going to ask you to stay. For good—"

She whips her head up to glare at me, though her downturned

bottom lip is starting to quiver. "I'm leaving. We're over. I don't want to talk about it. Nothing you can say will change my mind."

With a grunt, she pushes the overflowing contents into the bag and zips it up, the piercing sound of metal on metal.

"Wait—we're *over?*"

She brushes past me with her bag thrown over her shoulder. Eyes forward.

I follow her out to the living room, determined to not let her out that door without talking to me.

"You have every right to be mad, to be hurt, but you have to hear me out. I don't want to take a step back. Fuck. I want to step forward. With you."

She turns on me, her expression full of fury. "I don't want to hear any more of your lies." Her nostrils flare at the same time a tear falls to her cheek. "I can't be here. I'm not strong enough for this."

I'm about to drop to my knees for this girl. Beg if I need to. I've never felt this desperate. "I'm not lying. What I said this morning—"

"You all but admitted it this morning!"

What the fuck does that mean?

I'm too distracted, her words confusing me, that I don't realize her hand is on the door until she opens it.

I rush over, grabbing her wrist. My hand slides down, grasping for hers, needing to feel her fingers intertwining with mine, needing to give me a reassuring squeeze so I know she's with me. Her and me.

She looks down to our hands together and for a second, I think she's going to. She'll hold it back and wrap her arms around me and I'll make sure we're okay.

Silently, her beautiful big green eyes watery and red-rimmed, she looks up and me and slips her hand out of mine.

Blood is pumping so loud in my ears I can't hear. Can't think. Adrenaline is making me shake. But I try to breathe. I lower my head to hers and say in as steady and soft a tone as I can, "Whatever it is, we can fix it. Just please don't go. Don't do this."

But I already know. The despair in her eyes conveys everything, echoing the twisting wrenching of my insides.

Without saying anything else, she leaves.

I don't know how long I've been standing here, staring at the closed door as the shadows from the window grids cross the floor and the room grows dark. My legs ache when I finally move.

I throw the sauteed mushrooms and half-dredged chicken in the trash.

♥　♥　♥

The nights are the worst.

During the day I can shut everything off. Focus on work. My bookkeeping has never been so up to date, my desk never so clean. That happens when I spend more time in my office than out in the shop tattooing. I can't stand the way my chest aches when I look at her demon and angel drawing near my station. Can't bring myself to take it down, either.

But I can't lock myself away from things that remind me of her at night.

My sheets still smell like her.

Lying in bed, surrounded by her, minutes turn to hours with painful consistency, a countdown reminding me with every turn of the clock that I am not asleep.

I'm not tired and yet I'm exhausted.

Time is steady—but each hour grows longer as I lie here awake. Even so, I am hurtled toward morning with frustrating speed. Time slips away along with my chance for respite.

The quiet nighttime noises mock me. What comes for others will not come for me.

I want to sleep. To go away for a while. To forget.

But I can't forget.

I can't forget the way her lips tasted, or how her body felt under mine. Or her laugh. Or the way she swirled her fingertips up and down my back to help lull me to sleep. Or the sound of her heart beating as I lay on her chest.

♥ ♥ ♥

The knock on my office door is fast and light before the door swings open.

I knew I should have locked it.

Taryn walks in, her thick eyeliner giving her eyes that permanently unimpressed look. Her half smirk doesn't help either.

"What's up?"

She crosses her arms. "So, you lose Anthony over her, one of the best artists in the shop, and then not even two weeks later, you're already tired of little Livvy? You dump her and she quits. I hope she was worth it. Doesn't seem like it."

I drop the pen in my hand. It hits the metal desk, the ringing echoes around the small space.

Unblinking, I take a deep breath, clenching my fist as I try to unclench my teeth.

Taryn takes an almost unperceivable step backward.

"I didn't dump her. And I'll be down another employee if you don't keep her name out of your mouth."

"Are you kidding me? Nah. I'm out."

"There's the door."

She's shocked into silence for probably the first time in her life.

"And to answer your question—yes. She was worth it."

♥ ♥ ♥

Wood's humming "I Kissed a Girl" by Katy Perry while stirring the noodles for his legendary macaroni and cheese.

I'm nursing a bourbon on the rocks, absentmindedly swirling the glass, the clanking of the ice almost hypnotizing.

"You got a text," Wood says, nodding toward my vibrating phone on the other side of the counter.

I perk up, a burst of bright excitement from somewhere inside of me that still has hope.

"It's not from her," he says.

I knew it wouldn't be, but I'm still disappointed. That high, the split second of dopamine making me feel even worse now that it's gone in comparison.

"It's from Bex."

I roll my eyes as I take a sip of my drink. "What does she want?"

He leans over, stretching so that he can still stir the pot and see my screen. "She's inviting you to dinner tomorrow."

"Pass."

"With her, Macy, Spencer, Jake, and...Livvy." He wiggles his eyebrows at me, his lopsided smile growing with each second I deepen my scowl.

"Even more reason to say no. She doesn't want to see me. She doesn't want to talk to me. I've called. I've texted. Everything unanswered. That's my answer. And I have to respect that."

Wood nods, wiping his hands on his 'manpron' then picks up my phone. "Cool, cool. Yeah, totally." He starts typing on it.

"Hey, what are you doing."

He smiles. "Just telling her you'll be there. It's at The Capital Grille. Fancy."

I set my glass down hard with a thud. "Wood. I said I wasn't going."

"Is that what you were saying? I must have misunderstood. Oops." He proceeds to grate a block of sharp cheddar cheese with a smirk.

"Give me my phone."

"No."

"I'm not going. I don't want to bother her."

"No. You're going. You two are perfect together. I've never seen you so happy and I'm not letting you fuck this all up because you're scared."

"I'm not scared."

"You've been scared to lose someone and get your heart broken since the accident."

I clench my jaw. He knows I don't like when he brings it up.

He puts down the cheese. "Fine. I'll do it. I'm going to be the bad guy and say it because you need to hear it. You lost your whole family. It's just about the worst thing anyone could go through, and it's not something you're ever going to get over. My mom still cries every Christmas and on Aunt Jenny's birthday and whenever she hears 'Wake Me Up Before You Go-Go' on the radio."

"Wood—"

"I'm not finished. But what happened doesn't give you an excuse to never open yourself up to love, to stop living your life because you're scared to get hurt again. They wouldn't want that for you."

"But what if she won't talk to me? What if she won't give me another chance?"

"What if she does? It's not like it could get worse."

I grunt and take another drink.

"You never told her about the surprise, did you?"

"I didn't get the chance."

"Well, here you go." Wood sprinkles his mound of shredded cheese over the pasta. "What should I wear? Do you think I'll need a tie? I should probably go with a tie."

"What are you talking about?"

He rolls his eyes. "For dinner. I'm going with. Obviously."

CHAPTER 23

LIVVY

"If your party has all arrived, I'll take your drink order." The server smiles. She has a soft voice and a pixie cut.

"Yes, we'll—"

"Oh, no, we're waiting on one more!" Bex cuts Spencer off.

The server nods. "I'll come back in a minute to check on you."

Spencer looks at Bex, and while his expression is calm and unchanging, I suspect he's imagining blowing her head up with his mind. He just has that vibe.

"I invited Noah," she says.

My heart stops.

It stops, and everything blanks. No thoughts, no sound, my vision goes white for a split second, and then everything comes rushing back in full force. My pulse revved up, blood coursing through my veins so hard and loud, I feel like I'm vibrating.

I'm sweating. I'm too hot. Everything is loud and throbbing, and I need to get out of here. I need to be anywhere but here.

I didn't want to come out in the first place, Bex had to practically drag me from the couch, force me to shower, and doll me up in one of her dresses and do my makeup.

She doesn't know what's been wrong with me. How could

she? I haven't told her about Noah yet. I will. I know I need to. She deserves to know he's a liar and a cheater, but I also know it's going to upset her. And I'm afraid she'll be mad at me.

I was going to do it when Spencer came back, before she went back to stay at Noah and Wood's place. But she decided to stay where I was, much to Spencer's delight.

Anyway, we get to move into our new place on August first, just a week away. So, I've been suffering in silence, trying to hide it. Admittedly, I'm not doing great.

He's all I think about. I miss him. I hate him. But I'm in love with him.

And I absolutely do not want to see him. I don't want him to see me.

I'm breathing too fast. It's too much. I can't.

I scan around the restaurant for the nearest exit. I've got to get out of here.

But it's too late.

Noah's walking toward us. And he's already got his eyes locked on me. He's wearing black on black. Black dress shoes, pants, a fitted black button-up that's snug around his biceps, and a thin black tie that only draws more attention to the tattoos around his throat and up to his razor-sharp jaw.

He's never been more beautiful.

"Hey, guys!" Wood comes from behind him as they reach the table. He's wearing navy slacks, a crisp white shirt that pops off his tan skin, and a gray tie. It's the most dressed up I've ever seen him, yet he still looks casual, effortless, like he's ready for his hundredth weekend in the Hamptons.

Noah sits in the only open seat. Directly across from me. Next to Bex.

I can't breathe.

I also can't look away from him. Heart pounding.

Wood is unfazed that there aren't any other spots at the table. He pulls a chair away from an empty table across the aisle, the legs squeaking across the floor, and adds it to the end of the table.

I keep my gaze focused on the other end of the table. Anywhere but at Noah.

But I can feel his eyes on me.

"Is everyone here *now*?" Spencer asks with pursed lips.

Bex nods.

"Fantastic," he deadpans, then waves the server back over. He nods toward Macy and says, "She and I will have the cabernet sauvignon."

"I thought you were more of a mojito girl, Mace," Wood butts in.

Spencer darts a glance at Wood with tight lips.

Macy's cheeks darken.

"Do you have a problem, Woodall?" Spencer asks.

"Not at all." Wood looks up to the server with a smile. "Well, I *am* a mojito girl, and that blueberry mojito sounds wonderful."

The server returns his smile and writes it down then looks at me. My cheeks heat. Surely everyone can tell I want to melt into a puddle and slither away.

His eyes are still on me. Burrowing deeper.

Don't look at him. Don't look at him.

"I'll just have water, thanks."

She goes around the table. Noah gets a gin and tonic. Bex orders a vodka soda. Jake gets a beer, but one of those fancy ones that's supposed to have undertone of caramel and hickory or whatever the fuck.

Our eyes meet. Fuck.

He doesn't say anything, but those eyes say everything. Those eyes that have haunted my dreams since I was a teenager and my nightmares the last week we've been apart. Dark blue, in shadow under heavy brows, sunken and ghostly. He hasn't been sleeping.

I look away, even though the heat from his stare burns on my skin.

"So nice of you, Noah, to join us for our seven o'clock reservation at"—Spencer pulls back the crisply ironed cuff of his shirt to glance at his shiny watch—"twelve past the hour."

"Actually, it was my fault we were late," Wood chimes in, with even more volume and enthusiasm than normal.

"Of course, it was. You've always liked being the center of attention without regard to anyone else around you."

Wood smiles at him in response. "I guess there's more than one way to be a self-centered asshole."

Macy sits with her hands in her lap, staring blankly at the tablecloth.

"I didn't realize you were even invited, Woodall."

"Oh, I invited myself. Isn't this fun?"

No one says anything for a beat. Jake takes a drink of water, the ice in his glass clinking around piercing the silence.

Noah's still cutting me with his eyes.

The drinks arrive at that moment, thank god. I'm regretting not getting alcohol. She starts taking our dinner orders and while Spencer is ordering Macy and himself the salmon—but cooked to no more than one hundred and forty-five degrees and with the white wine butter sauce on the side—Noah leans across the table.

"Liv," he whispers.

I pretend not to hear him.

He knows I did. My pulse is racing. But I keep my head turned and my eyes trained on the server who comes around for my order next.

My voice comes out all weird, and I clear my throat and smile. *Smile so you don't cry.* I order and hand her the menu, all the while never looking back at Noah.

His tattooed fingers drum on the white tablecloth in my peripheral vision.

Ignore him.

"How was your day, Mace? Did you work today?" Wood asks.

Macy, mid-sip of wine, coughs and puts her drink down to

answer. "Um, yes. I assisted with two vaginal births and one of our NICU babies got to go home today. It was a good shift."

"That's amazing. I couldn't do anything like that. I'm not good with blood and needles and stuff." Wood shivers.

"What *are* you good at these days, Woodall? Partying?" Spencer asks flatly.

"Among other things." Wood smirks.

Bex laughs wildly at something Jake said. I must have missed the joke, though I, admittedly, wasn't paying attention to their conversation.

Keeping my eyes averted from the man sitting across from me —the rich, dark scent of his cologne bringing back memories of twisted bedsheets and roaming lips and hard—I reach for my glass of water.

But my hand smacks the glass, knuckles knocking it over. It crashes to the table, water splashing across the white cloth, ice spilling out to the sound of shrieks and gasps. Everyone is standing. Water drips over the edge onto the floor.

Noah and I reach for the glass at the same time, his fingers brushing my skin instead. I recoil from him, refusing to meet his gaze. The server and another young man come to help with a rag.

"Please, miss, let us take care of it."

I back away, everyone's eyes on me, an overwhelming sob beginning to rise in my chest. Tears brimming to the surface, I turn and dart toward the bathrooms.

Panting, I shut the door to the single-use restroom, turning the bolt, but not hearing the telltale click of the lock. Great. Broken.

Of course, I'm not lucky enough for there to be a window in here. Just walls covered in a dark and moody maroon floral wallpaper. I lean over the sink and stare in the mirror, willing my breathing to slow.

My skin is pale and my stomach churns.

There's a gentle tapping at the door. "Livvy," Noah says from the other side, his voice deep and low and a little strained.

No, no, no.

"Liv, are you okay? Can I talk to you?"

I loved when he called me Liv, and now I can't stand it.

With a soft click, the doorknob starts to rotate.

I rush to the door and snatch it open, letting the door swing wide and hit the wall. Noah's there, arm outstretched, hovering in the dimly lit hall.

"I don't want to talk to you," I say, heart beating wildly, hating how my voice cracks on the *you*.

He takes a step back, his throat bobbing against the tight collar of his shirt and tie. "I know."

I step past him and back toward the table.

"Livvy, wait—"

But I don't wait. I won't give him the satisfaction of seeing how much he hurt me. I won't cry. Even as my vision starts to blur and my eyelids sting holding the tears back.

I sit at the table, head high. It's been cleaned up, a new, dry tablecloth put down and a fresh glass of water at my place.

Everyone quiets as I scoot my chair in.

Bex leans in. "Don't worry about it. Are you okay?" she whispers across the table.

"I'm fine."

She sits back and smiles, but it's half-hearted. She exchanges a weary glance with Jake next to her.

Then Noah joins us. Every line of his face hard. His dark brows brooding. Soft lips in a pout. He wraps his tattooed fingers around his gin and tonic and takes a sip. Silently staring at me.

He wants to talk?

Okay.

Let's talk.

Let's put it all out in the open. I'm sure my sister would love to hear about how you took my virginity along with everything else while you were fucking her, too.

Everyone is quiet.

There's an energy in everyone's silence. A buzzing just under the surface.

Bex is sort of bouncing as her eyes shift between Spencer and Jake. Then to Noah.

I fist the thick cloth napkin on my lap.

Noah catches me looking, our eyes meeting for the quickest of seconds. I hate that I can see the longing in his face. I hate that I'm sure it's mirroring mine.

I turn away.

Macy looks at Wood's almost empty mojito while her glass of wine sits full.

Here goes. I'm going to do it. I'm going to tell Noah I found out about him and Bex. Then I'll have to beg her for forgiveness and hope she doesn't hate me.

I take a sip of water first, heart pounding, hand shaking, fingers threatening to drop the slippery glass again.

Jake loudly clears his throat. "I have something to tell you all," he says, straightening. He nods toward Spencer. "It was my brother's idea to come out tonight to celebrate me getting selected for a prestigious position in the oncology department at the hospital. It's been several grueling weeks of interviews and panels."

Spencer raises his wine glass and gives a curt smile.

"But I have another exciting thing to share," he takes a deep breath before he continues. "When I arrived in town, Spencer let me stay with him while I was in limbo, looking for a permanent place. He also specifically said to stay away from this one." Jake points a thumb at Bex who smiles back at him. "So much so, that he said he'd kick me out on my ass if he caught me messing around with her."

"Christ," Spencer mutters under his breath.

"He knows I have a weakness for blondes." Jake beams at Bex, almost blushing.

What is going on?

"Well, I'm sorry, Spence, but I didn't stay away."

What. The. Fuck?

"What?" Spencer's expression is unreadable, though his lips look thinner than normal and he hasn't blinked this whole time.

Macy's face is contorted in confusion.

Noah doesn't seem fazed at all.

Wood stirs his mojito with his straw.

"Anyway," Jake continues, putting his arm around Bex's shoulders. She leans into him. "Now that I have a secure, permanent job and I'm getting my own place, we can finally tell you all that—"

Bex bounces with a giant grin and cuts in, "We're in love and we're going to move in together!"

Spencer's nostrils flare, but he doesn't say anything.

Wood shouts, "Congrats!" then slurps the rest of his drink.

Spencer stands, throwing his napkin to the table. "Are you fucking kidding me?"

"Wait—what?" Macy tilts her head, her mouth hanging open.

"I know"—Bex makes a cute little cringey face—"I won't be going in on the apartment with you guys." She looks at me apologetically, but I still haven't processed half of what's going on.

"No." Macy shakes her head. "I mean, I thought you were hooking up with Noah."

Jake turns to Bex. "What?"

She shakes her head.

"What?" Noah shouts. "No, we're not hooking up. I'm in love with Livvy."

"WHAT?" Now it's Bex's turn to shout.

Jake and Spencer are up, in each other's face at the other end of the table. Staff is starting to circle us with concerned looks.

Wood asks one of them if he can have another mojito.

"Wait," I say quietly. "You two were never sleeping together?"

"Fuck no! Why would you ever think that?" The pleading in Noah's voice rips a new hole in me.

"Bex told us you were."

Everyone's eyes turn to Bex, except for Jake and Spencer, their voices getting louder and getting more and more stares from staff. A manager comes by and asks if everything is all right. We all smile and nod. Even Spencer gives a tight-lipped smile as he and Jake nod.

After he leaves, Noah turns on Bex, a dark shadow passing over his expression, his chest heaving even as his words come out steady.

"What the fuck is this, Bex?"

"Yeah," Macy chimes in. "Why would you tell us you've been sleeping with Noah if it's a lie?"

Bex's cheeks darken. "We didn't want Spencer to find out about us yet, and I was stressed about the whole pregnancy scare thing and Noah's name was the first one that popped into my head. I didn't think it was a big deal. He's my ex, and exes sometimes hook back up, and I didn't think he was with anyone at the time—" Her eyes widen like what Noah said just dawned on her. "Oh my god, Livvy, is that why you've been so sad and crying all the time?"

I haven't moved, haven't breathed in what feels like minutes. My limbs feel like concrete.

"Fuck! I'm so sorry!" Bex gets up and starts to round the table toward me, but Noah grabs her elbow, stopping her instantly.

"No." The word comes out like a snarl, his eyes almost black. "I'm going to have a word with you later, but right now—" He makes hard eye contact with me. "Right now, Livvy and I are going to go talk. Alone."

CHAPTER 24

NOAH

I can't even see two feet in front of me, only red. My mind is swirling and I'm vibrating so much I want to crawl out of my skin. I've never wanted to wring someone's neck, but Bex might find I'm a new person.

Later.

Livvy first.

She winds down the dark hall and back into the same bathroom as earlier. I follow her, shut the door, and turn the lock. I have to unravel my fists to do it, they ache from being clenched so tight, my palms dented with marks from my fingernails.

My vision is still blurred, darkness creeping in on the edges, heart rate elevated, blood pumping full of adrenaline and ready for a fight.

But as soon as I turn around and see Livvy standing there, tears running down her face, it clears. Everything else melts away. She's the only thing that matters right now.

"I'm so sorry," she says, letting out a sob.

"Angel." I wrap my arms around her instantly and she reaches up around my neck without hesitation.

I scoop her up and set her on the counter and hold her tighter, basking in her warmth, the scent of her hair as I bury my face in it. She nuzzles into my chest and I'm never taking this feeling for granted again. This is where I belong. This is where she belongs. With me.

The front of my shirt is wet, but her sobs have subsided to hiccups.

After a few minutes, it's quiet again.

Her face is still smashed against me when she says, muffled, "So, you haven't been sleeping with my sister?"

"No, Liv." I say it softly, still holding her, but the thought makes me want to smash this sink with my fist.

She lifts her head, looking up at me with tear-streaked cheeks, red eyes, and a runny nose.

She's beautiful. She's mine.

"And nothing happened at the lake house?"

"The lake house?" I contort my face trying to figure out what she means.

She wipes her face with her palm. "I saw a text on Bex's phone. She asked you not to tell anyone about what happened at the lake house."

"Oh, that. I caught Bex and Jake together at the lake house. She didn't want anyone knowing about it. I didn't ask why. It wasn't my business."

Livvy starts crying again. "I'm sorry I didn't talk to you. I wouldn't have believed it if Bex hadn't said it to my face. I should have—"

"Shh." I wipe her eyes with my thumbs and kiss her forehead. I kiss her nose and then both damp cheeks as her stuttering breaths start to ease. "You should have talked to me," I whisper against her lips.

"I know," she breathes. "I should have trusted you."

"I wish you had. But I gave you reasons not to."

"No." She shakes her head. "You didn't, I—"

I take her face in both my hands. "I did. I was getting scared.

Scared when I realized how in love with you I am. I started pushing you away because I was afraid if I let you all the way in, I'd just get hurt when I lost you."

But that was a lie. She was already in. Embedded so deep there's no way to disentangle her from my heart. No way to forget her. And I knew the day she walked out my door last week I was fucked.

"You're in love with me?" She sniffles. Her black eyelashes are wet, sticking together in little spikes around her big, green eyes.

"Yes." And for a second, my heart stops, my lungs deflate, and I'm alone and vulnerable, about to crumble to dust.

Until she says, "I love you, too."

I can't help but smile, and she smiles back. Breathtaking.

I crush her to me, kissing her hard. Our teeth clank together because we're still smiling while we kiss like idiots.

"Ow." She breaks out into a giggle.

I pull back, still holding her face, and look into her eyes. "I'm sorry you ever had a reason to doubt—to think that I had eyes for anyone else. I don't. There is only you. You're everything. Promise me you'll come to me next time. Whatever it is, I know we can fix it, but you have to talk to me, angel."

"I promise." She curls her fingers around my hands, a silent tear falling.

"You've got to trust me. Trust in us."

"I do," she whispers, eyes closed.

"And I promise I won't push you away again. Ever. I'll always fight for you. I want you by my side. Forever."

She looks up at me, eyes watery but happy. I've never said forever to anyone. I thought I'd feel vulnerable, scared, weak. But I feel strong and free and happy. Safe and secure in this thing I have with her.

Livvy stretches to kiss me, then pulls me in hard for a deeper kiss. She tastes sweet with the slightest hint of salty tears, and I'm going to do my best to make sure she never cries sad tears again—not over me, at least.

She breaks the kiss, panting, our breaths heated. Her nipples are hard and perky in her little satin dress with the tiniest straps. Knowing she isn't wearing a bra and knowing how perfect she is under this dress has been torturing me all night.

I slide a hand up her leg, pushing her dress up to her hip, squeezing the soft flesh of her thigh, the curve of her hip and around to her perfect ass.

She moans at the touch. It makes my cock jump.

"Do you think you can be a good girl and be quiet for me?"

She nods, starting to pant.

"Or do you want to make noise? Do you want everyone out there to know you're being fucked?" I can tell by the way the pulse in her neck quickens she's as excited as I am about the thought.

I'm hard as a rock and I rub my palm over my slacks to ease the throb.

I yank her dress up to her waist and spread her legs with my hips. With both hands on her hips, I pull her butt to the edge of the counter and kneel, keeping my eyes on her. I kiss the insides of her thighs before burying my face between them. I'm too impatient to go slow. I need her. Now.

I kiss her panties, breathing in the scent of her and listening to her breath quicken before hooking a finger in them and pulling them to the side to reveal her pretty little pussy.

I know what she likes. She likes long, broad strokes of my tongue to start, nice and slow. She likes when I tease her, not quite reaching her clit. And then when I do, I get the satisfaction of moans as I make gentle circles. I go faster, putting a little more pressure there, making it swell. She fists my hair with one hand while the other is white knuckled on the edge of the counter as I suck hard. I switch between sucking and licking, driving her wild. She gets louder, her thighs crushing my face.

She says my name and I know she's there.

Normally I might draw it out, but I need inside her—I need to fuck her—so I let her come for me. And she does, hard and fast with shaky breaths and quivering legs and the sexiest "fuck" I've ever heard.

I stand and she puts both hands on my face, pulls me in and kisses me hard.

"I need you," she says, still panting, our foreheads together.

"I know you do, angel."

I've already retrieved the condom from my pocket and her breath hitches when my belt hits the bathroom counter. I push my pants and boxers down just enough to expose my hard cock, then roll the condom on, grip her hips, and slam inside her.

"Yes," she groans.

She throws her head back, her neck exposed and the line of her body arched back in pleasure as she holds onto me, fingers digging into my biceps and legs tight around my hips. She doesn't need to hold on. I've got her.

I hold her hip down firm and her other knee tight to my side as I fuck into her. Not too fast. She gets louder as I go harder. She wants it a little rough.

"Noah...fuck. More."

I'll give her more. I'll give her everything. Anything. It's hers.

She's incredible. Hot around my cock. Lips parted, red lipstick smeared across her cheek. Breasts bouncing behind the silky fabric of her dress. And all the while she's moaning and gasping and saying my name.

Then she looks at me. Looks me right in the eyes while I'm fucking her and she knows I'm hers, at her mercy. She owns every inch of me.

"Say it," I say, barely restrained.

"I'm yours," she says, panting.

"Mine," I growl.

I'm undone in a second, emptying myself inside of her and

holding on to the counter for support as I shake from the force of it. She wraps her limbs around me as I begin to come down.

A high-pitched gasp pulls me from my post-orgasm trance, and I whip my head toward the sound—toward the opened bathroom door where Macy is standing, her hand over her mouth.

CHAPTER 25

LIVVY

He's still inside me, cock pulsing, shuddering through the final waves of his climax as Macy stands wide-eyed.

"Okay. It is what it looks like, this time," I say with a shrug and a nervous little laugh.

Macy turns around quickly. Noah buries his face into my shoulder, shaky, unable to compose himself quite yet.

"Sorry!" Macy squeaks. Hand over her eyes she says, "If I could just get a paper towel—"

"Oh." I reach over and pull a couple from the dispenser and hold them over to her. "Here."

She feels around blindly, finally grabbing them and saying, "thank you," then clattering away, the door banging closed after her.

"I swear I locked the door," Noah whispers against my neck, another aftershock making him shiver against me.

"I think it's broken," I laugh.

"And you knew. Naughty." He kisses my lips, then my nose, then my forehead as he pulls out of me, the perfect ache left in his place.

While he disposes of the condom I hop down and straighten

my dress and wet a paper towel to wipe my face. While I'm fixing my smudged lipstick, he comes up behind me in the mirror. His tattooed hand plays with the strap of my dress before caressing my bare shoulder.

His dark figure behind me, all in black, covered in black ink, bends as he kisses the spot where my shoulder meets my neck.

I try to focus on my reflection, but he's warm and solid behind me, pressing against my back as he slides his hand around to my stomach. He's hard again.

"Mine," he snarls against my neck and keeps kissing me.

I arch back against him, making him groan, his chest vibrating, and suddenly I'm liquid for him again, needy. Greedy for him. He's all mine.

"We better get back before I bend you over and fuck you again," he says with an edge to his voice, a breathy desperation that tells me how much he'd like to do that and how much he's holding back.

I wiggle my ass against his erection, and he chuckles, moving his lips up to my earlobe. He nips it between his teeth. "I'm going to take my time with you later."

"Can't wait," I say, watching him behind me in the mirror, tilting my head to give him better access to my neck as he kisses and sucks.

His arms encircle me, shirtsleeves shoved up to his elbows, fingers digging into my dress. He surrounds me, consumes me, and it's better than thirteen-year-old little Livvy could have ever dreamed up.

Reluctantly, he takes my hand and leads me out of the bathroom and back to the table.

My panties are soaked under my dress, clinging to my skin. Noah squeezes my hand and looks down at me with a smirk like he knows exactly what he's still doing to me.

But before we get to the table, it's clear Spencer and Jake are still deep in an argument. Macy pleads with them to take it outside, looking around in distress, tidying up what looks like another spill. She touches her boyfriend's arm but he shrugs her hand away with a sneer.

Finally, he and Jake exit the restaurant with Macy and Bex following.

We approach the table cautiously, Wood the only one left, sipping on his third mojito.

"So, how did that all go?" Noah asks quietly.

"Bro, tonight has been amazing. Best night I've had in a long time. I'm so glad I came." Wood leans back in his seat with his signature lopsided grin. "Oh, and the night just got better."

Our server along with two others arrive with trays full of food. Our head server does a good job of hiding her mild horror at our empty table.

"Will the rest of your party be back shortly?"

"Nah, I don't think so," Wood says. "Don't worry, I'll take it all." He pats his flat stomach. "Are you guys going to sit and eat, or should I have your dinners boxed up for later?"

Noah looks at me with a wicked glint in his dark eyes. "I'm not very hungry. What about you?"

I shake my head. Food is the last thing on my mind.

"All right." Wood waves the server back over. "Go ahead and box everything up except mine, and I'll take the check and another mojito."

She says right away, and he gives her a smile and a wink.

"I'm going to have to leave her such a big tip." He chuckles. "I'll bring the food home later? To our place?"

I nod and Noah smiles. "Yeah," he says.

Wood looks back and forth between us and down to where our hands are clasped. His grin widens. "So...does this mean you'll be staying with us again? For good?"

Noah's gaze hasn't left my face. "If she wants to. I want her to."

My throat constricts and my chest tightens at the same time

tears threaten to well up again. I'm afraid I won't be able to speak. So I just nod. I nod and smile so wide my cheeks hurt and finally squeak out, "Yes. Yes, I would like that."

"Good," Noah says.

I glance back at Wood. He's sitting with his elbows on the table, resting his chin in his hands, dopey smile on his face. "Don't mind me," he says, wiping his eyes. "I knew you two would work things out." He looks down and slices his steak, sneakily wiping away another tear. "I'm getting a little tired of it, honestly."

"Of what?"

"The whole serial dating, one-night stands, booty-call thing." He takes a big bite off his fork but continues talking anyway. "It's not very fulfilling. I think I'd like something more, you know?"

Noah squeezes my hand and just as I'm about to tell Wood how great I think that is, Wood's phone buzzes, rattling against the table.

He looks at his phone, his face lighting up. "Ooh, Audrey. Change of plans." He shovels another piece of steak into his mouth and starts texting. "I have a date."

"So, the whole *wanting something more* you were just talking about..."

Wood grins at us. "Bruh, Audrey is, like, really fucking hot, though. I'll start looking for something more next weekend."

"Should we tell them you need another meal boxed up?" I ask.

"What? No way. This is my warm-up meal." Wood beams.

"All right, see you back home," Noah says, barely hiding the chuckle in his voice.

Wood points at me as we step away. "Hey, waffles in the morning?"

I nod excitedly.

"Knew it!" And with a couple of shots fired from his finger guns, we wave and walk out of the restaurant.

Outside, the sun has gone down behind the surrounding buildings, throwing everything in a hazy blue shadow. The orange glow of the sun in the distance means the streetlights haven't come on yet, hovering somewhere between day and night.

The rest of our group is under the covered roundabout. Spencer is hastily exchanging his keys for a twenty-dollar tip with the valet. He gets in the driver's side while Jake holds the passenger door open for Macy. As soon as she gets in, he peels away. No time for her to even get her seatbelt on or wave goodbye.

Noah squeezes my hand as we approach Bex and Jake. Jake gives us a little nod and unwraps his arm from around my sister. "I'll, uh, give you guys a minute to talk." He kisses Bex on the cheek and tells her he's going to pull the car around.

He leaves and we all stand there for a minute, quiet. The air is heavier as dark clouds roll in on a warm breeze. She looks back and forth between us and down to where I have a death grip on his hand.

"I fucked up," she says, exhaling.

"Yeah, you did," Noah cuts, barely restrained fury rippling off him like thick swirls of black smoke.

"Don't be a dick. I'm apologizing!"

"You told my girlfriend I was hooking up with her sister," he spits, his grip on my hand becoming tighter.

I should say something. But my heart is racing, and I don't like fighting. Bex was always the fighter, not me.

Bex's eyes widen. "Girlfriend?" She turns to me.

I nod, still trying to find words.

"Shit, Livvy. I should have realized." She comes to me with arms open. Noah reluctantly lets go of my hand so I can hug her back. "I was so caught up in my new relationship, I wasn't even paying attention to you. I'm sorry."

She squeezes me, and even though she's restricting my lungs, it finally feels like I can breathe.

"I should have told you," I say, grimacing. "I was scared."

She pulls back, keeps a hold of my arms. "Why?"

"Because of what you had said—about never dating a family member's ex."

"I did say that, didn't I?" She almost laughs. "I wouldn't let something like that get between us."

"So you're not mad, about me and Noah?"

Bex tilts her head. "It's a little weird, but he and I were together a long time ago. I'll get over it. I just want you to be happy. I've always only wanted that for you."

She smiles, getting impossibly prettier, her crystal blue eyes twinkling as a cool rain drop hits my nose, then she narrows her gaze at Noah. "If you hurt her, I will fucking kill you."

Noah chuckles, wrapping his arm around my waist and pulling me up against his side. "I know."

"I'm not kidding. Straight up murder."

"I believe you."

Jake pulls up to the curb as more rain drops start to fall.

"Love you," Bex says, smiling at me and flipping Noah off.

"Love you, too." He returns the gesture with both middle fingers as she gets into the car. She and Jake drive off as the patter of rain hitting the pavement surrounds us.

Noah wraps me in his arms, and I nuzzle into his warm chest. "Sorry my sister threatened your life."

He kisses the top of my head. "I'm not worried about it. I have no intention of hurting you. I'm going to keep you and take care of you, forever."

I look up at him, the man of my dreams, and he's promising me forever. It doesn't seem real.

He smiles down at me. "I have something else I need to tell you. Actually, let me show you.

♥ ♥ ♥

We walk for several blocks, the rain letting up as the clouds open and dissolve away to a beautiful night sky.

At first, I think he's taking me to the shop. We pass the bar, which is still dead this early in the evening. Then, as we get to the doors of the shop, he keeps on walking, arm around my shoulders.

He takes me to the next door down, the coffee shop.

"After you," he says, holding the door open.

"What are we doing here?"

"You'll see."

I walk in, Noah quietly behind me, his hand on my lower back, steering me away from the counter and over to the booths up against the wall. I glance all around. The lighting is dim, moody. Everything painted in muted tones of brown. It's not very full. The few people sitting around murmur softly while their ceramic mugs clink against little saucers. Soft key clicks come from someone working on their laptop in the corner, earbuds in.

Noah puts both hands on the sides of my face and tilts my head back, directing my eyes upward.

And there, on the wall, in this quiet corner coffee shop, is the nude drawing I did of him in the loft, framed with a simple white mat against the aged, brick wall.

I stare blankly up at it, mouth open. I'm frozen and it's like everything around me is fuzzy, out of focus, sounds muffled like I'm under water.

"Are you mad?" Noah gnaws on his lip. "I know I did this behind your back, I wanted it to be a surprise—"

"I'm not mad. I... I don't know what to say."

"It's not an art gallery, I know, but I thought it might feel like a step toward it one day. You're so talented, you deserve to have your work seen."

It's unreal. I can't stop looking at it. My little drawing, up on the wall. It looks like...art. Real art. "I can't believe you did this for me. So, this is the sneaking you and Wood were talking about?"

"Yeah."

Oh.

He rubs the back of his neck. "I called the other day to have them take it down, but he told me someone made an offer on it, full price, as long as it's the original."

I glance at the little tag in the bottom corner. *Twenty-five hundred dollars?* "You sold it?"

"I told him to hold off on it. I didn't know what to do. He said if you decide to sell, he'd like another piece to hang in its place. He also has a sister shop across town he wants a piece for."

I'm overwhelmed. "This is amazing." Tears start welling up in my eyes as he bends down to bury his face in my hair as he pulls me to his chest. "Thank you," I whisper.

He smells faintly of gin with that piney undertone and I breathe him in, knowing he's mine. I still can't believe it. Noah Dixon. Loves me.

He did so much just to help make a small part of my dream come true. But *he* is my dream come true.

CHAPTER 26

NOAH

SEVERAL MONTHS LATER

"**A**re you ready?" I motion for her to come. "You can do it."

Livvy nods, walking toward me in her new neon pink bikini. Two cute little bows obscure the wing tattoos on her hips, but her newest tattoo is on full display. Finally fully healed so we can get back in the water.

It spans almost knee to hip on her left thigh—my favorite tattoo I've ever done. Not only because it's on the woman I love and she designed it, but also because it represents us, and it's a piece of me that will be with her always. An angel, nude, draped in beautiful wings in the embrace of a wicked demon, kissing her in reverence.

She steps to the edge of the pool, toes curled over the side. With a chest-puffing breath and a big smile, she jumps into the deep end, water splashing in all directions.

Not going to lie, my heart skips a beat every time her head goes completely under the water, but I'm getting better.

Livvy pops back up, that smile still on her face. My perfect drop of sunshine. Heaven personified.

She swims over to me in the shallow end, and I kiss her on the lips. It never gets old—her smiling at me, kissing me, when I know she's mine.

"Show me," I say.

Her grin widens and she bounces a little, pushing off the bottom of the pool then shooting away from me. Head down, she does a beautiful freestyle to the other side of the pool, strong kicks. She turns around just like I taught her and swims back to me.

She gets another kiss when she reaches me.

"Good job. You're doing so good," I say.

Her cheeks darken.

I slap her butt. "Keep going."

She does a backstroke this time to the end and back. Another kiss. Another lap. Another kiss. Ass grab. Another lap. Another kiss. Boob fondle.

And then she does it. Five laps. Ten lengths of the pool.

"I did it. Were you counting?" She's a little out of breath, water dripping down her face, beads shimmering against her pale skin.

"I was. You did it. I'm so fucking proud of you." I kiss her harder, grabbing her waist, pulling her in against me at the same time she wraps her arms around my neck.

"You know what that means," she says with a mischievous grin.

I groan as she giggles. "I know what it means." But an agreement is an agreement.

"Do you know what else it means?" she asks, snaking her hands down my back and around to my lower abdomen.

"What else?"

"It means you might be too sore later, so we should do this now." She drags her fingertips over the front of my trunks. My cock, already at half-mast just from watching her in this damn bathing suit, responds immediately, swelling and hardening under her touch.

"Oh, I like this idea much better." I hike her up and she yelps as we both almost fall backward.

I slide my thumb under the triangular scrap of fabric holding back her breast and pull it to the side to reveal one perfect pink nipple and dip down to suck it into my mouth.

She gasps, holding the back of my head to her, digging fingertips into my scalp, urging me to suck harder.

Resisting the impulse to pull at the bows on her bottoms to get them out of my way, I slip two fingers between her thighs instead.

"Whose pussy is this?" I snarl just before taking her nipple between my teeth.

"Yours," she pants. "All yours, Noah."

My cock gets impossibly harder when she says it, throbbing against the waistband of my shorts. And then her delicate hands are pulling at them, freeing my cock and then wrapping her fingers the length of it. I frantically push my trunks down with one hand, the other two fingers deep in her warm cunt, sucking her distended nipple harder until she's moaning uncontrollably.

"Sit on my cock, angel. I need to be inside you."

My good girl doesn't hesitate. She holds onto the edge of the pool as I line us up and then she impales herself on me.

She groans as I slide in, and I hold her hips down and push up into her the rest of the way.

"I love the way you fuck me," she whimpers. "You feel so good inside me." She clings to my shoulders, bouncing up and down.

I pull at her top again so I can see those pretty nipples as her breasts bounce. She undoes the knot around her neck and flings the bikini top out to the middle of the pool, still riding my dick. Her eyes roll back, her lips darkened and puffy, skin flushed all over. I love it.

I love her.

"You're always so good for me. So perfect." I grip her thighs, just under her ass and walk us out of the pool, never leaving the perfect warmth of her body.

I lay her down on one of the bright white and yellow lounge chairs, kicking my trunks off somewhere between the pool and here. She lies back, tits out, cheeks pink, skin glowing, and I'm about to lose it.

She reaches for me and I yank the ties on her bottoms and toss them aside then come over her, covering her body with mine. I kiss her hard as I lift her knee, spreading her out and pressing her down as I thrust in and out of her, nice and slow and deep.

My naked ass is pointed directly at the security camera, and I don't give a fuck.

"Do you like fucking this pretty little pussy?" she breathes between kisses.

"Fuck." I can't handle it when she says things like that while I'm inside her. "I'm coming."

She pulls me in deeper, squeezing me with her legs as I tense and release inside her, filling her up. As the muscles in my ass and hamstrings are spasming, Livvy runs her hands through my wet, tousled hair and kisses my face. She sighs contentedly as I slide my still-erect cock out of her, covered in both of us.

Her pussy lips are spread open, dark pink and puffy, little round clit poking out between them and my cum oozing out of her. It's the hottest fucking sight on the planet.

I love getting to fuck her raw. "Do you like feeling me fill you up and drip out of you? Just like we used to chat about?"

"Yes," she breathes.

I dive down, lapping her up.

"Fuck," she cries out as I suck on her clit and I swallow up all the mess. "What are you doing?"

"I'm cleaning you up. And you haven't come yet."

"What about this morning in the shower?"

"I've always got to keep you an orgasm ahead, angel."

"Oh." She throws her head back, her legs falling open, and I get to work.

♥ ♥ ♥

"Are you ready?" The wheels of the stool squeak as Livvy sidles up to me, and I hear the familiar snap of latex gloves as I lie face down on the black leather table.

"I can't believe I'm letting you tattoo my ass."

She giggles. "I've been practicing." Then she gives my bare ass cheek—the one without the stencil on it—a little smack.

That reminds me. I snag my phone and hit Wood's number, putting it on speaker.

It rings a couple times. "Sup, bruh," Wood answers.

"Hey, I'm going to need you to log into your parents' security system and erase the video from around noon to one o'clock today."

"Did you have sex in the pool?"

Livvy snickers in the background.

"I can hear you, Livvy," Wood says, the stern edge in his voice completely exaggerated. "I thought I told you to stop having sex in the pool."

"You're one to talk."

He sighs. "Fine, but you owe me. Again."

"Thanks, brother." I end the call. "Ready when you are, angel."

Livvy inhales then exhales slowly. It's her first tattoo on a person. For all I know, it might be her last tattoo, too. She's been spending less and less time at the shop, and more time at home painting. She's got paintings up at seven stores now, and they keep selling. And I couldn't be happier about it. Or any fucking prouder.

"Don't be nervous. You'll do great. Besides, it's just my ass.

You're the only person who's ever going to see it. Maybe Wood if he catches me bending you over in the kitchen again."

I can't help it. She keeps sexting me during the middle of the day until I'm so needy I have to sneak up for a quickie between appointments. She knows I have a weakness for her dirty texts.

"He scrubbed the counter for half an hour after that." She laughs. "Thanks, I am a little nervous. But not about the tattoo, about something else. Something I need to tell you."

"What do you need to tell me?" I start to roll over, but she pushes my hip back down and smacks my butt again.

"Hold still or you're going to have wobbly lines."

The loud buzz of the tattoo gun drowns out any other sound and then her hand is holding my ass cheek still and taut.

The first contact of the needle with skin is always the most jarring. It's been a while for me, but the memories rush back and it's familiar again. Almost comforting. Still hurts like a mother-fucker, though.

She pulls a line, then wipes. Another line. Wipe. She's gentle, not too heavy-handed, slow and steady. After a few more wipes, she pauses the machine.

"You waited until I couldn't move to tell me on purpose, didn't you?"

"Maybe," she says innocently. "It's not that big of deal, I just didn't want you to hear it from anyone else. Don't be mad, okay?"

Oh fuck. I chuckle. "What is it?"

She hesitates and I'm suddenly sweating.

"I texted Anthony the other day."

My heartrate spikes as adrenaline rushes through my system.

She laughs. "Relax. Your ass is clenched."

"Sorry." I unclench my ass.

"I just wanted to apologize to him for how things went down and maybe..." She takes a deep breath and then says in a rush. "See if he would come back to the shop."

Every bit of tension leaves my body, and I can breathe again. I almost laugh. She didn't see the way he left. "How did that go?" I ask.

"Not great. He seems to think you two were always in competition for who was the best artist in the shop. And then when he and I went out, you felt like you needed to compete with him for me, too. That you stole me away from him, just so you could win."

I'm about to push off this table, tattoo be damned, so I can assure her that while, yes, I was jealous as hell, I wasn't trying to win her like she was some prize.

But she cuts me off. "But you didn't steal me away from him, or anyone. That would have been impossible."

"Why is that?"

"Because I was already yours. I've been in love with you since the first time Bex brought you around and I hid at the top of the stairs just to catch a glimpse of you."

"Really?"

"Yeah."

I thought maybe she'd had a little crush on me when she was young, the way she'd blush and run away, but it all makes sense now—the way my soul knew she was mine before I did.

"Wait—so the crush you told me about as Angel, the one you'd had for years—was that me you were talking about?"

Her laugh is light and airy. "Of course it was, silly. It's always been you."

It brings a smile to my lips. "I'd thought maybe it was some idiot from art school or something. Whoever it was, I hated him."

She laughs harder.

"I love you," I say. I never get tired of telling her how much I love her. My angel. She saved me in more ways than one.

"I love you, too, Noah Dixon. Now, shush so I can concentrate on your ass."

ABOUT THE AUTHOR

 Rae writes romances she hopes will have readers squealing, kicking their little feet one minute and blushing the next. Biscuits and gravy enthusiast. She'd love to travel the world but is also an unapologetic homebody. You can find her under a cozy blanket next to the fireplace at home in the Pacific Northwest with her husband, three children, and entirely too large dogs.

For more info and a complete list of books, visit
www.raekennedyauthor.com

 instagram.com/rae.kennedy.author